Head of State

Richard Hoyt

TOR

A TOM DOHERTY ASSOCIATES BOOK

For Jacques de Spoelberch

HEAD OF STATE

Copyright © 1985 by Richard Hoyt

First Printing: September 1985

A TOR Book

Published by Tom Doherty Associates
49 West 24 Street
New York, N.Y. 10010

ISBN: 0-312-93310-X

Printed in the United States of America

The fact is that a smell of decomposition began to come from the coffin, growing gradually more marked, and by three o'clock was quite unmistakable. In all the past history of our monastery, no such scandal could be recalled, and in no other circumstances could such a scandal have been possible, as showed itself in unseemly disorder immediately after this discovery among the very monks themselves. Afterward, even many years afterward, some sensible monks were amazed and horrified, when they recalled that day, that the scandal could have reached such proportions. For in the past, monks of very holy life had died, God-fearing old men, whose saintliness was acknowledged by all, yet from their humble coffins, too, the breath of corruption had come, naturally, as from all dead bodies, but that had caused no scandal nor even the slightest excitement.

—*The Brothers Karamazov*, Fyodor Dostoyevsky

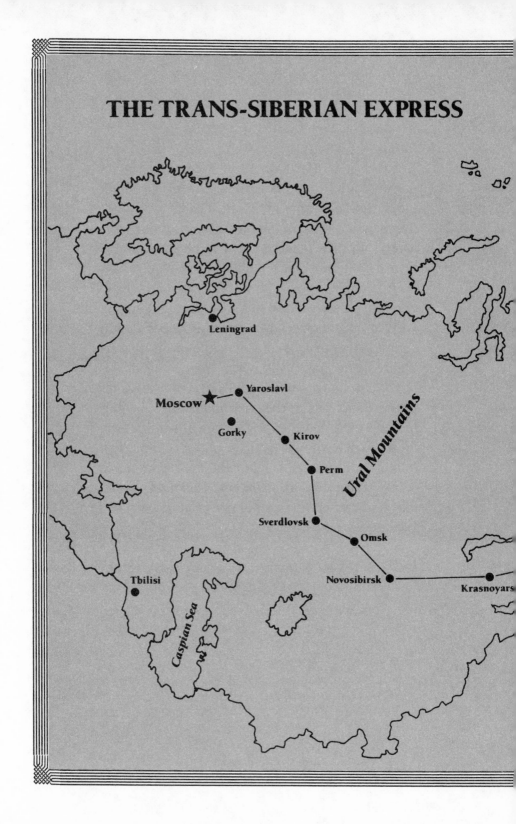

THE TRANS-SIBERIAN EXPRESS

Leningrad

Moscow ★ ● Yaroslavl

● Gorky ● Kirov

● Perm

Ural Mountains

Sverdlovsk ●

● Omsk

Tbilisi ●

Caspian Sea

Novosibirsk ● Krasnoyars

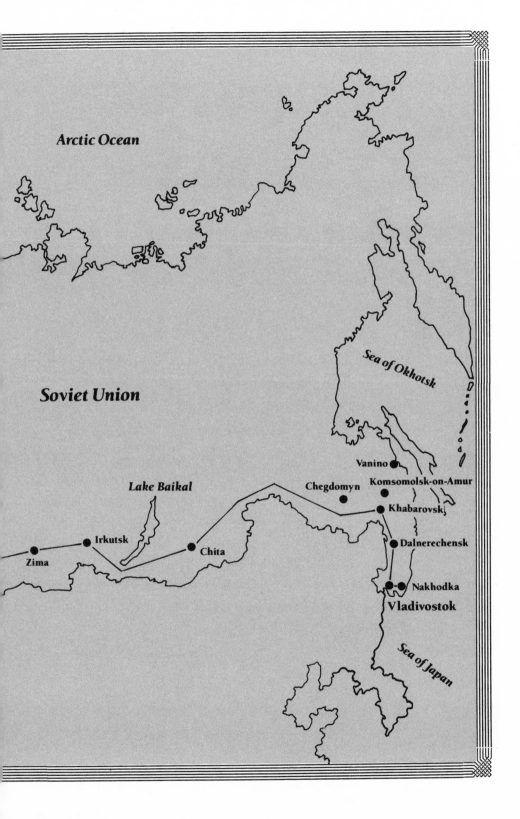

Arctic Ocean

Soviet Union

Sea of Okhotsk

Lake Baikal

Vanino

Chegdomyn

Komsomolsk-on-Amur

Khabarovsk

Irkutsk

Zima

Chita

Dalnerechensk

Nakhodka

Vladivostok

Sea of Japan

Book 1

One

THE JANUARY TEMPERATURE PLUNGED TO TWENTY DE-
grees below zero on that sad day in 1924. But the bitter
wind in Gorky was of no consequence to those hardy
Russians as they set about to bury the one who had led
them in those first historic, exhilarating hours, and in
whose shadows the world was destined to live. The
bearers were rotated so that more might share the honor
of feeling his weight. As they were replaced, they fell in
among the mourners who followed silently behind. They
carried him along a snow-packed trail through a forest of
birch and aspen.

The Russians had a four-hour walk ahead of them, yet
they did not cover their faces. They were carrying the
weight of history. They were determined to shoulder it
proudly. They breathed in great clouds of white. They
bore the crimson coffin slowly along the trail. A terrible
wind lowed among the birches as dark clouds gathered
in the northwest; it would snow later in the day. They
did not wince, did not falter. Their eyes were sad. They
believed he had been a messiah and so was immortal,
yet they had not imagined his coffin could be so heavy.

The mourners did not feel the cold working its way

3

up through the soles of their boots; they were Russians and so knew the cold. Their solemn countrymen gathered among the trees to see the beginning of the melancholy journey.

Three windows had been cut in the coffin so his head could be seen lying in calm repose. He had a high, intelligent forehead. His cheekbones had a hint of Asia about them. His jaw was defiant, unyielding, his mouth unforgiving. His hard, furious eyes were closed. He looked calm, at peace in the end.

He had redeemed them and imprisoned them at one and the same time, although they did not believe that, would not believe it; such treachery was too outrageous for them to comprehend, they even who had known the czars. He had given them deliverance, and their bodies and souls were his. Their children would be his as well, and their children's children; such were the consequences of his remorseless passion.

The bearers heard the steam engine well before they got to the Gorky station. Out there, alone in the forest, with the windowed, crimson coffin on their shoulders, they heard the engine up ahead, waiting. The engine inhaled with a high-pitched wheeze and exhaled heavily: *sssssh, WHUH! Ssssssh, WHUH! Ssssssh, WHUH!* Scoop of frigid air, release of spent steam. Scoop of frigid air, release of spent steam. *Sssssssh, WHUH! Sssssh, WHUH!* Tiny at first, muffled by the snow, the sluggish rhythm got louder and more insistent as the bearers approached the station.

Thus it was that Vladimir Ilyich Ulyanov—known as V. I. Lenin—was being taken to his rest.

One of the men at the station waiting to say good-bye was named Salomon Ginsburg. He wore a Russian-style fur hat—a *papakha*—pulled down over his ears and a heavy woolen scarf pulled up over his mouth and nose. He wore a heavy blue overcoat and shifted from foot to foot to keep his feet warm. He wore spectacles in the manner of intellectuals and in fact was one, a historian.

When Ginsburg saw the peasants waiting for Lenin, he saw poetry. Ilyich himself had disdained peasants; to him, they were ignorant cattle.

For keeping Lenin's company and for being Lenin's friend, for standing by Lenin's side and fighting Lenin's fights, Salomon Ginsburg had toiled for three years in one of the czar's lumber camps east of the Urals. Ginsburg had surrendered one of his little toes and part of one ear to frostbite, and his kidneys, pummeled for the pleasure of one of the czar's guards, had never recovered.

Ginsburg was a passionate revolutionary but did not himself want to rule. He was like their friend Trotsky in that regard. Ginsburg had not taken part in Lenin's government, although he remained close to Lenin. A week before he died, Lenin had confided in Ginsburg that the great experiment had gone wrong. They had ignited a revolution to free peasants from oppression and had themselves turned to the same old despotism. Lenin told Ginsburg he wanted Trotsky to be his successor and had put that on paper. Lenin had said he didn't trust Stalin: "He loves power for the sake of power, Ginsburg. You've seen him. You know. Turn the country over to him and you'll lose everything. Everything, Ginsburg."

Ginsburg put his gloved hands under his armpits and shifted from foot to foot to keep warm. He saw the red coffin emerge from the woods, riding the shoulders of the solemn bearers.

At last the bearers approached the station, a small building made of uneven white bricks that looked as though they had been laid by drunks or jokesters. The engine seemed even more loud and demanding. A billow of white steam rose above the red station roof with every sighing *WHUH!* of the awaiting engine.

The mourners on the platform parted respectfully as the coffin approached. As the coffin passed, however, they pressed forward, leaned to get a better look. They wanted to be able to tell their grandchildren: I was there. I saw.

Ginsburg coughed slightly and said, "Good-bye, Ilyich," as the coffin passed by. Without another word, he turned his back on the gathering and walked alone into the trees, thinking about his son Avraam. Ginsburg thought about Stalin and a rush of fear coursed through his body, swept across his face.

Eighteen months later, Salomon Ginsburg, on a walk along the shores of the Gulf of Finland, was taken into custody by Stalin's secret police. He was taken into a bare room and beaten until his face was a bulbous potato, purple with bruises. Ginsburg signed a paper that he could not read because he had been blinded during the beating. Then he was dumped into the river Neva, where he drowned.

The bearers slowed on the icy platform. Nobody spoke. Nobody fussed or argued.

A single red railroad car awaited to carry the coffin to Moscow. The passenger car was attached to an enormous black steam engine. The engine had been cleaned for the occasion, and its blackness stood in startling contrast to the white of the snow and the red of the car. *Sssssh, WHUH! Sssssh, WHUH!* The steam rushed forth, billowing white in the frigid air.

The engineer of the steam engine had never met Lenin, but he loved him still. He was a Ukrainian and his name was Yuri Korenkho. He had been chosen for Ilyich's last ride—sent out from Moscow—because he had been Trotsky's engineer in 1919 and 1920, when Trotsky beat off the White Russians and foreign mercenaries who threatened to topple the Bolshevik government. Korenkho believed. Sure, the Bolsheviks were brutal, but that was the way of life in Russia. The czars had been worse. And now that the foreigners were driven out and the Bolsheviks were secure, Korenkho was certain life would get better—better for his little son, Serafim, better for everybody. Lenin had made it all possible.

Korenkho leaned out in the cold air and watched for the wave of the hand signaling that Ilyich's coffin was aboard and secure. There it was, a wave of the hand. Korenkho turned and pulled on a lever that released the brakes with a great savage gust of steam that made people step back on the platform.

Yuri Korenkho pulled the throttle out one notch, and the engine began to move slowly. Take your time, the party officials had told him. Let the people see. Korenkho felt proud and honored to be the engineer on this run. It would be a lovely story for little Serafim when he was older.

Korenkho saw to it that the engine moved slowly, slowly down the tracks. *FOO! WHAH!* the engine said. *FOO! WHAH!* The great iron wheels moved on heavy thighs. *FOO! WHAH! FOO! WHAH!* Oh, the pain, the pain. Outside, young workers with shovels ran alongside throwing sand onto the rails in front of the locomotive's great iron wheels. They wanted to be able to tell people they had sanded the rails for the locomotive that took Comrade Lenin to Moscow and to posterity.

When the young workers fell behind, exhausted, running awkwardly in their heavy boots, the funeral train came upon an icy stretch of tracks, and as the wheels of the engine spun momentarily, the *FOO! WHAH!* speeded to a sudden *Fffffffffhhhhhhhhhffffffffffhhhh!* then, on dry steel, slowed to the *FOO! WHAH!* dirge.

Salomon Ginsburg had reason to fear the consequences of Lenin's death that day. Yuri Korenkho did not, yet he too paid for Stalin's insecurity. Four years later, Korenkho was summarily pulled from his family in Odessa—he had a wife and three small children—and sent to the railyards at Krasnoyarsk in Siberia. Korenkho was one of twenty thousand Ukrainians sent to Siberia in one forced move. The Bolsheviks told the Ukrainians

*the people needed railroad workers in Siberia and put
Korenkho to work sledging spikes into ties on roadbeds
that took a terrible beating from the weather.*

*Korenkho eventually contracted a savage case of dys-
entery that would not go away. Rather than fuss with
such a bothersome wretch, the Bolsheviks simply shot
him.*

Up ahead, peasants bundled in coats, with woolen
scarves wrapped around their faces, closed in by the
tracks to say good-bye to Ilyich.

So it was that Ilyich was taken to Moscow. The
outpouring of emotion in Red Square during the next
few days startled even the Bolsheviks.

The Soviets built a platform in the House of Trade
Unions—which later became the State Historical Museum—at the north end of Red Square. The temperature
plunged to twenty below zero, and a snowstorm pushed
through Moscow, as uncounted thousands of Russians
gathered to pass by Lenin's body. Hour after hour after
hour they filed wordlessly by his coffin and saw Ilyich
lying there, one hand closed, one open, his head on a
white pillow. At the end of three days and three nights,
the Soviets, feeling they were called upon to do something dramatic, hastily dug a vault under the Kremlin
wall facing Red Square.

On the morning of Sunday, January 27, 1924, Lenin's red-draped coffin was placed by the vault as the
Russian people gathered in the huge square, waving red
handkerchiefs and wearing black armbands trimmed with
red. They laid scarlet funeral wreaths by the coffin.
Bands played mournful dirges. Minor officials, railway
workers, factory workers, and union men made passionate speeches glorifying Lenin and extolling his virtues
and character.

The noise began at exactly four o'clock that day.
Naval guns opened up, firing salvo after salvo. The
army turned its seige guns loose: boom after boom

erupted from Red Army bases across the country. Sirens wailed in the factories and on the streets. Foghorns boomed. Steam whistles screamed on locomotives and aboard ships. People rattled cans and shook bells and kicked barrels. The din reverberated in every village and city in Russia and across that hodgepodge of annexed, captured, or stolen lands and territories known collectively as the Union of Soviet Socialist Republics.

The demonstration continued unabated for three shocking, elemental, emotional minutes, and at the end of it grown men wept.

Two

THE ARCTIC AIR WAS NUMBING COLD THAT SUNDAY NIGHT, and if logic had prevailed, the eight pallbearers would have ridden in two cars and shared body heat. But no, there were four cars assembled for the ride out the main gate of the Kremlin to Red Square. Joseph Stalin, the general secretary of the party, would have preferred eight cars with himself riding last, but that would have violated the collective sense of propriety. Stalin assumed the responsibility for determining the order of departure and arrival. He had decided that he and Felix Dzerzhinsky, who controlled the secret police, would arrive last. Lenin had hated pomp and ceremony. Stalin rather liked it, in fact insisted on it.

Stalin scrawled the order on a piece of paper and gave it to his driver, who was chief driver. None of the others said anything. Grigory Zinoviev made a snuffling sound. Stalin and Dzerzhinsky had the secret police; what could Zinoviev do? What could any of them do?

It was less than a kilometer from inside the Kremlin to the place by the wall where they would carry Lenin's frozen body. Stalin settled in on the seat of his limousine and waited for his car to join the procession. He folded his hands neatly on his lap.

Stalin knew there would have to be an autopsy. But he wasn't worried. He would shoot any physician who didn't agree with his decision that Lenin had been felled by a stroke. Stalin had thought this over since he had learned that Lenin was losing his grip and telling people Stalin loved power too much. When Lenin had begun saying that Leon Trotsky, a Jew, should inherit the leadership, Stalin had decided it was necessary to put a quick end to Lenin's illness. Lenin had to die someday—everybody died someday. Stalin had seen no reason why he shouldn't hurry things up a little.

A majority of the members of the central committee were Jews. Stalin didn't like Jews. If they gave him trouble, he'd have them shot.

The heavy cars entered from the north end of Red Square, moving slowly down a roped-off passage through the mass of bundled Russians. Soldiers with megaphones shouted at the mourners to stand back. Other soldiers blew whistles at anybody who touched the ropes. The soldiers outside the vault had moved the crowd back to accommodate the automobiles. Lenin's bearers were to arrive in a fashion later made famous in America by movie actors on Oscar night. The workers and peasants watched the heavy cars moving slowly over the ice. Each of them wondered: Which one is Stalin? Which one is Dzerzhinsky? Stalin ordered men flayed. Dzerzhinsky did the flaying.

As they turned right on Manyejhnaya Square, Stalin and his comrades could see a sea of mourners coming up Volkhonka Avenue from the west, down Kalinina Prospekt, Gertsena Avenue, and Gorky Street from the north, and Karl Marx Prospekt from the east. The white city was given color by the browns and grays of their winter coats.

Mikhail Bakunin, Lev Kamenev, V. M. Molotov, Mikhail Thomsky, and Zinoviev were bearers because they were Lenin's revolutionary comrades. Ianis Rudzutak was a union official; his only reason for being there was that he was favored by Stalin. Felix Dzerzhinsky, the head of Cheka, Stalin's secret police, rode with Stalin. But Dzerzhinsky opened his door just a fraction before Stalin. This was not an accidental gesture; they arrived together but everybody knew they were not equals.

The bearers wore impeccably tailored black winter coats and sable *papakhas*. They stood silent for a moment, humble but proud.

The very last to step out into the terrible cold was Joseph Stalin. As he did so, the clouds parted briefly to reveal a pale white half moon. Stalin was not a man who could bring himself to bow his head in mourning— even as one of Lenin's pallbearers. He stood tall. The awe and fear in the peasants' eyes was a radiant glow to him, a charming warmth. While others' bones were cold that night, Stalin felt nothing.

Stalin looked at the sea of faces before him and could hardly believe their affection for Lenin. The problem was that they were religious. The Bolsheviks did not want competition from gods and so had banned religion. So now this: the peasants had seized upon Lenin. This upwelling of emotion had shocked Stalin. He couldn't send all these people to Siberia; that would be an inauspicious beginning for his rule. What would he do?

Stalin hadn't pursued power over the Kremlin so assiduously without knowing something of its history. He knew, for example, that Lenin's tomb was not far from Lobnoye Mesto—the Place of the Skull—a stone mound from which the heralds of the medieval Muscovites had read the laws. The Muscovites believed their city would one day become the Third Rome and inherit the earth. Then, they believed, the laws of Russia and its conquered territories, of the entire earth in fact, would be read from that mound. They believed Lobnoye Mesto was the center of the earth, and would radiate a secret power for eternity.

There was a skull within this mound, they said. This skull was the source of the secret power. Protect it and the power was theirs. Lose it and their power was gone. The skull was priceless beyond imagination.

Lobnoye Mesto was just off the southeast corner of Red Square—a matter of yards away from the base of St. Basil's Cathedral. The czar's men had beheaded state criminals at Lobnoye Mesto. The czars—Ivan the Terrible, Peter the Great if he was in the mood—had watched from a high tower. Stenka Razin, the Cossack chief who had led the peasants of the Volga in revolt, had been beheaded at the mound.

Joseph Stalin, thinking of Lobnoye Mesto, gathered with the other bearers. Stalin had received ecclesiastical training as a young man and so knew the power of myth and symbol. Outwardly—as many people later recalled—he was somber that night; his face was properly melancholy. Inwardly he felt a strange, wonderful mixture of joy and expectation.

Quickly and confidently, Stalin assumed the head position at the right-hand, forward side of the red coffin. He would enter Lenin's vault as Lenin's right-hand man, Lenin's trusted lieutenant and disciple—the man who would assume the responsibility of Lenin's socialist vision. The eight men bent as one and hoisted the coffin shoulder high. Joseph Stalin could hardly feel the weight. Lenin's corpse was no burden at all.

Joseph Stalin studied the report on his desk before he addressed the small man in the neat jacket. His name was Dr. Leonid Ilyich Latsis. He had been trained in Paris and until the Revolution had lived in Petrograd. He had embalmed royalty. He was the best available in Moscow.

"I want you to tell me about Lenin's body," Stalin said. "What will happen to it when it thaws out?"

"The bacteria will take over and the corpse will begin to decompose," Latsis said. When he had visited the

Winter Palace he had worn a tie. He wondered if he should have worn a tie for Stalin. Was a tie too pretentious for a member of the proletariat?

Stalin said, "How long does this take? Tell me exactly what happens."

"In a few hours there's apt to be a greenish tinge here," Latsis said. He put his hand on the lower part of his abdomen. "By the second day dehydration sets in. The green skin spreads from the abdomen. Is Comrade Lenin on ice?" Latsis wondered if it was proper for him to ask questions. He didn't want to be shot for some violation he knew nothing about.

Stalin seemed not to mind. "Yes, he is. Tell me, can you stop this process by embalming?"

"Embalming?"

"Yes."

Leonid Latsis sensed danger. What was he being asked to do? One did not fail Joseph Stalin.

"Well, it can't, not really," Latsis said. "The embalming we do, with formaldehyde, is only intended for a couple of days, until the bereaved have a chance to see the body, no more. We make the corpse look nice. We put color on its face. Then we bury it, and nature takes its course."

"I was thinking of something more permanent," Stalin said.

Latsis knew he was in trouble. "Well, I suppose we could do the body in sections, put the formaldehyde in the femorals and brachials as well as the carotids."

"Explain that," Stalin said.

"The carotids are arteries on your neck—here, under your jaw. You pump a formaldehyde solution in the arteries and blood comes out the veins. You do it up, then down." Latsis raised his chin up and, using his forefingers as needles, pointed first up, then down, on either side of his chin. "The brachials are under your arm, here, and the femorals are on the inside of your thigh." Latsis showed Stalin the location of his own brachials and femorals. He paused. "We can put lanolin in the solution and that'll help some. The best way to preserve him for a long time is to keep him cold enough so the bacteria can't live."

"On ice?"

"Yes. You could freeze him. We have found mastodon flesh preserved in the permafrost."

Stalin didn't like that idea. "How about a vacuum? Couldn't we put him in a vacuum? Do bacteria live in vacuums?"

"Some of the worst kinds," Latsis said.

Stalin was not pleased by the drift of the conversation. He'd been expecting something better. This was the twentieth century, after all. There were submarines, radios, and airplanes. Stalin didn't think it would do to have people parading through an ice room to see Lenin lying there like a side of venison. Stalin said, "I want you to pump him full of the most effective solution possible and do whatever you do to make his face look normal. Then I want you to go back to your laboratory and find out how to make it permanent. I'll see to it that you get all the dead bodies and assistants you need."

Latsis was trapped. "Yes, sir . . ." He cleared his throat and opened his mouth but said nothing else. Latsis read the journals in French and German. There had been no advances that would accommodate Joseph Stalin. This was 1924, sure, but to do that, preserve Lenin perfectly, permanently, why there was just no way. None.

As the undertaker left, Stalin made a note that viewing Lenin should be done by permit only, so that the viewers' body heat might not encourage bacteria.

Latsis and his fellow doctors did their best with Lenin's body, but changes in the corpse followed inevitably according to the laws of nature. Deterioration set in. To call attention to a need for progress, Latsis was summarily shot. His colleagues were removed from the project and exiled from Moscow. More doctors were brought in. For two years Russian physicians tried to do something to Lenin's face, which was now wrinkled from dehydration.

In 1926, Stalin brought another man of science before him, Dr. Ilya Zbarsky. Stalin said, "Lenin looks like an old man. He looks like he's scowling. I want this stopped."

Zbarsky said nothing. Everybody knew what had happened to Latsis and his associates. Lenin looked like he was scowling because his skin had dehydrated and shrunk. That had happened to King Tut, and it had happened to V. I. Lenin. It was impossible to boil Lenin in water and plump him up like a raisin.

"I know they make wax figures that look like real people," Stalin said. "There's a museum in London. I want you to get an artist and have the artist give him a proper face."

Zbarsky was relieved. Stalin was making a little sense for once. "It could be done," Zbarsky said. "We can have Lenin's skull, Lenin's skin, but with a thin wax overlay. Wax his face, his neck, and his hands. That's all that anybody can see. We can put a red light on him. Red will give him a youthful appearance."

Stalin smiled. "There's no real difference between makeup and wax if you get right down to it; wax is thicker and looks better, is all. I want you to have it done quietly and announce that you have discovered the secrets the Egyptians used to embalm the pharaohs. Announce that Lenin's body will last for eternity."

Thus it was that Lenin's face regained its middle-aged appearance in 1926. Joseph Stalin, without anybody being the wiser, had shifted the location of Lobnoye Mesto as casually as a carny shifting a pea under a walnut shell.

In 1930, a mausoleum of red Ukrainian granite and Karelian porphyry was built over Lenin's vault. Then Lenin's body disappeared from sight for a few months. It was announced that the Kremlin's sewers had overflowed, and the mausoleum would be closed while these repairs were undertaken. When the mausoleum was opened a few months later, Lenin's body—defying all the laws of nature—had entered an even younger incarnation. Lenin's fierce, resolute middle-aged face was gone. He had become a young man, calm, contemplative, remote from the struggle that had raged in the wake of his death.

A left-wing German physician was given a quickie tour of the tomb to inspect V. I. Lenin. The secret police ensured Stalin's pleasure by threatening to shoot the doctor for the wrong answer.

Premier Stalin shook his head in amazement: the dumb kraut—the Fritz—had proclaimed Lenin authentic without even touching him. Stalin was so amused by the success of his nonsense of Egyptian embalming that he decided the USSR needed its own pyramid. He proposed that the country build a thousand-foot pyramid in Moscow, and top it with a dramatic statue of V. I. Lenin.

This was the first of a series of proposals for a Lenin monument that eventually ended up with Ivan Dmitrov's celebrated statue of Lenin in Oktyabrskaya Square.

Three

SIXTY-THREE YEARS LATER, A SMUGGLER CROSSED INTO eastern Turkey from Soviet Georgia with Contact David's proposition for the Central Intelligence Agency.

Four

JUST AS IT WAS A NOTE THAT DREW THE AMERICANS INTO the story, three years earlier a note had instructed Isaak Ginsburg to appear at 2 Dzerzhinsky Square for a "preliminary interview" so that his request to emigrate from the USSR might be processed by Soviet authorities.

The notice was so designed as to allow for an individual's name and the government's particular concern. It began with a blank space. Here someone had typed "Isaak Avraamovich Ginsburg." The text of the form followed: "Your presence is required at 2 Dzerzhinsky Square." There was another blank space where someone had typed "2 P.M., 26 February." The form continued, "for the purpose of." A typist had completed the blank line that followed with "preliminary review of your application to emigrate to Palestine."

There was another blank line, a short one, where the typist had entered "I. Podoprigora."

Below I. Podoprigora, the form read "Committee for State Security."

The form did not say that Irina Podoprigora was the personal secretary of Colonel Felix Jin of the Jewish Department of the Fifth Chief Directorate of the KGB.

19

The Fifth Chief Directorate was responsible for the internal control of the Soviet population. There were separate departments for the control of troublesome nationalists in Latvia, Estonia, Lithuania, Georgia, and Armenia as well as separate departments to deal with Moslems, practicing Christians, and intellectual malcontents. All these except for the Jewish Department were handled on a regional basis. There was a central control for these regional units that reported to a party committee and the Secretariat.

Such was the importance of the Jewish Department that it was national rather than regional in organization.

For years the Soviet Union had attempted to rid itself of Jews by systematically repressing the Jewish culture—chiefly by prohibiting the use of the Yiddish language. Ginsburg himself knew only isolated phrases. The government had also imposed an impossible tax on Jews who wished to emigrate, but had eventually removed that obstacle on the grounds that it was too obvious.

The government's stated concern was the loss of scientists and engineers who had been educated at state expense. The Soviets did not like it when one of their botanists turned up at Oxford University. They were furious when a Jewish émigré—working on a computer that enabled him to beam paragraphs around like Captain Kirk on *Star Trek*—wrote a novel excoriating communism as it was practiced in the Soviet Union.

Sometimes the Kremlin assented to pressure from the Europeans and let a few Jews out. The way Ginsburg saw it, if he were lucky enough to be on the list at the time, he might get to go. If not, he knew, he risked an asylum or the gulag.

Two young military officers—an older and a younger lieutenant—these were ranks having nothing to do with age—sat next to Isaak Ginsburg in the metro as he rode toward the old KGB headquarters at Dzerzhinsky Square. They had an animated conversation about Soviet preparations for the Seoul Olympic games. The officers agreed that the Americans had made fools out of themselves in the last Olympics, strutting gold medals won against no competition. The Soviets had done the same thing in Moscow, but that was different. Things would be different in Seoul as well. The East Germans would unleash their swimmers. Bulgarian weight lifters would show their power. Russian boxers and gymnasts would clean up.

The younger lieutenant said that if the Americans didn't have black athletes, they'd lose to Albania.

The older lieutenant wondered if a Zionist athlete had ever won a medal. He couldn't think of any.

Ginsburg emerged from the train at the metro stop opposite the Moscow Hotel and found his way to the sidewalk above—on the north side of Karl Marx Prospekt. There was a metro stop just down the street on Dzerzhinsky Square, but he wanted a few minutes to think about possible answers to inevitable questions. It was a cold day with a pale blue sky. He had been over the details of his situation several times, each time flopping his adversary's logic.

As Ginsburg saw it, if they were going to send him to a camp, they'd have sent soldiers, not a request for a preliminary interview. The KGB probably interviewed everybody who applied for permission to emigrate.

Across Ploschad Pyatidesyatiletye Oktyabrya—Square of the Fiftieth Anniversary of the October Revolution—formerly Ploschad Manyejhnaya, pilgrims to Lenin's tomb spilled from old buses parked there as Soviet security officers went through the morning ritual of forming them into a double line.

One after another the buses unloaded: peasant women in head scarves, children in uniforms, old men. They were herded through the gate into the park area to form a queue that in another hour would be moved along a white line on the bricks of Red Square. This line led to Lenin's tomb at the base of the Kremlin wall. A man with a battery-operated loudspeaker shouted, and the people who had gotten off the buses did as they were told, moving in groups this way and that.

Ginsburg walked east on Karl Marx toward the Bolshoi, where by night the most beautiful ballerinas in the world danced on long legs, small backs arched, their wrists and arms of willow.

A long block west of the Bolshoi—two long blocks from the Kremlin itself—lay Dzerzhinsky Square. All Soviet citizens knew that it was at Dzerzhinsky where—as medieval cartographers said of unknown, and therefore feared territory—dragons lay. The old KGB headquarters was on the one side of Dzerzhinsky; adjoining it on the right was Lubyanka Prison, built by German slave labor.

Number 2 Dzerzhinsky, which had been erected by the czars, was a high, romantic clutter of arched, barred windows and decorative columns. The main KGB headquarters was no longer at Number 2. It had been moved to the outskirts of Moscow, to a curved building in the International Style of architecture that resembled nothing so much as the CIA's headquarters in Langley, Virginia. In fact, it sat outside Moscow's outer ring road much as the CIA's headquarters sat just off Washington's Beltway.

The halls of power were in the new KGB building. Ginsburg assumed the officers at Dzerzhinsky would be young, enthusiastic, and on their way up, or old, embittered, and on their way down. Ginsburg could be impaled by either horn: ambition or indifference.

Ginsburg descended a short flight of stairs to the pedestrian passageway under Karl Marx and came up on the other side. There were several hard-faced young men on the broad sidewalk in front of the gray stone building. The young men were athletic inside their well-cut suits. They had necks as hard as wood.

Two men closed in around Isaak Ginsburg as he approached the main entrance to the storied building, the original Moscow Center. Ginsburg felt a flutter of anxiety and pushed open the revolving door. He immediately faced a woman behind a desk. The woman, whose reddish-purple hair had been colored by henna, motioned with her hand for Ginsburg to stop.

A man at her side said, "Raise your hands."

Ginsburg did as he was told, and one of the young men who had followed him inside frisked him for weapons. He stepped back.

Ginsburg hesitated, then lowered his hands. He looked down at the parquet floor, then up at a large oil of Lenin that dominated a pale green wall.

The man snapped his fingers impatiently, and Ginsburg dug the envelope with the summons from his jacket.

The red-haired woman held out her hand for the summons and studied it momentarily. She opened a desk drawer and took out a form with a small photograph clipped to one corner. The photograph, Ginsburg saw, was a copy of one that had been part of his file at Moscow University. She looked at Ginsburg, then at the photo, then at Ginsburg, then at the photo. She did not want to lose her KGB perks through carelessness. She was thick of body, serious of expression. She reread Ginsburg's summons.

"Jin," she said. She looked up at Ginsburg; she picked up the receiver of her desk telephone and dialed a number. "One for Comrade Jin," she said.

Fifteen seconds later, a tall, serious man in a brown suit appeared. His shoes echoed *click, clack, click, clack* on the parquet floor. He took the summons, read it, looked at Ginsburg, and said, "Jin?"

"Yes," the woman said. Ginsburg followed the man to an elevator, which they took to the third floor.

The man walked down the hallway, motioned Ginsburg to stop, and knocked softly on an office door. When the door buzzed, he opened it. "Comrade Jin," he said.

Ginsburg heard a voice say, "Yes?"

"Citizen Isaak Ginsburg, comrade."

"Send him in and wait outside," the voice said.

Ginsburg stepped inside, knowing—as he saw Felix Jin—that his life would never be the same.

Jin was small and dark-complexioned. He had a high forehead and intelligent eyes that had a suggestion of an eye fold. His black hair was neatly parted. He was slender, fastidious in his manner but not effeminate. He was young for a colonel—in his early thirties.

Colonel Felix Jin said, "Go ahead, you can sit." There was a single chair opposite his desk.

Ginsburg sat.

"Would you like a cigarette?"

Ginsburg shook his head no.

Jin said, "You're wondering, so I'll tell you. My great-grandfather was Mongolian. My father was a mathematician. My mother was Russian, a ballerina at the Kirov. A man named Jin cannot afford mistakes." He paused and added, "And you are a Jew."

Ginsburg said nothing.

"Far better to have a one-syllable surname," Jin said. He removed a file from a metal cabinet as Ginsburg stared out the barred window at barred windows on the other side of the building's central courtyard. The office was smaller than he had expected. It was the same green as the entrance hallway and was lit by a single, large white globe on the ceiling.

Jin opened the file on his desk and began reading. "A good dossier," Jin said. He looked at Ginsburg, looked at a photo in the file, looked back up at Ginsburg. "You want to emigrate to Palestine?"

Israel, Ginsburg thought. He said, "Yes."

"I thought you called it Israel."

Ginsburg cleared his throat.

Jin smirked. "A poet, it says here. It says your grandfather was a poet." He looked at the folder. "Salomon Ginsburg. Drowned in the Neva River."

"Yes."

Jin said, "Allegedly a friend of Lenin's. Is that true?"

"That's what my father said."

"Tell me about your poetry, comrade. What kind of poetry do you write?"

"Lyric poetry, I guess you would call it. I write about small moments."

Jin read more of the file, the KGB's assembled life of Isaak Ginsburg. "This says the Writers Union doesn't like your work."

"I think I am a good poet," Ginsburg said.

"Ahh, pride," Jin said. "You were denied membership in the Writers Union. Therefore you are not a poet, comrade. Writers are members of the Writers Union."

Ginsburg didn't know what to say.

"They cite this," Jin said. He held up a chapbook of Ginsburg's poems that had been circulated in manuscript at Moscow University. "You play a stupid game, Ginsburg. 'Journey to Lobnoye Mesto.' You think we can't read. Poems about blighted trees that are not trees. Do you think we are so stupid that we can't understand parable and metaphor?" He flopped the chapbook back into the folder.

"I don't think you have thought this over sufficiently, Ginsburg. You're a university graduate, qualified to teach the English language. We educate you, then you want to go to Palestine. Do you think that's fair?"

"I think I would be better off there," Ginsburg said.

"You are an arrogant Jew, Ginsburg. A parasite. If you are Salomon Ginsburg's grandson, you've slandered and denigrated everything that he stood for. I think what you need is a chance to learn how to love your country. What do you think?"

Ginsburg didn't answer. He wasn't meant to answer.

Felix Jin said, "Two years in a camp, then. For parasitism. This will give you time to think about your pretentions, Ginsburg. No poetry. You will not write poetry while you are confined. Is that understood?" He made an entry on Ginsburg's file. "There," he said, "this will make clear what I have in mind. Your camp commandant will see that my wishes are carried out."

Ginsburg was stunned. "I thought this was to be a preliminary interview."

"Preliminary to your being sent to a camp. Do you expect us to waste the people's time when we have everything we need in your file here?" Comrade Jin punched a button, and the door to his office opened instantly. Jin said, "Lock this man up. He is to be sent to Siberia as soon as it can be arranged."

Ginsburg felt the guard take him by his arm. He was to be taken now. A camp! Both Ginsburg's parents and his younger brother had been killed in a train derailment, so it wasn't as though he had a family to say good-bye to. Still, it was a shock. He had come believing this was to be a first step. Numb, disbelieving, he allowed himself to be led down the hall.

Five

THE RUSSIAN WINTER MADE A FINAL RUSH ON MOSCOW the first week of March; the snowflakes rushed hypnotically against the windshield as Leonid Akimovich Kropotkin negotiated the center of the tracks that were developing on Kalinina Prospekt. The Kropotkins lived close to the Kremlin in one of Moscow's finest apartment houses. This was owing to Kropotkin's position in the foreign ministry. Kropotkin refused to use the metro like other people. He owned a Volga and liked to be seen in it.

It was part of the emotional minuet of their married lives—the steps rehearsed and familiar after six years of marriage—that Leonid and Natalia Serafimovna said little on their way home from the party. Natalia waited for the alcohol to fuel her husband's suspicions of her infidelity. He would begin with the accusations. If she said nothing, he would take it as an admission of guilt. If she tried to defend herself, he would become enraged. This opening movement was inevitable. It was always the same. Always. It never varied.

Thus began marital violence as the Kropotkins practiced it. Doomed couples the world over have their own dances, played to different tunes and themes.

Kropotkin seemed more drunk than usual, so Natalia, who knew well the pain of his temper, vowed silence in response to his lead.

"I see you found young Korzov charming company tonight, Natasha." Kropotkin geared down carefully to avoid swerving on the hard-packed snow. When the Volga had been slowed safely, he glanced at her.

Natalia said nothing. The folds of his broad face made him seem suddenly older to her, drunker, meaner.

"If it weren't for me, you'd probably be in a camp like your father. You certainly wouldn't be the most favored *znachok* designer in Moscow. Speak to me."

"Oh, Lyonya." Natalia wanted him to please, please stop. Why couldn't he get horny like other men? Sonia Akimova said her husband got amorous when he was loaded. Sometimes he had a hard time getting it up, Sonia said, but he was always game to try. Not Leonid. Leonid turned mean.

"You shop the best shops because of me. You travel to the Netherlands and the United States because you're married to me. And how do you behave?" He paused. "How?"

Natalia said nothing. Leonid's speech was slurred, a sign he was entering the final stages, teetering above the terrible abyss of mad rage.

"Like a slut is how. A cunt."

"Lyonya." Her voice was small. She was frightened. She had reason to be.

Kropotkin was suddenly calm as they neared their apartment. He parked the car, saying nothing. She followed him inside, still frightened but hoping that the music of paranoia had somehow subsided.

It hadn't. In the elevator he said, "Korzov's an insipid adolescent. Why you're attracted to them is beyond me." By "them," Kropotkin meant younger men. He was twenty-two years older than Natalia and felt his added years gave him character that all younger men, by definition, somehow lacked. It never occurred to him that while some men gain character with age, others lose it—or never had any.

The truth was, Ivan Korzov was forty-four years old and apparently so ambitious as to be indifferent to women; Natalia Kropotkina's women friends suspected him of being a homosexual. Natalia knew her husband: an insecure, flaccid, fifty-four-year-old party suck who had risen above the destroyed careers of competents who favored a more flexible Soviet foreign policy. "We talked about the American elections," she said.

"With Korzov?" Kropotkin was disbelieving, derisive. He unlocked the door of their apartment. He turned, laughing, showing the gold caps on his teeth. "What does Ivan Korzov know about the Americans? Does he shave yet, could you tell?"

"Korzov says the reactionaries will win the presidency again because the American public doesn't trust the Democrats with the economy."

Kropotkin said, "The reactionaries will win again because American companies will see to it that they win. They'll buy the election." That was the correct answer. Korzov had sounded soft. Kropotkin was curious. "Korzov said the Americans don't trust the Democrats? Really?"

Natalia was suddenly concerned that she might inadvertently get Korzov in trouble. "Someone said that. Maybe it wasn't Korzov. Someone said the American public doesn't trust the Democrats. What does it matter who said it? I wasn't interested in Ivan Korzov."

"No? You don't know who said something like that? How could you forget?"

"I talked to a lot of people tonight, Leonid."

"Sure you remember; it was either Korzov or it wasn't. If it wasn't him, who was it? It was Korzov."

"I didn't say that."

"And you wanted to go to bed with him."

"No, Leonid."

"Sure, you did." Kropotkin went into the kitchen and returned with a bottle of vodka and a glass. He poured the glass half full of vodka and took a hit. "I think we should talk, you and me."

"No, please."

Kropotkin finished the glass of vodka and dragged her into the bedroom by the elbow. "Take your clothes off," he said.

Natalia Kropotkina sat on the bed and bent to begin with her boots. She braced herself for the first blow. It came hard, alongside her ear. She cried softly and the next blow came—this one from the other side.

Kropotkin said, "No yelling or you'll regret it."

Natalia said, "Please, Lyonya, not the face this time. I've got a show coming up next weekend."

"Take them off."

As she removed her boots, Kropotkin again struck her on the sides of her head. He threw her against the wall as she pulled her sweater over her head. This was not any kind of agreed-upon sexual drama or mutual exploring of fantasies. In fact, it was not sexual at all. It was Leonid Kropotkin's madness and his wife's pain. He enjoyed it for reasons that were perverse and deviant, not ideological or institutional. Leonid Kropotkin's demons were private and Freudian, found among unfortunate, unacceptable men in all cultures.

Either way, Natalia suffered.

In the end, Natalia Kropotkina was naked and bruised. Her nose was bloody, but she had not suffered the black eye that was her worry, and which was almost impossible to hide with cosmetics. She winced with every breath from a broken rib. This was the eighth or ninth rib that had been fractured from having been slammed against the edge of a dresser. She had lost track of the broken bones.

Kropotkin said, "Now put your clothes on and get out."

Natalia, wincing each time she had to bend or twist her torso, dressed herself and left the apartment to spend the night with her friend Sonia Akimova. Kropotkin's penis was limp on these occasions, paralyzed by vodka; he liked to be left alone to curse women and nurse his hatreds in private.

On the way down the hall to the wing where Sonia and her husband lived, Natalia wondered suddenly what it would be like to shoot Leonid. She hated him. Wanted him dead. Wanted to kill him, although this shocked her because she had always accepted domination. She saw him yelling at her, pushing her. Then she pulled a pistol out of her handbag and shot Leonid and watched him die with a surprised look on his face.

That was what Natalia thought about on her way to Sonia Akimova's.

The Akimovs lived in a hideously cramped, one-bedroom apartment. The Kropotkins had three bedrooms, due to Leonid's influence—he "needed" a study at home.

Sonia Akimova opened the door, knowing who it was because of the time of night. She knew the reason as well. This was not the first of Natalia's early-morning visits. Sonia went to get cigarettes and a bottle of Ukrainian brandy while Natalia curled up on the sofa and wept softly. Neither woman said a word. The only light was the glow of cigarettes. Natalia told Sonia what had happened, what Leonid had done.

Sonia inhaled slowly so that she wouldn't have to say anything. Natalia's stories and questions were always the same. What could she say?

Natalia wiped away her tears with the back of her arm. "It's sick, I know. But there's nothing I can do, nothing. I can't leave him—he'd destroy me with a snap of his fingers."

"You'll have to get your rib taped so you can stand to be on your feet at the showing," Sonia said.

"Ribs heal."

"Yes, Natasha, but the scars remain." Sonia Akimova embraced her friend to help the mending begin yet one more time.

Six

Isaak Avraamovich Ginsburg and the other *zeks* rode like cattle in the empty boxcar that left Moscow the fourth of March. Except for a crack where the edge of the metal door had been twisted in a derailing, the *zeks* could not see the Russian landscape. They didn't care especially. With few exceptions, they knew, the Soviet landscape varied little from Vladivostok on the Sea of Japan to Vyborg on the Finnish border.

Once in a while a bored, doomed *zek* peered through the crack at the forests of white-barked birch trees and the snow. There were aspens, too, with their pale, off-green bark. And spruce.

Isaak Ginsburg met the coughing *zek* on that terrible run to Zima. The train rattled east from Moscow, headed for the Urals, then Siberia: Sverdlovsk, Novosibirsk, and beyond. Zima itself—two hundred miles north of Mongolia—was just west of Irkutsk on the shores of Lake Baikal.

There were forty-two prisoners in the car. Some were first-timers like Ginsburg. Others, like the coughing *zek*, were veterans of the Gulag Archipelago. They knew all about the islands of suffering. They knew Zima would be a dunghill; it was intended as their purgatory.

The coughing *zek* kept to himself yet never strayed far from the largest group in the boxcar. The cougher was a veteran. He coughed until he was weak, then coughed more. It was as though he were trying to turn his torso inside out. He could not stop. Could not. His face went tight with each spasm. His rheumy eyes appeared to see nothing, yet Ginsburg sensed they saw everything.

The boxcar had once carried used tractors, and there were tire prints of black grease on the splintered floor. The veteran *zeks* knew that if they arrived at Zima with black smears on their blue-gray trousers, they would have to answer for it. And it was likely, they knew, they would have to serve their entire sentences with the same annoying grease smears.

There was a crude stove made from a barrel in the center of the boxcar, but it was not used for the first two days. The *zeks* avoided the greasy tire prints, huddling together in the corners to conserve body heat. They cupped their balls with their hands to keep their hands warm. They massaged the toes of one foot with the heel of the other.

The second morning out, Ginsburg took a turn at the door crack, peering out at a frigid Russian morning. Smoke rolled from the chimneys of unpainted peasant huts with roofs of tarpaper or corrugated tin.

Before the *zeks* were shipped from Moscow, a barber had shorn their heads with an enormous pair of Polish-made shears. This was so their heads could be painted with an insecticide to rid them of parasites. They were not bald in the sense of being properly shaven. They simply ended up stupid-looking; scraps of hair stuck up here and there like weeds. Their ears stuck out. They pulled their caps down over their ears, both to keep their heads warm and because they were doing their best to remain dignified in the face of routine humiliation. The *zeks* knew they looked pathetic and so were embarrassed. Except for their memories they owned nothing at all, not even a head of hair.

When he returned from watching the Siberian winter through the crack in the door, Ginsburg knew what he had to do. He had to remember what was being done to him. He would be a witness. He wouldn't have access to pen and paper; he knew that. He had to endure a two-year sentence; Jews had suffered far worse for trying to emigrate. He would need a device of some kind. He began, saying the words softly, turning them over so he could hear their sounds, as a cabinetmaker notes the grain of wood:

Strangely, there were no tears
as we stood before the shears.
On the terrible train I sucked frozen bread.
It was an awful dread.

Ginsburg repeated the lines three times. He would memorize quatrains. Ginsburg was a modernist—a style possible only for underground poets in the Soviet Union—and considered rhyming poems old-fashioned at best, doggerel at worst. He didn't care. The point was solely to help him remember. The rhyming would do that.

Late into the third night, the coughing *zek* said the temperature had dropped to twenty degrees below zero. He said he could calculate the temperature from how long it took spit to freeze. He spat and watched it freeze, counting:

"Oh-deen, dvah, tree, cheh-tee-reh, p'yaht"—one, two, three, four, five.

When the spit had frozen, the *zek* fell into another spell of coughing. An hour later the train stopped, and they were given firewood and coals for the stove.

When the train began moving again, the coughing *zek* eased toward Ginsburg and said softly, "We would have frozen to death if they hadn't given us some wood. After all the work it took them to shear us, they didn't want us to freeze to death. They're efficient that way. We're cheap labor. You'll get just enough of what it takes to live, no more. You'll see.''

The *zeks* formed a line that snaked its way around the stove, into a frigid corner, then back around the stove again. The first rule of the cold was to keep moving. Ginsburg followed the coughing *zek*, who walked with an odd, shuffling, flat-footed gait. As Ginsburg approached the stove the second time, he tried another quatrain:

> We warmed ourselves on imagined fire,
>   the raw edge of desire,
> until our piss splattered like yellow glass and we were
>   given birch to burn,
> Russian style, we lined up for the heat. Each *zek* got a
>   turn.

They stayed awake that night. Those who slept would sleep forever. The train stopped several times. At each stop the *zeks* heard the voices of women traffic controllers giving instructions to engineers and workers in the rail yards over huge loudspeakers. They were wonderful voices, still soft while giving instructions. Ginsburg tried to imagine a woman to match each of the voices.

The fire was cold by dawn, and they knew there would be no heat from the rising sun, a pale orange as it rose through the gloomy industrial haze above a Siberian town up ahead. The sky was a dry, frigid blue above the pall.

Five of the *zeks* had fallen asleep by the time the Soviets gave them more wood. When the fire got going again, the sleeping *zeks* didn't bother to wake up. The other *zeks* stepped over the frozen bodies as though they didn't exist.

They were given their food for that day late in the afternoon—a tepid, cloudy soup that featured small bits of fat. Ginsburg drank his gratefully. The coughing *zek* consumed his soup quickly, dining by the feet of one of the dead men. The workers who delivered the soup noted the bodies when they collected the bowls and the huge pot.

When the soup people had gone, the coughing *zek*— sensing it was safe because the bodies had been left behind—began quickly stripping the frozen corpse of its clothes. The other experienced *zeks* did the same thing; they were upon the frozen *zeks* with feral quickness. Now dressed in an extra layer of clothing, the veterans dragged the pathetic bodies to one corner of the car and stored them with their spines and wood-hard buttocks toward the center of the boxcar. Nobody wanted to look at their faces.

At the next stop the train halted again, and they were given more wood. The men who delivered wood pretended they didn't see the frozen, naked bodies in the corner of the boxcar.

When the fire was going again and the temperature in the boxcar was bearable, the coughing *zek* took Isaak Ginsburg aside. "You should not memorize your poetry out loud where other *zeks* can hear. There are people who would use it against you. It's bad enough on the outside; in the camps it's worse."

Ginsburg knew the *zek* was right.

"You don't know these men," the *zek* said. He was scolding Ginsburg, master to apprentice. Ginsburg had a lot to learn if he were to survive.

Ginsburg said, "I wasn't thinking."

"You're a Jew, aren't you?" The *zek* coughed.

Ginsburg nodded yes.

The *zek* said, "Trust no one. Be invisible."

The clanging and banging of metal on metal got louder as the train hit a rough stretch of track. The *zek* seemed lost in thought as they both considered the racket. He was overcome by another attack of coughing. Ginsburg knew he wanted to say something more.

"Go ahead, tell me," Ginsburg said.

The *zek* coughed. "Those poems . . . they're so you can remember, am I right?"

"Yes, they are."

The cougher lowered his voice to a bare whisper. He looked at Ginsburg with his sad eyes. "If I make it to Zima, I'm going to kill myself, first chance I get. I've been in one or another of these camps for sixteen years. When you've been gone that long, there's no reason for them to send you back. Everybody's forgotten by now. I'm tired of coughing. I'm dying. It hurts too much to continue." He coughed again. Ginsburg started to object, but the *zek* took him by the arm. "This is best for me, believe me. What are you here for?"

Ginsburg smiled. "Parasitism."

"You're here for being Jewish and a writer."

"Yes."

"For how long?"

"Two years."

The cougher considered that. "That's not bad. I'd count on more time than that if I were you."

"How much more time?"

"You can always figure on a couple more years. They'll get you for something. They'll do something to you. It's usually more time." The *zek* fell silent. "But not always," he said. "It could be something else. Sometimes more time is preferable."

The cougher looked around to see if they were clear of eavesdroppers. "I had a friend once in one of these camps. His name was Dr. Serafim Korenkho and he shared a potato with me when we were both starving." The *zek* paused. "Later they sent him to one of their extermination camps. I promised him when I got out that I'd tell his daughter what happened to him."

"His daughter?"

"Natalia. The last Serafim heard she was married to a man named Kropotkin who's in the foreign service. She's an artist. She designs *znachki*."

"*Znachki!*" The ubiquitous *znachki* were patriotic

lapel pins that featured Lenin's head or commemorated socialist accomplishments.

"Serafim said some artists are good at doing horses or dancers; his daughter is good at doing Lenin. He said Natalia's designs must be approved by a committee of party members. The Kropotkins live in Moscow, although they have lived overseas, in New York, Serafim said, and Holland. She would be about your age."

"What happened to Korenkho? I want to hear the rest of it." Ginsburg was curious about Natalia Kropotkina.

The melancholy cougher considered that. He looked around. "After a while ears get curious." He walked away, flat-footed.

Later he returned to finish his story.

The coughing *zek* removed the second layer of clothing that he had stolen earlier from the frozen corpse. He held the clothing out to Ginsburg. "Put this on."

Ginsburg said, "No."

"I said to put it on," the cougher said. "This is my choice. It is what separates men from dogs, I think. I may have forgotten the difference." The cougher smiled sadly. "I still have this right." When Ginsburg took the clothing, the cougher squatted and removed his shoes. He gave Ginsburg both pairs of socks, pulling them off two at a time. "See, no toes," he said. "Lost 'em two years ago. Socks don't do me much good." He embraced Ginsburg, then lay down on the icy floor of the boxcar. Without looking up, he said, "Believe me, I'm tired. I want to go to sleep." The *zek* repressed a cough.

Ginsburg knew the cougher had decided. There was no turning back.

The *zek* said, "I ask a favor."

"Certainly."

"I want you to keep my promise to Serafim Korenkho."

"Done."

The cougher sighed. "Thank you, my friend. Best to

stay well clear of me so as not to remind the others that you have three pairs of socks.''

Ginsburg did as he was told, and after a while the coughing *zek* stopped coughing, and his body was stripped by one of the living, a younger *zek* who had watched in frustration as the veterans beat him to the corpses the first time around. This time he was ready. He worked quickly, and when he came to the cougher's toeless, bare feet, he cursed and glared at Ginsburg; his eyes were furious.

The *zeks* arrived at Zima in the midmorning with a pale sun providing no heat at all. A terrible wind buffeted the train while they waited at the siding. Finally a truck backed up to the door of the boxcar. Two workers wearing heavy coats and breathing in great, frosty puffs stepped inside the boxcar and set about collecting seventeen frozen, nude corpses, including the one who had coughed his last the night before. The workers, who had Asian faces, seemed not to care that they were dealing with human beings. They slung the Leninist jetsam into the back of the truck, where the corpses hit with a hollow thump and tumbled to rest, arms and legs sticking this way and that.

The workers were in a hurry to get in out of the cold. When the bodies were on board, they slammed the rear door shut and raced for the shelter of the cab. The truck departed for the camp furnaces with an impatient grinding of gears and plunged across frozen potholes at high speed, the driver seemingly oblivious to the damage he was causing the truck. In the back, the frozen corpses banged and rattled like wooden chairs.

The twenty-five remaining *zeks*, grateful to be alive, were loaded onto a second truck.

Isaak Ginsburg had not only arrived at Zima alive, but with all his toes as well. He .was the only *zek* from his car who could say that. Ginsburg almost wished he had lost at least one toe. He was too lucky. Something awful would happen to make up for his intact feet. Since religion was officially prohibited in the USSR, the Russians were given to superstition. Ginsburg was no different. He had a sinking feeling in his stomach.

Just what would the punishment be? he wondered as he bounced along in the back of the truck. What would make up for his having arrived at Zima with toes that would still move the next day?

A corporal with an AK-47 slung over his shoulder flung open the truck door and shouted, "Out, out, out!" He had an unemotional peasant's face. He watched them with the indifference of a sated lizard. Two privates watched, also with reptilian eyes and AK-47s. The stiff, shivering *zeks* began to climb slowly off the back of the truck. The terrible wind knifed through them. They were weak. Their joints ached.

Standing on the back of the truck, waiting for his turn to lower himself to the ground, Ginsburg saw they were only a couple of miles east of Zima; the camp was on the edge of the sprawl of peasant huts that led to all Siberian towns. Ginsburg could see the train station from the back of the truck. As he lowered himself to the frozen earth, he heard the horn of a train just south of the camp. In fact, he saw it.

It was red with a yellow stripe down its side. The air horn of the Trans-Siberian Express went *hnnnnnnaaaaaa* as the train passed the camp, slowing for the white station house up ahead. There would be a fifteen-minute stop at Zima while the brakes were checked with the thump of a carman's hammer and the diesel was replenished.

"Form a line! Form a line or you'll be shot!" the corporal shouted.

The *zeks* quickly formed a line.

Seven

CAPTAIN YEVGENNI MIKHEYEV, COMMANDANT OF THE people's lumber camp at Zima, watched the *zeks* as they were unloaded from the truck. Mikheyev wore polished black boots. The hem of his immaculately tailored gray officer's coat fell to the middle of his calves—a design for Siberian winters. His aide had treated his *papakha* with lanolin, and it glistened in the cold morning light.

It was the misfortune of Captain Mikheyev's *zeks* that their commander had succumbed completely to the warming succor of the Leninist vision, thus relieving himself of the burden of conscience. Mikheyev was numbed beyond recovery by the coarseness of his profession. He was insensitive to irony and contradiction. Having lost whatever it is that separates men from beasts, Mikheyev ended up a casual brute, pathetic in his way, different from gorillas and baboons mainly in that he had larger genitalia.

Ordinarily Mikheyev preferred to sleep in on Saturday mornings and rub his face against Anna's soft, flubbery white breasts. When she was in the mood she let Mikheyev twist her nipples while she made horny little noises in her throat. Unfortunately, regulations required that a camp commandant meet each shipment of *zeks* personally, in immaculate military dress. Mikheyev expected his career to rise without a hitch; he followed regulations.

The corporal gave the truckdriver the information he needed to complete the forms necessary to conclude the transaction. When the corporal got the *zeks* squared away into a line of lonely, cold, and frightened men, he said, "Captain Commandant Yevgenni Mikheyev will have a word with you."

Captain Mikheyev lit a cigarette, inhaled, and took two steps forward. He spoke so quietly, his prisoners could hardly hear him.

"My name is Mikheyev. I own you while you are here. You have work to do and you will do it. You will work twelve hours a day, seven days a week with the logs there." Mikheyev gestured at the logs. "On the seventh day you will work longer so that the camp may be kept clean."

Mikheyev smoked. He took his time, making the shivering *zeks* wait. "If you disobey the rules, you will be flogged, put into solitary confinement, shot, or whatever other punishment occurs to me. You'll find that this punishment varies according to the severity of the infraction and according to my mood. You may be assured that I can be quite imaginative."

Eight

THE COMPANY REPRESENTATIVE WHO RECEIVED CONTACT David's message, Rennie Kriss, was allegedly an agent of Trans-Global Enterprises Ltd., a British importer of Middle Eastern handicrafts. Kriss, who grew up in Australia, had what could be palmed off on nonnative speakers of English as a British accent. Kriss insisted that the message be sent to Company headquarters in Langley, Virginia, via courier rather than coded cable.

Nine

Natalia Kropotkina's friend Sonia Akimova was in a contemplative mood when she swung her green Lada into the parking space to the rear of St. Basil's Cathedral. The warming May sun shone on the cathedral's colorful domes and made Moscow almost balmy. The two women walked to the southern end of Red Square and made their way through the visitors toward GUM, the Queen Mother of Soviet department stores.

Natalia had good reason to be in bad spirits. The selection committee had awarded her the pin commemorating Ivan Dmitrov's monumental Lenin statue in Oktyabrskaya Square, only to overturn the award for reasons that were obscure. Those who claimed to know said Natalia was becoming an individualist and so needed taking down a notch.

The reason for Sonia's moodiness was less clear.

GUM formed the eastern boundary of Red Square, and sat almost opposite Lenin's mausoleum. This was the heart of Moscow—right in the middle of Intourist hotel country—and so foreign visitors mingled among Russians. Intourist guides told the foreigners that a visit to GUM was a must, like the V. I. Lenin Museum, the

45

State Historical Museum, the Pushkin Fine Arts Museum, the Bolshoi, and so on; GUM was a Soviet showcase.

At GUM, Soviet citizens were treated to the cornucopia of Leninist economics.

Because of her marriage to Leonid Kropotkin, Natalia had a card that admitted her to the privileged sanctuary of reserved shops in GUM. These shops for the extra-equal comrades were on the third floor, past a long bank of shops that were empty and closed. Natalia was able to take one guest with her—in this case Sonia. Sonia couldn't buy anything, however; Natalia had to do that.

For her part, Sonia had a friend, Ekaterina, who had a contact inside GUM; the contact knew about the arrival of decent items that were scarce even for the party elite.

"Katya's never been wrong yet, has she, Natalia? Not once." Sonia had access to theater tickets that Ekaterina did not have, and so was the frequent recipient of Ekaterina's GUM tips, this one for wool sweaters. "Irish wool," Sonia said. "Polish at worst. A lot of sizes, Katya says."

"Maybe you'll find something," Natalia said. Sonia was slender but large-busted, and a Russian sweater in combination with a Russian bra made her look like a 1950s American movie starlet.

Sonia hated having her breasts stick out like the ends of rockets. "Well, maybe this time. I'd like something handsome and a bit loose, you know. Maybe something like those sweaters we saw in the Finnish magazine." Sonia had cooled on the shopping trip at the last minute, and Natalia had had to talk her into coming. Now Sonia was cheering up again.

"After we shop, what do you say we have a drink at the National? I got my card renewed." This was a treat for Sonia, Natalia knew. Every time they went to GUM, they visited the bar in the National, where it was possible to have an Old Crow. Sonia loved American whiskey and the intimacy of the bar where foreign guests had a drink after a day of sightseeing.

"Let's try something different this time—the Rossiya. We're in a rut, don't you think?"

Natalia was surprised but tried not to show it. Sonia professed to dislike the Rossiya. "Sure. Wherever you like."

"You have a card for the Rossiya too, don't you?"

"I've got a Rossiya card."

Sonia looked pleased. "Good, then the Rossiya it is." She followed Natalia through the entrance of GUM and under a net hung to catch plaster that was crumbling from a decorative arch.

Sonia said, "You want to look at the *znachki* before we go upstairs?" She knew Natalia would be eager to look at the largest collection of commemorative pins for sale in the Soviet Union. This shop, in the southeast corner of the courtyard nearest Red Square, had 350 numbered pins mounted on a wall behind glass.

"Oh, sure," Natalia said. Seventeen of the pins that featured Lenin were hers, including the top two bestsellers in the Soviet Union for three years running. The *znachok* shop in GUM always made Natalia feel wonderful. It wasn't hard to spot Natalia's pins: they were the class of the lot.

Natalia Kropotkina found it impossible to go shopping at GUM without remembering the department stores in the Netherlands and the United States where her husband had been posted—first at The Hague, then at the United Nations. Having had a bite of that wonderful capitalist apple, she wanted more. When Natalia returned to the Soviet Union, she had been appalled at the lines and deprivation she had formerly taken for granted.

Natalia's only hope of going back to the West was through Leonid, and she knew it.

Natalia Kropotkina had shopped in Bloomingdale's,

and so no longer believed the Soviets' claim that GUM was the best department store in the world.

If the Soviets had claimed GUM was the grandest-looking, or had the most curious architecture, they would have had an argument. On the outside, the store looked like a gilded warehouse of industrial charm. On the inside, however, GUM was lovely. Tiers of classic Roman columns rose impressively—if decoratively—around two long, rectangular courtyards that formed the dramatic center of the GUM architecture. Between the columns were the facades of small shops, three floors of them.

Shoppers strolled along elegant Victorian balconies overlooking the ground floor. It was possible to lean against the black iron rail and watch shoppers queuing up at the wine shop, the ice cream stall, and the bakery near the entrance. High above the hubbub of shoppers there was a vast rounded skylight made of hundreds of small panes of glass. Thus shoppers enjoyed the sunshine that suffused the civilized courtyards with a natural, warming glow. The shops beneath the skylights were painted pale blues and greens. Cooling colors for the long waits, went a Moscow joke.

Natalia Kropotkina knew that American entrepreneurs would have turned the lovely GUM building into a truly fabulous store—fashionable, possibly filled with trendy eateries. In New York, Natalia had been in stores with fashion shows, stores with disco music and flashing lights to add a festive, gay atmosphere.

The Leninists would say this was extravagant, she knew, wasteful. Still, it was wonderful to watch people have a good time and to shop free from want. It was almost as though the Russians were closet masochists, preferring sacrifice and deprivation to laughter and joy.

The shops in the lovely GUM building were determinedly, steadfastly utilitarian. A state monopoly had no reason to charm or please its customers, and so each shop had the decor and warmth of a garage sale. Each little cell, whether it offered blouses or underwear, was seemingly indifferent to quality and fashion. There were four walls, a ceiling, tables for display—that was it. If you wanted a coat, there was a coat shop, drab wraps hung on metal racks. A customer looked at herself or himself in a plain mirror and either bought or chose not to buy; the state didn't care. If you wanted shoes, there were bins of shoes. In GUM you waited in line always. There was an unsmiling clerk to take your order. There was an unsmiling clerk to total the bill on an abacus.

Following Sonia into an underwear shop, Natalia remembered the fabulous lingerie for sale in Dutch and American stores. Natalia hadn't been able to believe it at first. She had bought everything she could get her hands on. Provocative panties with strings that untied at the hip. Translucent panties to please imaginative capitalist men. Little shifts that didn't cover enough of your breasts. Bras that didn't feel as if you were wearing birdcages or chain mail on your chest.

None of this did any good with Leonid, however. Natalia only succeeded in arousing him to anger, not passion. He could only worry that some other man might have seen her looking this splendid or would in the future. It apparently never occurred to him to give the strings a pull and see what would happen. Natalia Kropotkina had a fabulous figure and knew it. She dreamed of meeting a man who would pull the strings unabashedly and enjoy. She could give him a little show. Turn him on. Why not? Was this a decadent, Western fantasy? she wondered. Was there something wrong with her? She thought about this at night, her hand at her crotch, middle finger moving, while her fantasy lover watched, pleased, encouraging her, making outrageous suggestions. All this while Leonid—his suspicions drowned by sleep—lay snoring heavily, dreaming what?

Last week Leonid had caught Natalia, dressed in a pair of her American panties, admiring the curve of her hip in her dressing mirror. He had thrown her against the wall so hard it knocked the wind out of her and brought a retaliatory thump from the apartment next door.

Natalia Kropotkina was curious about Sonia's sudden preference for the Rossiya over the National and was somehow disturbed by it. They had just stepped outside GUM, by the gray juice machines, when Natalia said, "I say we have our drink at the National, Sonia. I hate the Rossiya." Natalia had the entrance permit; there was nothing Sonia could do.

Sonia looked stricken. "I thought we had already decided."

"I don't like the Rossiya," Natalia said. She turned in the direction of the National and began walking with a stride that said she had made up her mind.

Sonia was suddenly agitated. She glanced at her wristwatch. "If you insist," she said.

Natalia led the way into the National through the revolving door, past the doorman who checked pass cards, and up a short flight of broad, carpeted stairs. At the top of the stairs, turning right toward the bar, she saw the reason for Sonia's nervousness.

Straight in front of the open door, at a window table overlooking the Square of the Fiftieth Anniversary of the October Revolution, Leonid Kropotkin sat, looking south toward Lenin's tomb. He was holding the hand of a slender, blond woman.

Natalia pretended that she had seen nothing. She was furious. At Leonid. At Sonia. After they were seated, she drank her Pernod in thoughtful, stony silence.

Later, as they walked across Red Square to Sonia's car, Natalia exploded, "How could you have, Sonia? How could you?"

"You saw him, then?"

"Yes, I saw him! How long have you been working for him? Just what is it he wants to know?"

"He wants to know if you're seeing another man. He says he's certain you've been seeing another man. He wants to know who. Today, he wanted me to keep you out of the National."

"You knew why, I take it."

"I guessed it, Natalia. I didn't have any choice. Your husband doesn't leave people choices."

"I know that," Natalia said. "Who is the woman?"

"If you could get tickets to the Bolshoi this weekend, you could see her dance."

What Sonia said was true; no doubt she hadn't had a choice in the matter. Natalia didn't want to know the form of coercion, whether it was a threat of punishment or promise of reward. What did that matter now? She knew, as a Russian, that friends were often required to spy on friends. Some of the stories of treachery were awful. Still, Natalia had not expected it to happen to her. Not her.

Her husband beat her and she was unable to fight back. Now this! Finding out that the jealous Leonid was himself an adulterer was nothing compared to the outrage of losing Sonia as a friend. Why did Leonid feel it was necessary to use Sonia? There had to have been a way that would have been just as efficient and caused less misery.

On the way back they saw a line suddenly gather on the sidewalk outside of a small food market. "Cucumbers, do you think?" Sonia asked. She pulled quickly to the curb.

Natalia joined the line without seeing what it led to. Sonia checked up ahead and came back to join Natalia, grinning. "Even better. Green beans. They're beautiful!"

"Green beans!" Natalia spoke with self-conscious gaiety. There was no reversing the clock for herself and Sonia.

Ten

It was Isaak Ginsburg's misfortune, when he was called before the commandant, that the May 9 anniversary of the Soviet Union's victory in the Great Patriotic War of 1941–45 was just three days away and Anna Mikheyev was entering the first day of her period. During the prior ill-tempered week, Anna's hormones had made her so jittery and tense that she couldn't stand to be touched. Mikheyev's hand on her breast felt like squeaky chalk on a blackboard. Anna's jumpiness had put Mikheyev in a foul mood.

No good could come from a meeting with a camp commandant. All *zeks* knew that. For a commandant to call a prisoner to his office and then not punish him was unthinkable; it invited unrest. A conscientious commandant, to insure a sufficient level of intimidation, always made a prisoner's humiliation public. This insured a smooth-running camp at a minimum of expense to the government.

Ginsburg was escorted to Mikheyev's office by two privates with AK-47s slung over their shoulders, and was ushered into the office without a word being spoken. Yevgenni Mikheyev looked up at a portrait of

52

Lenin on the wall and made a sucking sound with his lips.

This was the first time Ginsburg had seen Mikheyev close up. Owing to a wide jaw and broad forehead, Mikheyev's face was shaped something like the figure eight with a blunted middle. His nose was both wide and short, but turned up slightly at the end. He had huge dirty blond eyebrows that needed plucking; an abundance of hair grew out of the bottoms of his ears. He had long, slack hair, also a dirty blond, that he habitually combed back with his fingers—a nervous tic of long standing.

Mikheyev's military tunic was covered with heavy campaign medals and bright ribbons. He seemed to have one of everything the Red Army had ever awarded, but he didn't look like the kind of man who would rise to command anything. Ginsburg wondered if he might not be the grandson of General Yuri Mikheyev, a hero of the seige of Leningrad.

The commandant looked down at Ginsburg's file on his desk. Ginsburg saw it was identical to the one Felix Jin had consulted—complete with his University of Moscow photo and the Writers Union objections to his poetry—and wondered if this rap sheet of his life, the summary of the party's complaints against Citizen Isaak Ginsburg, a slandering, possibly psychopathic Jew, an individualist, might not follow him for the rest of his days.

Mikheyev made a great show of comparing the photo in the file with the dark-eyed man standing before him. When he was satisfied they were the same, he said, "Prisoner Ginsburg." This statement set out the nature of their relationship. "I am the grandson of General Yuri Mikheyev, but I suppose you've been told that."

"Yes," Ginsburg lied. He wanted to say his grandfather was Salomon Ginsburg, who had been there with Lenin, but he held his tongue. Intellectuals like his grandfather had brought about a successful revolution against the czar. Joseph Stalin did not trust independent imaginations, which was why he had murdered just about every one he could find. This fear, still prevalent at the Kremlin, was the reason Ginsburg was at Mikheyev's office in Zima.

"So you know I do my duty. My grandfather did his duty. I do mine. Your file says you are a parasite. You libeled your country with your scribbling. What do you have to say for yourself? Answer now, don't just stand there."

"I wrote about small moments, comrade, not politics."

"That's not what the president of the Writers Union says. It's right here, Ginsburg. Do you mean to argue with the president of the Writers Union? Are you saying he doesn't know how to read poetry?"

"I don't mean to say that at all—"

"Well, then?" Mikheyev interrupted.

"I—"

"Felix Jin says you are not to write poetry during your sentence, Ginsburg. Right here, he says it: 'This man is not to write or recite poetry during his incarceration.' " Mikheyev tapped his finger on the line where Jin had made his notation. "I know of Felix Jin," he lied. "A thoughtful man. Have you been writing poetry, Prisoner Ginsburg?"

Isaak Ginsburg knew he was about to pay for having arrived at Zima with ten toes. "No, comrade," he said.

"You're a liar. You were overheard reciting it aloud on the train coming here. Do you deny it?"

Ginsburg said nothing.

"Answer me, *zek*."

"I was remembering old poems, not writing new ones," Ginsburg said.

"Well, you're a liar, Ginsburg. You were overheard reciting poetry on the train from Moscow." The commandant ran his fingers through his blond hair, then opened a pack of Russian cigarettes. He lit one, watching the *zek* in front of him. Mikheyev was suddenly furious.

"Twenty million people died for our country in the Great Patriotic War." Mikheyev had been watching heroic war movies and patriotic documentaries all week on television. "Twenty million!"

"I was given to understand I was not to compose."

"Twenty million!" Mikheyev shouted. "Lying parasite! And you criticize!"

The commandant scribbled a note in Ginsburg's dossier.

Mikheyev took a handkerchief from his pocket and blew his nose. "The problem is you think too much, Ginsburg. We need to give you something to think about other than poetry," he said. He mopped up the moist leavings at the bottom of his nose.

Mikheyev pondered, and then his face brightened. He looked pleased. "Let's see, I'll give you a week to heal before you ride the train back. That ought to do it. You need to be up and around if you expect to ride the train to the relocation center at Gorky, eh, Prisoner Ginsburg?

"Two weeks in solitary confinement. One week before you leave, you'll be made to pay for libeling your country and ignoring the conditions of your sentence. It will be done at the dispensary by Dr. Aleshkin. An imaginative cut—Aleshkin has the skill, I'm sure. You should be well enough to travel in a week." Mikheyev did not want questions. "If I catch you writing poetry again, I'll have your fingers smashed. What I am going to have done to you will make you understand that the knife is more powerful than the word, just as the state is superior to the individual."

While Ginsburg watched, aghast, Captain Mikheyev picked up a ball-point pen and detailed the sentence in Ginsburg's file so that the camp surgeon might perform the unspecified surgical punishment two years hence.

"You'll be a far different man when you leave than when you arrived, Ginsburg. I guarantee. Now leave."

The *zeks* at Zima were housed in a low building with a corrugated tin roof. The building had four wings, one of them longer than the others, so that it was shaped like a crucifix. The compound was surrounded by a fifteen-foot-high barbed-wire fence. Ten yards beyond that there was an even higher wooden fence; the outer fence was topped by three strands of barbed wire. There were towers on all four corners of the compound and a tower in the center. The central tower contained a huge searchlight.

There was a storage area for great piles of logs to the west of the fence—toward Zima. To Ginsburg this was a mountain of logs. The logs were guarded by yet another barbed-wire fence.

Ginsburg had two years to consider Mikheyev's sentence. He could not write; that was out of the question, he knew. Ginsburg was determined that Mikheyev would not rob him of his passion and imagination. The question was, what would he become on his release? How would he live each day?

There were no trees inside the compound and the twenty-foot-high wooden fence blocked out the leafing birches in the spring. The lovely images and moments of truth that had been the pleasure of Ginsburg's life were gone. He didn't try to recover the loss. It didn't occur to him even to try in his colorless world.

Ginsburg's unspecified surgery triggered endless speculation and macabre jokes among the *zeks*: just what would happen to Ginsburg? The punishment would require a week's time for Ginsburg to heal—enough to travel, however much the pain.

Aleshkin, the doctor, would do what had to be done. Just what could that be? What? The worst was unthinkable.

Ginsburg plunged himself into his work in order to forget and so that the time would pass more quickly. Work hard and the time would go faster, he believed. The *zeks* worked twelve hours a day, seven days a week. Ginsburg hooked a chain around a log so that a boom might swing it into a new pile. He did this wearing bulky gloves in the bitter winter and shirtless in the summer.

If the wind was right, the *zeks* could hear the women giving instructions to engineers and brakemen over the loudspeakers at the Zima railroad station.

The *zeks* memorized the voices of those who worked the various shifts and gave them names: Sasha, Anna, Olga. Olga worked graveyard and had a warm, soft voice. Ginsburg thought Olga's instructions were wonderful as they rode gentle breezes, floating across shacks and mud in the spring and summer, across the snow and ice in the winter.

Ginsburg wasn't Olga's only admirer among the prisoners at Zima. Olga's soft voice was, by common agreement of the *zeks*, far superior to those of Sasha, who worked days, and Anna, who worked swing. Anna had a harsh voice. She would be heavy-hipped, the *zeks* reckoned: she would trudge when she walked.

The *zeks* survived off a chunk of bread and a cup of water in the morning, some rice with a chunk of fat at noon, and a watery gruel at night that was supposed to be borscht. The borscht featured a hunk of fat on Tuesday and one thin slice of sausage on Thursday. One *zek* was detailed to ration the slices. On Sunday the *zeks* got a cup of tea and that was wonderful, a treat. Sometimes, in late fall and early winter, they got crumbs of potato or bits of beet in their borscht. Their only utensils were their fingers.

In two years Ginsburg had fresh vegetables just twice: two slices of cucumber on May Day. This bounty was to celebrate the working people of the world, and was observed, as were all their meals, by a six-foot-high portrait of Lenin on one wall of the mess hall. Ginsburg weighed 170 pounds when he began. At the end he weighed 118 pounds and had loose teeth.

Ginsburg shared a six-foot-by-five-foot wooden cell with a squat Georgian named Lado Kabakhidze, a widower whose daughter Nina was a conductress on the

Trans-Siberian Express. Kabakhidze was serving time at
Zima for black-market activities. He had gotten caught,
he said, for swapping the people's cheese for Greek
shoes smuggled across the Black Sea in a Turkish fishing boat.

Kabakhidze said he had originally been sentenced to
four years, but this had been extended two years by
Mikheyev, who, in a fit of rage at the camp's mediocre
production, claimed that Kabakhidze, among others, was
a lazy shirker of his duties as a prisoner.

Ginsburg and Kabakhidze passed their few leisure
hours playing chess on a board scratched onto the wooden
floor of their tiny cell. They used scraps of wood for
their men. They used their thumbnails to mark their
wins, losses, and draws on the wall. They took turns
cleaning the tin can that was their toilet. And they
talked.

One night when they were alone, and cold, and listening to the silence of the Siberian winter, Ginsburg told
Kabakhidze of his promise to the coughing *zek*. He told
Kabakhidze how the cougher had given him his second
layer of clothing and both pairs of socks and had curled
up to sleep his last.

"It was on our last night on the train, Lado. The
cougher sought me out and put his arms around me and
told me to keep moving; we would share our heat. We
were on the edge. I thought I would die that night."

"You're still alive," Kabakhidze said.

Ginsburg smiled, remembering. "Because of him.
And he was alive, he said, because of a physician
named Serafim Korenkho, who shared a potato with him
when they were both starving. In saving the cougher's
life, Korenkho saved mine."

"That's something you don't forget, Isaak."

"The cougher told me Korenkho was sent to Slansky
because he refused to experiment on human subjects.
There's a slate mine there, and that's where the cougher
knew him. About three years ago, Korenkho was trans-

ferred to an underground uranium mine at Asht, in the Tadzhik Republic. The cougher said they make no effort to protect the *zeks* from radiation in the uranium mines, in the uranium enrichment plants, or when they clean the nozzles of atomic submarines.''

''You come out with cancer,'' Kabakhidze said. ''Those are death camps, Isaak.'' He adjusted himself under his blanket. ''I had a friend once, Isaak. But that's a long story.''

''The cougher wanted me to know so I could remember.''

''What happened to Korenkho?''

''A *zek* who knew him at Slansky told the cougher he saw Korenkho a couple of years ago. This *zek* was pulled off his train to help load and unload supplies that had arrived on the same train. The supplies turned out to be medical equipment destined for a clinic that was surrounded by dormitories.''

''At Perm, this was?'' Kabakhidze asked.

Ginsburg studied Lado's profile in the near darkness. ''Yes. How did you know?''

''It's one of those stories you hear if you spend enough time in the camps. My friend may have ended up there. The story is they do research on cancer victims. They don't need rats or monkeys. They have all the real people they need to test their drugs and operations.''

''The *zek* told the cougher he saw Korenkho sitting in a room watching television with some other patients. He was pale and was sitting with a tube draining black fluid from his lungs into a bottle on the floor. After the trucks were unloaded, the *zek* was taken back to the station and put into another carload of prisoners.''

Kabakhidze said, ''That's the place. Has to be.''

''The cougher's friend said the clinic is located on the east side of Perm, that is east of the Kama River. He said there's a huge bluff north of the railway tracks with apartment buildings on top of the bluff and a valley of log huts below. That's where the clinic is, at the northern end of the valley. The cougher wanted Korenkho's daughter to know about the potato. He wanted her to know the kind of man her father was. The cougher was starving and Korenkho shared.''

"You don't forget somebody like that."

"The cougher said Natalia Serafimovna is married to a man named Kropotkin. She designs commemorative *znachki.* Can you believe that? After what they did to her father?''

"People do what they must do, Isaak."

"She's about my age and has a Moscow residence permit.''

"If Mikheyev doesn't extend your sentence, you'll be getting out of here before me. You should look up my daughter, Nina.'' Lado Kabakhidze fell silent, then he said, "I hate this fucking cold, Isaak. If Mikheyev extends my sentence again, I'll die here. It was warm in Georgia; they grow lemons there. Nina looks like her mother did when she was young. Did I tell you that?''

Eleven

Isaak Ginsburg's scheduled March 4 release date came and went with no word from the camp administration. Each day Ginsburg awoke, wondering if that was to be his day. When the guard unlocked the cell door for breakfast and work on March 12, he said, "No breakfast for you this morning, Ginsburg. You are to report to the infirmary at three o'clock today. Where are you scheduled to work?"

"Helping unload the train." Ginsburg swallowed. A wave of anxiety washed through his body and he felt giddy.

The sergeant wrote a note on a small pad and gave it to him. "Give this to your shift foreman. You're to remain in the yards today. We'll send someone for you."

Within a half hour all the *zeks* and guards at the Zima lumber camp knew this was Isaak Ginsburg's day. The other prisoners watched Ginsburg out of the corners of their eyes.

Isaak Ginsburg walked to the infirmary in the company of two young men carrying AK-47s. He wondered, as he made his way along the muddy trail, if he shouldn't make a break for it—try for a burst of 7.76mm slugs in his back.

Ginsburg didn't run. He was taken to the infirmary, which was in a short wing of the compound. The commandant's office was just down the hall together with the offices of his chief administrators. The infirmary people ordinarily had little to do except amputate frozen fingers and toes and dispose of dead *zeks*. Ginsburg was a special case.

The chief medical officer at the infirmary was named Fyodr Dmitrevich Aleshkin. The onerous task of carrying out the commandant's instructions had fallen upon him. He hated it, but it was either do this or face similar treatment himself. While poor red-headed Aleshkin had never been what you would call the model of the healing physician, he was nonetheless a civilized human being and did his best for the *zeks* at Zima.

Aleshkin's hand trembled visibly and he cleared his throat as he ushered Isaak Ginsburg into the barren room where operations were performed. The operating table, Ginsburg saw, had wheels on it. It was portable. "Ginsburg, is it?" Aleshkin asked.

"Yes," Ginsburg said. He could hardly breathe. He hoped he wasn't going to faint. He willed himself to stay on his feet. Get it over with. "What are you going to do?"

Aleshkin ignored the question. "If, uh, you'll take off your clothes, please."

Do what you have to do, Aleshkin, Ginsburg thought. He put his cap on a nearby chair and bent to remove his shoes, wondering if he could straighten up again or if he would fall flat on his face. He began unbuttoning his shirt.

Aleshkin said, "We'll knock you out. You won't feel anything when you wake up because of the drug. When you wake up, Captain Mikheyev wishes to talk to you. After a couple of hours, there'll be quite a lot of pain. You'll be very sore."

Ginsburg's mouth was dry.

"I'll try to do a good job," Aleshkin said. "In time you'll heal. I'll give you some medicine."

Good job? Heal? There was no sense pestering Aleshkin with questions, he knew. Aleshkin had his orders. "Please get on with it," Ginsburg said.

Aleshkin said, "Yes."

Ginsburg climbed up on the table, which had a pad on it, covered with a sheet. That was the first time he had been on a sheet in two years. He lay back as if he were in a dream. Someone took his forearm, and Ginsburg felt a needle. A warm wave flushed across his face. He hadn't felt this good in two years, warm, drifty, ethereal.

All this for the offense of having memorized doggerel in a freezing boxcar.

Ginsburg realized this barbarity was part of the discipline his well-intentioned grandfather Salomon had helped bring about. Ginsburg felt his arms being tied down. He saw that Aleshkin had another hypodermic.

He heard Aleshkin saying, "I don't have any choice in this matter, Ginsburg."

Ginsburg said, "Without choice we are dogs, Aleshkin. Without choice we bark at the moon. When it sets, we bark even louder. Do what you think you have to do. Get it over with." He watched as Aleshkin slid a second needle into his arm.

Isaak Ginsburg awoke in Captain Mikheyev's office. He was still on his back, his arms still strapped to the table. There was a huge poster of Lenin on the wall. This wasn't the usual hard-jawed, determined Lenin. This was a casual Lenin wearing a blue cap with a small bill. Ginsburg was still drifty, confused. He looked at the portrait.

The cloudy figures and figureless voices in the rising fog rolled something else into the room. Another table? Ginsburg turned his head to the side. There was a cloth draped over something small in the middle of the table. He heard a voice. Aleshkin? "He'll be clearing in a few minutes," the voice said. Yes, Aleshkin. Someone else spoke. Mikheyev? Isaak Ginsburg saw the commandant standing there in his trim officer's tunic.

"Well, Ginsburg, how does it feel?" Mikheyev asked.

Ginsburg felt no pain or discomfort anywhere, and said so. He was still woozy from the drug.

Aleshkin said, "I told you. It's the Sodium Pentothal."

Ginsburg could still see and hear. He could talk. He had his tongue. So much for one fear that had plagued his nightmares for months. He clenched his fists. His fingers were present. He moved his ankles; he still had feet.

"Are you clear now?" Mikheyev bent over the operating table.

"I'm clear," Ginsburg said.

"Good," Mikheyev said. "Show him, Aleshkin. He'll want to see."

Aleshkin removed the cloth from the center of the second table, uncovering what was there, staining the sheet with blood.

Isaak Ginsburg looked and started retching.

Mikheyev stepped back. "Yes, Ginsburg. They're yours. Say good-bye to your balls, poet."

Ginsburg retched and gasped, turning his head so his throat would clear. It was ghastly. He couldn't move. He closed his eyes, refused to open them.

Aleshkin said, "We'd better unstrap his arms or he'll choke."

"Sure, sure." Mikheyev stepped aside so Aleshkin could free Ginsburg's arms.

Ginsburg grabbed for his genitals. They were bound in bulky surgical dressing.

Mikheyev said, "You'll heal, Ginsburg."

Ginsburg turned on his side and continued retching. He was at once exhausted and filled with horror and rage. He vomited until there was nothing left in his stomach to come up. He continued to retch, caught in painful spasms. He could hardly breathe. Ginsburg started easing his hand back toward the bulky dressing.

"There'll be some discomfort when the anesthetic wears off," Aleshkin said.

To that Mikheyev added, "You'll have to clean up after yourself, you know."

Ginsburg glared at him in rage. His mouth moved but he was unable to speak. He refused to look at the other table.

"Yes, those are your balls, Prisoner Ginsburg. You've probably never seen them from this angle. Maybe we'll feed them to your fellow *zeks*. Siberian oysters."

"I . . ." Ginsburg's wit failed him.

"Would you like a bullet?"

Isaak Ginsburg wiped his mouth with the back of his arm. He started crying suddenly, bawling. He couldn't help it. He looked pathetic and knew it. "Yes," he said.

"Well, ask him." Mikheyev gestured at the portrait of Lenin. "Say, please, Comrade Lenin."

Ginsburg looked at the poster. What did it matter? Everything would be over in a few minutes anyway. He said, "Please, Comrade Lenin." Ginsburg wanted to die very badly.

Mikheyev said, "Well, good. Here, how would you like it? In your mouth? I can blow your brains out if you'd like. All you have to do is open your mouth."

Mikheyev removed the revolver from the holster on his hip and put the muzzle into Ginsburg's open mouth.

Ginsburg could feel the barrel against his teeth, could taste the metal.

"Now?"

"Yes." Ginsburg could hardly say the word around the metal barrel.

When the hammer slammed down on an empty chamber, Isaak Ginsburg jerked rigid.

Yevgenni Mikheyev burst out laughing. He laughed

and laughed until he was weak and had to lean against his desk. "Wasn't that wonderful, Aleshkin? Wasn't it wonderful? Did you see the look on his face?"

Ginsburg stared at Mikheyev.

Mikheyev said, "It was a joke, Ginsburg. A joke. Tell him, Aleshkin."

"Those balls belong to poor Suslev, who died of pneumonia last night. We would have done this earlier, but we didn't have a body."

Ginsburg grabbed for his bandaged crotch.

"Everything's there," Aleshkin said. "Numb, but there. I deadened them with a shot." Aleshkin looked as if he, too, were about to be sick.

"They could have been yours, couldn't they, Ginsburg?" Mikheyev was still amused. He picked up Ginsburg's file from his desk. He would use his adjutant's office to detail the punishment as was required by regulation. Mikheyev had a spotless dossier. He followed instructions to the letter. This would be a wonderful entry. He couldn't wait.

Yevgenni Mikheyev hoped that his record of efficient and imaginative punishment would be noticed by his superiors and he would be rewarded with a posting in European Russia.

Isaak Ginsburg momentarily forgot about revenge. There was no matching Mikheyev's barbarity. All Ginsburg wanted to do was get the fuck out of the Soviet Union.

Twelve

ISAAK GINSBURG AND THE OTHER *ZEKS* RECENTLY RELEASED from the gulag were returned to civilian life by a Soviet administrative unit in Gorky. The prisoners waited in line in a low, white-brick building dated 1972 in red brick. The party insisted that buildings be dated in the Soviet Union so that the progress of Leninism might be noted. According to the plaque next to the main entrance, the relocation center stood beside the path down which bearers had carried Comrade Lenin's coffin in the bitter cold of January 1924.

Ginsburg was now officially cured of parasitism, having spent two years at Zima. What he would do and where he would live was at the leisure of the state. Ginsburg was at the mercy of the St. Peter of Gorky; he or she, a bureaucrat, would decide whether or not Ginsburg would return to Siberia or be sent to warmer climes.

Captain Mikheyev's damnable joke had made him even more resolved to get out of the country. Ginsburg stood. He stared. He moved one foot forward. He stood. He stared. He stood on one foot, then the other. He contemplated the path worn in the linoleum by countless *zeks* who had shuffled down this queue before him, each one, like himself, awaiting the decision of another government bureaucrat. He took another small step.

In the Soviet Union everybody learned to wait in line. Ginsburg reflected on this fact. This was a form of socialist training: everybody was equal in a line. Mothers waited in line to deliver babies. Wives waited in line for cucumbers. Children waited in line to kick a ball or to receive a test score. Men waited in line to buy vodka so they could forget about waiting in line.

Ginsburg waited for more than three hours before he reached the woman in a gray uniform sitting at a large table surrounded by stacks of folders. St. Peter was a woman. The name K. Trofimova was stenciled onto a rectangular piece of cardboard tacked onto the front of the table. Comrade Trofimova, who wore a Lenin pin on her lapel, waited to pass judgment on the next sinner against the people.

Trofimova took her time with her paperwork on the *zek* before Ginsburg. She stacked the file in the proper stack. She made a neat little check on a list of names. She put the notebook in its proper place. She made a quick notation in a larger notebook. She had bright blond hair with brown roots. Her large breasts pushed at the front of her gray uniform. She seemed pleased with her decision. She looked up at Ginsburg.

"Ginsburg, Isaak Avraamovich," he said. He wondered if K. Trofimova's Lenin pin had been designed by Natalia Serafimovna.

Trofimova regarded the tall, dark-eyed man. He had an intelligent face and had somehow maintained his dignity through whatever it was he had experienced. His hair, just growing out after a recent hacking with crude shears, looked ridiculous, worse than a soldier's if that were possible. Trofimova found it hard not to smile. She turned to the list of names and found his. Without looking at him, she said, "A Jew. I make the decisions.

If you protest, I'll send you above the Arctic Circle. Is that understood?''

Ginsburg said, "Yes." If he were a gymnast, or a hockey player, or a chess master, he'd have a chance.

Trofimova retrieved Ginsburg's file and opened it on the desk before her. Even upside down, Ginsburg could read the summary of Mikheyev's awful joke. Trofimova hadn't gotten that far when she glanced up at Ginsburg. "You have a university education?"

"Yes." Foreign service officers traveled abroad; that was out. A KGB agent. Ginsburg repressed a smile.

"And you wanted to be a poet."

"Yes." Like Osip Mandelstam, he thought.

"You are a Jew."

"Yes." The Soviets didn't want Jews, didn't like them, yet wouldn't let them leave.

"You Jews think too much."

We Jews replaced the czars with Jins and Mikheyevs, Ginsburg thought. "Yes," he said.

"You wanted to emigrate to Palestine."

Ginsburg said, "I'll gladly go wherever you send me."

It was only then that Trofimova came across Mikheyev's final punishment. She cleared her throat and kept reading.

Mikheyev had printed his summary in neat letters so Ginsburg was able to read it easily, even upside down. Mikheyev had included everything in his description of the " 'castration' of the prisoner, I. Ginsburg." Aleshkin had used an injection of novocaine to deaden Ginsburg's genitals. Ginsburg's vomiting was recorded in one neat sentence. His plea to be shot was noted. At the end, Mikheyev said, "The punishment was one-hundred-percent effective. Under its threat the prisoner ceased slandering the state; he did not, to my knowledge, write or recite poetry in his two years at Zima. Prisoner Ginsburg was returned to civilian life unharmed, ready to resume a useful and productive life."

Ginsburg read the last sentence and shook his head.

Trofimova reread Mikheyev's description of Ginsburg's special punishment twice through, then turned the book slightly on the table. She pointed at the long paragraph. "Is this true?" she asked. She looked at the form again.

"Yes," Ginsburg said.

"Is this exactly what happened? Tell me." She turned the folder so he could read it better. This was a violation of regulations, but she didn't care.

"Yes, what it says is true. That's exactly what happened."

Comrade Trofimova started to speak, then closed her mouth.

The men in the line waited patiently. If they complained, they risked return to a camp.

Ginsburg waited, outwardly patient. He thought of Yevgeny Yevtushenko. In the early 1960s, when Nikita Khrushchev was pushing de-Stalinization, had not Yevtushenko been allowed to read his poetry in New York?

Trofimova said, "All these men in this line today are being assigned as laborers. Because of your education there is a need for you in several cities. None of these are in Europe. They are in Siberia or the Urals." She unfolded a map. "There are possibilities in these cities." She pointed to several cities on the map.

Ginsburg hesitated. He studied the map. Sverdlovsk at the eastern foothills of the Urals was the closest to Moscow. He couldn't imagine there were many writers in Sverdlovsk.

Trofimova said, "You must choose, comrade. I am doing you a favor."

There was an opening in Novosibirsk—New Siberia— the largest city east of the Urals. The Soviets called it the Chicago of Siberia, but there was a nearby community of academics. "Novosibirsk, please," Ginsburg said.

"Novosibirsk?"

"Yes."

Trofimova removed an assignment sheet from a neat stack of forms and began filling it out in a small, neat hand. She made out a travel order. She filled in a form that told him where to report in Novosibirsk. "They'll tell you what you'll be doing when you arrive," she said without looking up. When she was finished she said, "Why did you choose Novosibirsk?"

"They say Novosibirsk has a wonderful opera house," Ginsburg said. "And a lovely circus too."

She glanced up at Ginsburg and caught his dark eyes straight on. "Do you like the circus?"

"The Soviet Union has entertainment for everybody: doves, ice-skating bears, clowns."

Comrade Trofimova looked at the *zek* behind Ginsburg. She said, "Next."

Isaak Ginsburg arrived in Novosibirsk the second week of April, twenty-six months after he had been summoned to Felix Jin's office. Ginsburg had to go through four lines in Novosibirsk: the first to register with the police; the second to find the location of his work; the third to decide where he would live; a fourth for a physical examination.

The first two lines went relatively fast. All the police bureaucrat did was compare the photo in the file with the man before the table. In the second, Ginsburg waited thirty minutes to receive a paper saying he was to be a bookkeeper in a grocery store. The female clerk said, "Report to work at eight o'clock Monday morning. Take this to the housing line. The woman there will have to know where you'll be working."

The keeper of housing in Novosibirsk was another woman, K. Krupskaya. Ginsburg waited in line, clutching six different papers, all required for housing. The first form gave him permission to travel to Novosibirsk. The second was a canceled travel voucher. The third said yes, he had checked in with the Novosibirsk militia. The fourth confirmed his employment as a book-

keeper in a grocery store. The fifth gave the location of
the grocery store and said he was to be assigned housing. The sixth listed biographical information including
his age, the fact that he was a Jew, and his education.

When K. Krupskaya saw Ginsburg's occupation, she
hesitated. She wet her lips. "Housing is very crowded
in Novosibirsk," she said. "We are working very hard
to correct this, but now space is limited." She studied
his job assignment again. "Downtown apartments, of
course, are out of the question. They aren't to be had."
She considered the employment form again.

She said, "We are building a major subway station
near the opera house here in Novosibirsk. The construction people have taken over a small building that they
use for office space and a place where they can weld
and do light repairs. There is one small room left in that
building, Ginsburg. It's very close to where you work."

"Anything's fine by me," Ginsburg said.

K. Krupskaya said, "The man in charge of the construction is an acquaintance of mine. He's a very conge-
nial man. Thoughtful." She studied Ginsburg.

Ginsburg grinned. His assignment to a grocery store
was a wonderful bit of luck. "I always help my friends,"
he said.

"His name is Georgi Kashva. If he doesn't like you,
he'll send you back."

"Kashva."

"The foreman. He'll want to talk to you. The room is
very tiny, but I'm sure you'll make do. You'll share a
kitchen and a bathroom with the construction workers.
You'll be moved within a year and a half; the building
will be torn down."

"Yes."

K. Krupskaya said, "You will then be reassigned at
our leisure, comrade."

"Yes," Ginsburg said.

"It won't be downtown next time," she added.

"I understand," Ginsburg said. He had lost four teeth

to the miserable diet at Zima, and explored the vacant holes with his tongue. He joined the line for his physical examination.

Isaak Ginsburg had to ease his way across a wallow of mud to get to the apartment building, which had metal scaffolding and planks leaning against the front wall. There was a pile of buff-colored bricks on one side of the main door. Someone had emptied his sinuses at the sill of the front door, and it was apparently the practice to tromp mud inside.

The crews had gone home for the day and there remained a single man, sitting alone with his muddy feet sprawled wide on the linoleum floor. He leaned against a desk on which there was a pile of papers, a yellow hard hat, and a crumpled paper bag.

"Kashva?"

"Yes." Georgi Kashva stood.

Ginsburg said, "My name is Isaak Ginsburg. I'm told that I should talk to you about living here."

Kashva pulled a pocket watch out of his pocket and checked the time. "My wife's expecting me. Listen, let me get to the point. This is a nice location and private, but I was kind of hoping Katerina would send someone who might be willing to help me out a bit. I've been using this room in the afternoons sometimes." Kashva twisted his wedding band. "Her name's Irina. She has kind of red hair."

"I can go for a walk or something."

"I really would appreciate it."

"I'll be working as a clerk in that grocery store down the street there." Ginsburg pointed with his head. "If I see something . . ." He left the second half of the sentence unstated.

"Really! That's the choicest grocery store in Novosibirsk. Isn't this a wonderful country? I give Katerina paint so she and her husband can redecorate their apartment. In return she sends me you. What do you want? I can get you anything.''

"For now, nothing. Maybe one day.''

"Ask when you're ready,'' Kashva said. "I know people.'' He opened the bottom drawer of the desk and removed a liter bottle of vodka and two water glasses that he proceeded to fill a quarter full.

"Here's to friends,'' Kashva said. "Call me Georgi.''

"Friends,'' Ginsburg said. "Isaak.''

They both emptied their glasses Russian style, tossing the vodka back in one gulp.

"That tastes like two more, Isaak,'' Kashva said. He poured another round.

"To fresh green peppers!'' Ginsburg said.

"Certainly.'' Kashva drank to fresh green peppers. They drank another round. They were both a little tipsy when Kashva took Ginsburg to his diminutive room. Ginsburg stashed his paper sack of belongings and walked outside with Kashva. On the way out Kashva said, "None of my construction people are to know about this. No one.''

"I understand,'' Ginsburg said. He parted with Kashva and, still drunk, went for a walk in the direction of the opera. Once he looked back and there was a man who seemed to be watching him. Was this man following him? Ginsburg could see the dome several blocks away in the late afternoon sun. The weather was balmy. A huge, dramatic statue of Lenin with others stood in front of the opera. There were three determined soldiers at Lenin's right hand, a robust young man and wholesome young woman on his left, signifying industry and agriculture.

Ginsburg watched an exuberant pair of newlyweds climb out of the back seat of a well-used Lada and start running toward the statue. Their friend took a picture of the couple placing flowers at Lenin's feet.

Thirteen

WHEN JAMES BURLANE FINISHED THE STORY ABOUT ISAAK *Ginsburg in* Newsweek, *he sailed the magazine across the room where it landed in a heap to join* Time. *Burlane was incensed. He couldn't see how magazine editors could stomach giving Ginsburg one line of copy, much less running spreads with his picture and quoting his bullshit poetry.*

Burlane got up to go play hackey-sack and break-dance with the kids down the street. He did this to maintain his coordination lest he come up against a Russian with quick feet. As a breakdancer, he was something to behold: his gangly arms yanking quickly, smoothly into odd contortions. He did this pretending he was gouging Libyan eyeballs or snapping Iranian necks. Burlane had had to move once when reporters from a local television station showed up to videotape him winning a neighborhood hackey-sack competition.

Later, he'd go for a drive to his special place in Virginia and practice keeping cans hopping in the air with his silenced .22 machine pistol. He'd have liked to have taken little Emilio, the local hackey-

75

*sack champ, who'd be thrilled to watch the cans jump,
but that was out of the question. Today, Burlane
decided, he'd pretend the cans were Isaak Ginsburg's
forehead.*

Fourteen

THE GROCERY STORE WAS A FEW DOORS AWAY FROM THE fanciest department store in town. There, a man could buy a pocket watch that had a sailing ship molded into the pot metal back and a red CCCP beneath the six on the face, or a woman might choose an almost stylish Yugoslavian lamp or a Hungarian vacuum cleaner that worked.

The ballet dancers who worked in the opera house lived in nearby apartments. The dancers received special treatment because they were proof to the world of superior socialist accomplishments. They were athletes as well as artists, and their vigorous training required a special diet: chocolate sometimes, or Western European beer. This food was obtained through Ginsburg's grocery store; it was handiest to the opera house. When the dancers wanted some black caviar and decent wine to toast the opening of a performance, that's where they ordered it.

The grocery store might have been fashionable, but it had a musty, pungent odor, the smell of earth. The smell was caused by cabbages in the summer, dirt-encrusted beets and potatoes in the fall, and stumpy, unwashed carrots on into the winter. There were seldom vegetables in the spring—occasionally an extra ration of green onions—but the odor continued, dank and acrid.

The manager, Anatoli Fedorov, was watching for Ginsburg and introduced himself as Ginsburg leaned over the vegetable bins, inhaling the aroma of dried mud. "Smells like Russia, doesn't it?" Fedorov said. "I take it you're Isaak Ginsburg." He shook Ginsburg's hand and took him back into his little office to talk.

Fedorov read from a folder with Ginsburg's name on it. This folder was similar to the file the housing woman had studied—a censored version of the file studied by Comrade K. Trofimova in Gorky and of the master file presumably stored in a KGB facility.

Fedorov said, "You graduated from Moscow University. Very impressive." He stopped.

"I've always been good at exams."

"It's a knack, they tell me."

"If you learn the subject, you'll do well on the exams. Learning the subject takes hard work."

Fedorov said, "I think I'm doing this backward. Maybe I should show you how the store works first, then get into the details of what you'll be doing. Have you ever kept books before?"

"No," Ginsburg said. "But I'm a quick learner."

"I think it's better to start out front. You'll need to know the clerks' records so you can keep a clean tally." With Ginsburg's file in his hands, Fedorov led his new bookkeeper on a tour of the small sales room. "The apartment houses are smaller in this area, so we aren't packed all the time. You will see some lines when we get hothouse cucumbers or onions in from Leningrad." Fedorov didn't say the cucumber lines sometimes turned the corner of the block outside.

"There seems to be enough frozen hake to satisfy everyone," Fedorov said. Because of its fishy taste and mushy texture, a little hake could satisfy a lot of people.

The government could afford to buy it because the Americans and Japanese scorned it.

Ginsburg wondered if Fedorov was working with the people who were following him. "Wonderful fish," Ginsburg said.

"And of course we're one of the few stores with a good supply of socialist sausages."

The sausages looked like bloated, bulbous turds. Ginsburg hesitated, with a pause that Fedorov would note were he working for the KGB's Jewish Department. "They look delicious."

"You spent some time in a camp, didn't you, Ginsburg? That's why you're here in Novosibirsk."

"Yes," Ginsburg said.

"What for, do you mind my asking?"

"I asked to emigrate to Israel. I spent two years in a lumber camp at Zima for parasitism."

"Did I tell you that my son, Yuri, and his cousin, Aleksei, are facing the university examinations next year?"

"Could you use a tutor? I can help."

Fedorov smiled. "There are ways I can return the favor."

A few days after he had settled in, Isaak Ginsburg became a tutor to Yuri and Aleksei, going to his supervisor's home every day to instruct the young men in approved Leninist explanations of history and economics.

Fedorov kept Ginsburg well supplied with vodka while he, Fedorov, read the newspaper in the next room. Fedorov grinned and got a little loaded himself. Ginsburg occasionally stayed on afterward to drink more vodka; he and Fedorov talked about Dostoyevsky and Turgenev, whom they each admired for different reasons.

A week after Ginsburg began his tutoring duties, Fedorov gave him a half-dozen beautiful yellow squashes from a small lot that had arrived unexpectedly from west of the Urals. The squashes were treasures.

Ginsburg gave them to Georgi Kashva.

A fortnight later, Ginsburg was able to pass along two bottles of special vodka to Kashva. These were shipped from Khabarovsk in the Far East and contained ginseng, which was said to improve a man's potency. "For you and Irina!"

The flow of gifts from Ginsburg to Kashva inevitably wound up in Irina's hands. Ginsburg never asked for anything in return. Irina was able to swap the good food for perfume, clothes, jewelry even. Kashva told Isaak that Irina got hornier and hornier with each gift. He'd never seen anything like it. He wanted to know if Ginsburg could get him some more vodka with ginseng in it. Kashva said he'd used up the last of his ginseng vodka to prepare himself for Irina's reaction to the American pantyhose she had scored with an earlier gift from Ginsburg.

Georgi Kashva felt indebted to Ginsburg for this bounty and one night, loaded on vodka, guilty, told him about his prized connection, a Georgian named Abu Ali. He said if Ginsburg ever got his hands on some extra rubles and wanted something really special, Abu Ali was the man. Abu Ali could get Isaak Ginsburg anything his heart desired.

Fifteen

ISAAK GINSBURG DIDN'T THINK IT TOOK A GENIUS TO READ between the lines of Soviet literary journals. The Soviets were once again under international pressure for being anti-Semitic and for refusing to let Jews emigrate to Israel; the Moscow Writers Union was in the market for a house Jew to show the world. The road to freedom ran through Moscow; the road to Moscow was paved with obeisance.

The KGB would watch him constantly, he knew, just as someone was watching him now. Let them.

Ginsburg made a list of the most likely hangouts for approved writers in Novosibirsk, and began prowling libraries and bookstores each night after he finished tutoring Yuri and Aleksei. He spent as many nights at a place as it took to know its clientele. He browsed. He circulated. He checked the bulletin boards. He stayed each night until closing. He read everything he could find by popular, currently approved Russian poets. He read everything he could find about Lenin—and that, on a Soviet bookshelf, was a lot of books.

In the end, the place he wanted was only twenty minutes away, walking at a good clip. It was an estab-

lishment library and so not infected by intellectual malcontents. Plus that, it offered something special: a small
room with a samovar so readers could step in out of the
quiet of the stacks and talk about books over a cup of
tea. It was the gathering place for the approved Novosibirsk literati.

The library was run by an enthusiastic old Communist
named Arkady, who was nosy and who immediately set
about to learn Isaak Ginsburg's reading habits. Comrade
Arkady kept lists of books everyone read in case there
was a deviant lurking undetected. Arkady thought he did
this on the sly, but all his regulars knew it and assumed
their reading habits were passed on to the KGB. Ginsburg
detected Comrade Arkady's curiosity on his third visit
and knew this was his place.

Moreover, once a month, on a Saturday night, the
members of the Novosibirsk Writers Union met there to
read poetry and talk about books. This session was for
members only.

Learning this, Isaak Ginsburg made himself a regular
at Comrade Arkady's library. One night, Ginsburg felt
Arkady's presence over his shoulder as he squatted near
the shelves reading a book of poems by Dmitri Lagunin,
who was a current Moscow favorite and much published
in Soviet literary journals.

"Isn't Lagunin wonderful?" Arkady whispered. He
had a red face and tiny little lines on his nose. His front
teeth had been recapped, and his mouth flashed gold as
he talked.

Ginsburg nodded gravely. "He has a wonderful ability to get to the heart of the communal spirit. You'll
notice he doesn't waste words. He gets it down there."
Ginsburg held his thumb and forefinger apart about the
distance of a small berry. "Like that. Like so," he
whispered. He thought, *That's the size of Lagunin's
brain.* Ginsburg held up Lagunin's book. "He's fabulous. Say, earlier I looked for Kuharin's biography of
Lenin, but I see you don't have it." If Lagunin was an

asshole, Ginsburg wondered what Kuharin must be. Kuharin was even worse.

"Ahh, you're a man who knows your Lenin," Arkady said. "You want Kuharin, I'll get you Kuharin." He grinned. "It may take a while, but I'll get you one. My name is Arkady Nikitovich Zhelanov, but around here they call me Comrade Arkady."

"Isaak Avraamovich Ginsburg."

Comrade Arkady's face changed almost imperceptibly. "It may take a while," Arkady said. He squatted beside Ginsburg and ran his fingers across the spines of several Lagunin titles. " 'The mother ties the sheaves with loving hands . . .' "

Ginsburg finished the line: " 'Sings the song of Lenin's land.' A wonderful poem."

Arkady pulled at his red-veined nose. "Say, you do know Lagunin!" Arkady seemed amazed.

"Isn't he wonderful? Gripping language," Ginsburg lied. "Special stuff."

"I'm getting a volume of Svetaylo in tomorrow. Do you know her work?"

Ginsburg, to Arkady's surprise and delight, recited one of Tanya Svetaylo's poems. "Isn't she nice? She knows her peasants, doesn't she?"

Tanya Svetaylo wrote about simple, happy peasants, and the joys of living in permafrost country. The party called her a socialist Rousseau although she wasn't anything of the sort. She was yet another slavish adherent to approved socialist dogma and everybody knew it. Ginsburg felt it was all but impossible for a stylish writer to be a party favorite; felicity of style generally went hand in hand with felicity of thought. Svetaylo avoided grace at all costs. She was about as elegant a writer as one of those ice-skating bears in the Novosibirsk circus.

Nevertheless, Svetaylo was declared a master stylist and so she officially was. The members of Ginsburg's old Moscow circle of friends used to speculate on the number of party dicks she must have sucked. Ginsburg masked his rage with a contemplative, thoughtful face.

Isaak Ginsburg began work on his new oeuvre in Comrade Arkady's library. He worked every night, carefully rewriting and polishing his work. Each page of his tablet was a maze of circled and crossed-out words, arrows, and carets.

One Saturday afternoon, Ginsburg again felt Arkady's presence over his shoulder.

"Oh, a poet!" Arkady said.

Ginsburg looked embarrassed. "I was once, but not anymore."

"What do you mean, not anymore?"

Ginsburg knew Arkady was straining his nearsighted eyes trying to make sense of Ginsburg's illegible scrawl and the confusion of copy marks on the page. "I write only for myself." Ginsburg did his best to look caught.

"Nonsense. When people write, they write for other people to read. You will read before the Writers Union. A word from me is all it takes."

"Well, I don't think so, thank you," Ginsburg said.

"Nonsense. Done!" Arkady said, and it was so: Ginsburg had no choice but to read before the group. "Most of the local writers will be there," Arkady said. "We'll drink some vodka. Maybe talk about books. There're some people I'd like you to meet."

"Certainly, then, if you think it would be all right."

"What do you mean, is it all right? Nonsense," Arkady said. "You come, Comrade Ginsburg. You finished with the Chaychev title?"

Ginsburg nodded. "I think Chaychev's a good judge of character. He's right: Lenin was a gentle man, not at all given to violence. The costs of the Revolution must have been hard on him." Ginsburg looked solemn.

Sixteen

CONTACT DAVID'S REQUEST AND THE ACCOMPANYING REPORT *by Rennie Kriss were forwarded to Ara Schott, deputy director of the CIA. Schott took Kriss's report to the office of the Director of Central Intelligence, Peter Neely—also known as the DCI. This was done in accordance with Neely's standing instruction; the President had a keen interest in rumors of discontent in the Soviet Union.*

The DCI adjusted the cuff of his jacket and considered the note. He turned soundlessly, effortlessly in his swivel chair, a chair so splendid as to elevate him from the mundane world of his underlings. Neely's subordinates called this chair Cloud Nine, but never to his face.

Neely was DCI because he was a friend of the President and made slick, sincere appearances before committees of Congress. Power was to his taste, but he was insecure in the nether regions of the cold war. "What do you think, Ara?"

Ara Schott had been chief of counterintelligence during the Townes affair. He was chief of covert operations now. After Schott had mastered the art of defending, Neely had put him on the attack. Schott was given neither to hyperbole nor to panic. "Heavens, I don't know," he said. "I think this is one for Burlane."

Seventeen

COMRADE ARKADY CLOSED THE LIBRARY AT NINE, AND the writers adjourned to the tea room. The Novosibirsk Writers Union had provided buckets of iced vodka, crackers, and red salmon caviar. The writers at the party didn't spend a whole lot of time talking about writing or about books. They speculated about the tastes of the new president of the Moscow Writers Union. They complained about the Novosibirsk allocation for the coming year; the previous year they'd been treated to Polish beer at their monthly gatherings. They gossiped about one of their colleagues, a novelist, who had been given a Moscow residence permit.

Anatoli Stalnov was president of the Novosibirsk chapter of the Writers Union. Ginsburg sensed that Arkady secretly hated Stalnov. Arkady doubtless wanted to be president of the Novosibirsk writers himself. Arkady had done the boring detail work for years—including organizing these readings—tirelessly and apparently enthusiastically.

Stalnov was a slender man, in his late forties, with thinning black hair that he combed straight over his head. He had heavy black eyebrows and intense, aloof

87

brown eyes. His administrative duties had all but eliminated his time to write, although he still referred to
himself as a writer. None of those who knew him dared
suggest otherwise.

Isaak Ginsburg had done a little research on Stalnov.

Stalnov's reputation as a writer dated to the late 1970s.
He had published three slender novels, one of them
mentioned by Leonid Brezhnev in a discussion of a
"socialist renaissance" in Soviet literature that was pub-
lished verbatim in *Pravda*. Brezhnev said the novel,
Mushroom Country, was a Leninist "lightning rod."
Stalnov was the object of attention for more than a year,
but the excitement stopped abruptly when Brezhnev died.
Stalnov was unable to get his stories published—lest
fashion be changed by the followers of Yuri Andropov.
Andropov's reign was short-lived, but it was too late for
Stalnov. He was destroyed as a writer.

Comrade Arkady introduced Isaak Ginsburg to Anatoli
Stalnov.

Ginsburg looked impressed on hearing Stalnov's name.
"You're not the author of *Mushroom Country,* are you?"

Although every aspiring writer in Novosibirsk had
read *Mushroom Country,* Stalnov acknowledged the au-
thorship with a grin. He was an official of the Writers
Union, so he did not have to admit it was his last
published story.

"It's a lovely little novel," Ginsburg said. "I like
your description of the taiga birch—'ghosts of Russians
past standing at our side.' That says something to us all,
I think." This was like spreading warm manure on
moldy bread, Ginsburg thought.

"Really?" Stalnov said.

"The ambiguity was wonderful," Ginsburg said.

"Well, thank you, Comrade Gendorov. Gendorov is
it?"

"Ginsburg."

Stalnov hesitated. He looked surprised. "A Jew, then."

"Yes."

Arkady said, "Isaak is going to read some of his poetry tonight." Ordinarily Stalnov would have picked the reader, but Stalnov had been away at his dacha in the Urals.

"I'll be looking forward to it," Stalnov said. It was obvious that he didn't look forward to it and wouldn't have said so if Ginsburg hadn't been a Jew who liked *Mushroom Country*.

Comrade Arkady was in high spirits. He was going to catch himself a libelous Jew.

Isaak Ginsburg looked confidently out at the writers who breathed salty fish-egg breath and whose eyes were reddened by vodka. He said clearly:

"I am a Jew,
    And once complained,
    But I learned to love at Zima."

Comrade Arkady looked confused. What was this? Anatoli Stalnov paid attention.

"Worked in the woods,
    Worked at the mill;
    Learned that forests matter more
    Than individual trees. Trees grow back."

Comrade Arkady watched the listening writers out of the corner of his eye as Ginsburg read on from the messy pad.

Anatoli Stalnov listened.

Isaak Ginsburg read four poems, pausing between each. Each poem was more intense than the one before. In the end, Arkady moved quickly forward, prepared to throw Ginsburg on his ear. He would have, too, had Stalnov not gotten there first.

Stalnov embraced Ginsburg. "Wonderful stuff, Isaak!

Wonderful! Is this true? Are you a Jew? Did this happen to you?''

"Yes."

"You!" Stalnov laughed. "I wouldn't have thought you were a Jew. A person can hardly tell these days." Stalnov could hardly believe his good fortune. He was glad he had gotten to Ginsburg before that stupid little asshole. Without asking, Stalnov took Ginsburg's manuscript. He looked at the title: *A Second Journey to Lobnoye Mesta: Afterthoughts.*

"In this case the source of the secret, eternal power is love of the socialist vision," Ginsburg said. "That's our invaluable treasure at the Kremlin. The journey is what I went through in understanding that truth."

"You're a Jew?" Stalnov asked again.

Ginsburg said, "Yes, a Jew."

"I would like to read the whole manuscript if I may," Stalnov said.

Ginsburg hesitated. "I don't want to get into any trouble. I didn't ask to read tonight."

Anatoli Stalnov said it was his duty as the president of the Novosibirsk Writers Union to read Ginsburg's new oeuvre. Whereupon he tucked the manuscript under his arm. There would be no argument.

Stalnov read *Second Journey* when he got home from the gathering. He did not stop until he had read the poems twice through. The poetry was good enough that the intrusion of Leninism didn't make any appreciable difference. Ginsburg had all the correct opinions, but before the reader got too bored, Ginsburg had something interesting to say. It was a wonderful skill to be able to bloat a poem with ideology and still not have the reader gag. Stalnov admired Ginsburg's talent. Used properly, Isaak Ginsburg could make the Americans and Israelis choke on their words, Stalnov knew. The worst were the goody-goody Dutch. Ginsburg would shut them up.

Stalnov finished his chore in the early hours of the morning and went to sleep a happy man; although Irma

Stalnov's gelatinous buttocks felt extra comfortable resting against his hip, his final thoughts were of Moscow women.

Three months later, Isaak Ginsburg received a letter from the president of the Writers Union in Moscow, the same organization that had declared him unacceptable and turned his samizdat manuscripts over to the KGB. Would Isaak Ginsburg like to read his poetry in the Bolshoi Theater? That could be arranged. There would be a reception in the Metropole Hotel afterward.

The letter said that Ginsburg should contact Anatoli Stalnov, who was to be Ginsburg's sponsor.

Colonel Felix Jin took a sip of tea and for the second time read the report from Novosibirsk on the poet Isaak Ginsburg. The file on Ginsburg had taken an unusual turn, two unusual turns as a matter of fact—although the first had no apparent relationship to the second. Jin couldn't remember a more interesting case, certainly not one more provocative in its possibilities.

The first item was that Ginsburg's name had turned up in the KGB investigation of black-market activities. Ginsburg was living in a building taken over by a construction crew working on the new underground in Novosibirsk. The foreman of the crew was Georgi Kashva, who was on the KGB's list of possible black marketeers. The matter of housing could be innocent enough, Jin knew: Ginsburg had had no choice in the matter.

The second twist, reported by a librarian in Novosibirsk, struck Jin as curious in the extreme. The librarian had included some of Isaak Ginsburg's poems. Jin contrasted the poems with Ginsburg's dossier spread on the desk before him. At the bottom of this dossier, the camp commandant at Zima, a Captain Yevgenni Mikheyev, had proudly detailed a bizarre joke he had pulled on Ginsburg. Even Jin was taken aback by the bogus castration, although he was an experienced KGB officer and thought he had heard everything.

Felix Jin wondered if it were possible for Ginsburg to write poems like these after Mikheyev's joke. Jin studied Mikheyev's notation and didn't think he himself could have done it. Had Ginsburg done some kind of psychological flip-flop? If he had, this was one for the textbooks.

The Novosibirsk KGB rated the librarian highly, but Jin wasn't so sure; the librarian was obviously anti-Semitic. Jin had no way of knowing how personality tics and jealousies might have skewed the librarian's judgment.

Colonel Jin knew he had to be judicious. The party was in the market for someone like Isaak Ginsburg. It would be suicidal for Jin to make any kind of allegation before he was sure of his facts.

Eighteen

Isaak Ginsburg and his compartment-mate Ivan Shepelev talked about wild mushrooms—Shepelev loved to gather big Urals *beliyes*—until eleven when they turned out the lights, pulled the shade on the window of their soft-class berth, and rolled over to sleep. Isaak Ginsburg lay there in the darkness listening to the rattling and banging of steel on steel. When he got to Moscow he would have to cut himself off from his former friends. If he was to turn himself over to the Soviets, he would have to be theirs completely. He twisted and turned and did not fall asleep for another two hours.

The next morning brought a humid, Continental day. This was the time of year Soviet photographers made shots for postcards and for magazines that circulated in the West: shots of buildings, bridges, monuments, and pretty girls. The summer leaves softened the hardship and poverty—like gauze or Vaseline over a lens.

Ginsburg shaved and stood in the aisle, watching the birches slide by. He didn't want to get involved with Shepelev. He paced the aisle and sat on one of the small seats that folded down under every other window. When there was a stop at a small town, he joined the others on the platform. After a while his feet began to tire; boredom closed in on him. He returned to the compartment and told Shepelev he was going to take a nap.

"The birches are so beautiful. I can't get enough of them," he said. It felt good to get off his feet. He closed his eyes and lay on his berth. The hot August sun felt good on his body.

Shepelev watched his sleeping companion.

Later, Ginsburg awakened to see Shepelev returning from the aisle. "Perm coming up," he said.

Ginsburg sat up and looked outside and there it was: the bluff of people's apartment buildings overlooking an awesome valley of shacks. It was just as the coughing *zek* had described. The apartments were great, featureless, prefabricated concrete obelisks, hives of tiny cells for those Perm workers lucky enough to escape the isbas—the log shantytown.

Ginsburg began gathering his things: a light bag with clothing in it, and a heavy bag with a strap that cut into his shoulder. "Good hunting, Ivan," Ginsburg said.

"And a good visit to you too, Isaak," Shepelev said. He gathered his two small bags and followed Ginsburg out of the train.

The train station at Perm was painted white, like that at Zima. The inside of the station was muddy, and echoed, and smelled like a root cellar. Isaak Ginsburg strode past soldiers in rumpled uniforms and peasants with medieval faces. The soldiers and peasants sat on old benches amid a clutter of bags, sacks, and baskets, and watched him. They were neither curious nor cautious. They waited for whatever was going to happen to them to happen.

Ginsburg strode past a group of oxenlike women wearing dark blue head scarves and Day-Glow orange vests over their dark blue blouses. They walked on heavy, slow thighs, looking down at their coarse brown shoes. They carried the crude birch brooms they had used to sweep the railbed and station yards. Ginsburg wondered what they thought of when they went to sleep at night.

Isaak Ginsburg knew that he had been followed in Novosibirsk. He wanted to look back to see if Shepelev or anyone else were there now, but he didn't.

The Lenin Hotel was less than a half mile from the railway station. It had been a sweltering, humid summer afternoon. Black clouds gathered to the west as he walked up the street.

At the hotel, Ginsburg changed his clothes. He walked down the hall to the bathroom. There was no hot water. Ginsburg brushed his teeth. Back in his room, he took a pint flask from the smaller of the two bags and had a slug of vodka as the first lightning popped over the river to the west. In a few minutes a wind kicked up and pushed rain against the window.

Ginsburg poured himself another drink as the thunder rumbled and gurgled, then crackled and popped. A startling bolt of lightning lit the street outside, followed by a booming crack overhead that sent Ginsburg out of his chair. In twenty minutes it was over, and Ginsburg went out to do what he had to do, wearing old trousers and a casual jacket with the heavy bag slung over one shoulder. The air was made fresh by the rain; it smelled good.

Ginsburg passed the railroad station and turned east on Brezhnev Prospekt, paralleling the tracks that ran east to west across the river. Brezhnev Prospekt was paved, but it was so dirty it was hard to tell, and the rain had turned the dirt to slime. Ginsburg stopped occasionally to rest and also to check the street behind him. He saw no one. Once he hung his heavy bag on the stub of a broken aspen branch and rested his shoulder, swinging his arm to get the blood circulating again.

Walk east, the cougher had said; stay north of the railroad tracks. Soon, unmistakably, Ginsburg was upon the valley of huts.

The pavement of Brezhnev Prospekt ended abruptly. Ginsburg made his way down a road that was a wallow of mud. The screeching of crickets replaced the sounds of city buses. He passed a maze of prefabricated metal garages that stored Ladas for the people lucky enough to own them. By some quirk of central planning, the garages in Perm were either purple or green. Judging from the muddy trails leading up the bluff, these cars belonged to people who lived on the top.

Just beyond the garages was a city of root cellars, mounds of earth, each with a small door and two vents on top. If the Americans should ever attack, the citizens of Perm were supposed to dart into a root cellar and settle in among the bags of beets and potatoes.

Ginsburg's feet were soon sticky balls of mud. After a couple of kilometers, he paused and whacked his foot against the white bark of a birch. As he cleaned his shoes, it occurred to him that each hut, no matter how dilapidated or pathetic, was surrounded by a fence. Each tiny garden plot, each crumbling isba was somehow staked out. In Russia, where everybody owned everything or nobody owned anything—depending on how you looked at it—everybody had a fence. Ginsburg remembered a line from the American poet, Robert Frost: "Something there is that doesn't love a wall."

Ginsburg smiled to himself and walked on with lightened shoes, the bag still cutting into his shoulder—although not as heavily as his determination to honor his word to the coughing *zek*. Ginsburg owed it to the cougher to see the Perm cancer clinic for himself before he told Serafim Korenkho's daughter, Natalia Serafimovna Kropotkina.

Isaak Ginsburg chose each step carefully. It was possible, in Perm, to drown in Russian mud.

Nineteen

ISAAK GINSBURG FOUND THE CANCER CLINIC AT THE FAR
end of the valley of isbas, as the coughing *zek* had said.
The administrative offices and laboratories were in a
low, white-brick building. The bricks were of various
sizes, and rose and fell like slow swells on a lazy sea.
Maybe the bricklayers had been hitting the vodka. The
clinic was in a lovely area, the center of a parklike
woods of birch and aspen.

While the Americans argued the efficiency and moral-
ity of using laboratory animals, Soviet researchers—having
the advantage of working with human animals—pushed
hard for the great socialist breakthrough in cancer.

The research subjects lived in smaller buildings made
of the same white brick. The dormitories were fenced,
but the gates were open, and Ginsburg saw men in
zek-like uniforms sitting on benches under the trees.
Ginsburg found an empty bench, relieved his shoulder
of the heavy bag, and watched the patients.

The patients didn't seem to regard Ginsburg's presence as unusual; no doubt residents of Perm strayed onto
the benches to contemplate the fluttering of leaves in a
light wind. The patients were younger men, most in

their twenties through early forties. Some were pallid, more sick than others. A few hardly looked ill at all.

A man with an athletic build walked toward Ginsburg. He walked alone, enjoying the leaden stillness of the cooling, wet air. He whacked the ground with a stick. He had an intelligent, alert face. He looked at Ginsburg, wondering who he was. "Hello, there," he said.

"Good afternoon. I'm told that you're all dying here. Of cancer."

The man looked surprised at Ginsburg's casual honesty. "Yes, we are. I got mine at Sovetabad. See what's happening." He lifted his cap. His head was bald.

Ginsburg shook his head slowly. "Did the cancer do that, or drugs?"

"Experimental drugs," the man said. "Some of us can't shit. Some shake. Some puke. Others are going blind. I lost my hair, although my leukemia seems to have steadied. I have leukemia. Jaan Birk is my name. I'm an Estonian."

"Isaak Ginsburg. Would you like some vodka?"

"Of course," Birk said.

Ginsburg took a flask from his jacket pocket and gave it to Birk who unscrewed it and took a hard jolt. Ginsburg said, "So, tell me. How did you get sent to Sovetabad?"

Jaan Birk took three small balls from the pocket of his crude hospital trousers and began juggling them with his left hand. "I was athletic when I was younger. Do you really want to know?"

"Sure."

Birk put the balls back in his pocket. "I was sent to Sovetabad because of a woman and a Russian. My father was an army sergeant who was killed in Hungary in 1956. My mother died of pneumonia the next year, and I was taken in by her brother—my uncle Viktor Konnen—who was an animal trainer for the circus in Tallinn. I went into the Red Army like my father." He took another blast of vodka. "It was very rare for an Estonian to be made an officer. My uncle Viktor was

proud of me. I thought it was the best thing that had
ever happened to me until I met Nadia.''

"Nadia?''

"Nadia was also the worst thing ever to happen to
me. She was a gymnast at the Institute of Physical
Culture in Leningrad where I was assigned. I was a
younger lieutenant. We fell in love and I asked her to
marry me, but she said no, she wanted to see if she
could qualify for international competition. It was her
dream to travel to foreign countries. The next world
championships were scheduled for Lisbon, then Munich
after that. She had been invited to train in Moscow.''

"Did she get to travel?''

Birk shook his head. "No, she didn't, and two years
later she said yes, she wanted to marry me. She had
given it her best, but she wasn't good enough. She was
grateful that I waited while she tried. She returned to
Leningrad and we were married. Then, it turned out,
there was this problem.''

"There always is," Ginsburg said.

"It turned out that in Moscow, Nadia had gotten cut
from the competition early on. She also caught the eye
of the first cousin of the director of the Institute of
Physical Culture. He intervened and she was allowed to
continue training. She said that at the time going to bed
with the Russian seemed a small enough price to pay.''

Ginsburg dug a bottle out of the heavy bag and
opened it.

"The Russian showed up a year after we got married.
He said he had arranged for her to be a trainer in
Moscow. She was to return to Moscow. She said no. A
month later I was arrested for 'libeling the Soviet people' and sent to Sovetabad.''

"And Nadia?''

"Nadia killed herself. As you see, I'm here waiting
to die. Before, I thought of myself as an Estonian who
was also a citizen of the Soviet Union. I will die an
Estonian only.''

"You will die then."

"We all die someday," Birk said. "I'm part of what the Russians call an experimental group. I live in a barracks full of ex-*zeks* who worked with uranium and plutonium. We've all got the same form of leukemia and they've got us on a drug that keeps it in remission. We spend our days cleaning, sweeping, raking, shoveling, pruning, and puking. Actually we're given quite a lot of freedom; we're allowed to visit our families on furloughs."

"I see."

"It's for our morale, they say. All that puking. They're going to take us off the drug in a year. This is so they can see how fast we deteriorate. The Russians are a wonderful people, Ginsburg."

"What?"

"Just like pulling the plug on a bathtub to see how fast it drains. We know a guy who's screwing one of the secretaries who works in the administration. She says our group's scheduled to be taken off the drug next summer—part of their research. We've got one more year of puking before they turn us over to the disease again. You were a *zek* too, weren't you. What happened?"

Ginsburg said, "I spent two years at a lumber camp in Siberia. At Zima." Ginsburg told Birk what Yevgenni Mikheyev had done to him at Zima. When he had finished, Birk said nothing. Both Ginsburg and Birk remained silent for a full two minutes. A slight breeze kicked up, stirring the leaves on the birches.

"Well, they got us both, then," Birk said. He took a heavy slug of vodka. "You know, a man in my position spends a lot of time drunk. There's not a lot else to do except puke. A person gets to thinking of ways to get even. Do you do that?"

"Every day at Zima. When I got out, though, all I wanted to do is get out. What are you going to do to them? Nothing."

"I've been thinking it would be fun to steal Lenin's

head from the tomb,'' Birk said casually. He laughed
and gave Ginsburg a crooked grin. "Wouldn't that be a
kick in the nuts? Swap it for a year of open emigration,
say.''

"Steal Lenin's head?" Ginsburg was disbelieving.

"Sure," Birk said. "I used to be an army officer. I
could do it. A little parting gesture from a comrade with
leukemia. Keep in mind, Isaak, that these are Russians
we're dealing with, not humans in the ordinary sense.''

Ginsburg could only grin and shake his head. The
proposition was so obscene as to be humorous. In fact, a
few years earlier a satirical samizdat had circulated in
Moscow in which a man hid himself in Lenin's tomb
after closing and stole Lenin's head—which turned out
to be stuffed with straw. Ginsburg remembered some
lines written by the American poet, T. S. Eliot:

> We are the hollow men
> We are the stuffed men
> Leaning together
> Headpiece filled with straw. Alas!

This was a far more outrageous proposal than merely
stealing a head. This was the Leninists' secret of secrets—
the new heart of Lobnoye Mesto, the skull that radiated
a secret power for eternity. The arrogance and conceit of
Russian destiny had not changed since the medieval
Muscovites, through all the czars, through Ivan the
Terrible, through Joseph Stalin.

If Jaan Birk stole Lenin's head, he would castrate the
Communists; there was no word more accurate than the
naked truth. Captain Mikheyev had stolen Isaak Ginsburg's poetry, and having thus neutered him, gave
Ginsburg one final lesson in the horror of impotence.

Ginsburg said, "Say, do you have a place to store a
little something?" He opened his bag wide enough for
Birk to see.

Birk was amazed.

There were a half-dozen bottles in the bag: Old Crow, Old Granddad, Bombay gin, and three bottles of Johnnie Walker Black Label scotch.

"Maybe this'll help you figure out a way to steal Lenin's head."

Jaan Birk said, "You don't think it could be done? I could do it. I may be a little drunk now, but there has to be a way. You figure out a way to get me some weapons and get the head out of the country, and I'll come up with a way to get it out of the tomb. Where did you get this stuff?"

"From a special store in Novosibirsk," Ginsburg said. "If the comrades in the Politburo drink well, I don't see why we shouldn't also. Everybody is equal in the Soviet Union, as we all know."

"I could figure out a way."

Ginsburg said, "I told you I shared a cell with a man named Lado Kabakhidze."

"With the conductress daughter."

"With the conductress daughter. If she carries my letter, it'll arrive unread."

Jaan Birk was amazed. "I think you're drunker than I am, Isaak Ginsburg."

Twenty

IN HIS NEW ROLE AS MOSCOW'S RESIDENT JEWISH POET, Isaak Ginsburg received invitations to an unending round of readings, openings, and parties. He was introduced to visiting French and Italian Communists eager for reassurance that the Soviet Union was the object of libel and was not, in fact, as coarse as it appeared in the bourgeois Western press. When a group of Marxist officials arrived from Liverpool, Ginsburg was summoned forth to read poems extolling the beauty and glory of the universal city. When journalists arrived from New York, Ginsburg read poems filled with Yiddish allusions and references to the Old Testament.

Ginsburg knew he would eventually meet the designer Natalia Serafimovna Kropotkina in the course of his social life. Dr. Serafim Korenkho's daughter had married well. Leonid Kropotkin was powerful and respected in the Communist party.

In late September, Ginsburg first saw Natalia at an exhibition of her lapel pins in the Hotel Rossiya, just south of Red Square and overlooking the Moscow River. Kropotkina had designed the fifteen-kopek pin Premier Spishkin had worn on his lapel when he spoke before the United Nations General Assembly. A rectangular pin, red bordered by gold, it was now on lapels all over the Soviet Union.

Paintings of Natalia Kropotkina's pins—the originals of her work—were mounted on portable panels that partitioned a conference hall into smaller, more dramatic viewing spaces. Spotlights mounted above the panels dramatized the pins on display.

At one side of the hall stood a long table with bread, caviar, vodka, and bottles of beer in buckets of ice. Natalia herself was surrounded by men with serious faces who nodded heavily, jowls waggling, as she gestured with a slender hand toward first one, then another of her works.

A sign by the entrance said N. Kropotkina's Lenin pins were wonderful examples of socialist commemorative art, art that brought people together. In a lapel pin, the sign said, art and pride in the great socialist accomplishments were one. The biography on the wall said N. Kropotkina had been compared to Rodin and Diego Rivera. By whom wasn't made clear.

Natalia was a small woman with long, jet-black hair that had been brushed to a luster. She was fine-boned, petite, with a pale complexion, green eyes, and heavy eyebrows. Ginsburg spent a lot of time looking at the *znachki* but did not approach the artist herself. It would be coarse to tell Natalia about her father at an exhibition of her commemorative pins. He decided to wait.

If Ginsburg thought he was anonymous, he was mistaken. Natalia Kropotkina saw him and was furious. Her father had died in a slate mine at Slansky and here this odious suck had intruded on her exhibit. Jews of her acquaintance had more pride than Ginsburg. Natalia wanted the slime out of the hall, out of the building. She wanted to scream at him, wanted to grab him by the arm and shake him, but restrained herself. Ginsburg was an official hero. To make a scene would call attention to her father and would be the end of her pin designing. Even Leonid wouldn't be able to save her.

Ginsburg was tall and slender with curly hair and brown eyes that caught her own momentarily. There was something about his eyes, a calm. Presence. But there was more than that. Guilt? No. Resolve? Perhaps. What? No matter. When Ginsburg left the room, Natalia Kropotkina stared at him in barely disguised hatred.

Isaak Ginsburg thought Natalia was beautiful. He had never seen such striking green eyes. He went back to his apartment and drank vodka and thought about Natalia Kropotkina and her father and the coughing *zek* and Mikheyev and Jaan Birk's outrageous proposal.

Natalia Kropotkina was torn between hatred born of loyalty to her father's sacrifice and the memory of the complex brown eyes that had briefly held her own at her exhibition in the Rossiya. In spite of herself, Natalia was curious about Ginsburg. She met him again, as she had known she would, in the second week of October at a party given by a director of the Bolshoi. It was a gathering of artists and writers and those party officials— including her husband, Leonid—who enjoyed the company of artists and writers. When she saw Ginsburg, he was alone, having himself some French brandy and pickled mushrooms.

Serafim Korenkho had died in a camp because he had opposed medical experiments on human beings. Isaak Ginsburg, apparently without pride, had become a party suck on a level to rival Leonid. Natalia wondered how Ginsburg could spend two years in a camp only to turn around and abase himself, so assiduously and blatantly toadying up to the worst party creeps.

Ginsburg had a wonderful feel for the Russian language. Not even Natalia could fail to appreciate that. But just how he was able to be such a worm was beyond her.

Natalia looked Ginsburg's way, then returned to her conversation with two officials of the Artists Union. She wanted to ask Ginsburg flat out why he was such a jerk.

She didn't care about the consequences; the consequences be damned. The problem was how to quietly tell the bastard off without incurring Leonid's suspicion.

Leonid was drinking hard. Natalia knew she should be careful, stay among women, chat with men only briefly. Leonid kept his eye on her, and now there was no Sonia for comfort and support in the early hours of the morning. Leonid had successfully destroyed that. There was only the couch, cigarettes, vodka, and the companionship of her refrigerator, which had been making a humming sound lately.

Later, on her way back from the toilet, Natalia angled in Ginsburg's direction. She wanted to spit in his face.

Ginsburg disarmed her with his eyes and said, "I know what happened to your father, Mrs. Kropotkina. A *zek* told me on the train to Zima."

Natalia wanted to swear at him, even slap his attractive face; she could hardly believe this. "You what?" she whispered savagely.

"I know what happened to Dr. Serafim Korenkho. My name is—"

"Isaak Ginsburg, I know. My father died of a heart attack in a labor camp in Slansky. He died honorably, comrade." Her use of "comrade" was a bullet. Natalia glared at him, hating him, wanting to tell him what she thought of him. Her father was dead. Ginsburg lived, a roach.

Ginsburg was calm. "He died honorably, yes, but not at Slansky. He died as the subject of experimental drugs at a cancer research clinic in Perm. The very thing he opposed, I'm told."

"He what?" Was Ginsburg a liar on top of everything else?

"Your father was sent to Slansky, then to a uranium mine. The *zek* on my train and your father were starving in an earlier camp and your father shared a potato with him. Your father saved the *zek*'s life, the *zek* saved mine—a chain of humanity so that we may remain civilized and never forget, Mrs. Kropotkina. Your father wanted you to know what happened to him at Perm.''

Natalia Kropotkina was stunned, yet she believed Ginsburg; the Communists were capable of anything. She glanced at her Leonid. He was looking at her. "My husband, you see. I want very much to know about my father, but—''

"Would you like to talk later, then? Your father would understand that this is a matter of honor for me as well as the man whose life he saved. Perhaps I am not so terrible as you might think. Sometimes we do what we have to do.''

Natalia didn't know what to say. She wanted to know about her father. Now she wanted to know Ginsburg's story as well.

"Believe me, I understand your rage, Mrs. Kropotkina, but I would like a chance to explain myself. Please.''

Natalia believed what Isaak Ginsburg had said about her father. She wanted to know the rest of the story, all of it. She was also transfixed by Ginsburg's physical presence. The possibility that Ginsburg was working for the KGB did not occur to her. For reasons that were elemental and primal, she knew he was telling the truth. "Let me give you the number at my studio," she said. "I'm generally there in the afternoons.''

Twenty-One

COMRADE SERGEI PAVLICHENKO WAS AN IMPRESSIVE FIG-
ure on the stage of the small auditorium. Pavlichenko
had all the trappings of a poet: a gray beard, a corduroy
jacket with leather elbow patches—French-made and
therefore stylish, but well worn and therefore Bohemian—
and an English cigarette that he waved passionately. The
party leaders wanted their poets to look like poets.

"We ask ourselves who we are, we Russians . . ."
Pavlichenko stroked his beard thoughtfully.

"We have magpie souls, black and white. Magpie
hearts. Who are we?"

Pavlichenko's voice rose angrily until he shouted the
question again. "Who are we?" The Soviets encouraged the clichéd angry-artist notion on condition that the
anger be directed according to their instructions. Pavlichenko, who liked shopping in privileged sections of
GUM, did his best to make the polemics colorful.

Isaak Ginsburg, who sat near the front of the hall with
the other writers and editors of the Writers Union, nodded in agreement at the correct places. Pavlichenko's

dramatic reading was a pathetic spectacle; everybody had to agree with him or risk being sent to a camp.

Pavlichenko started to sweat. Before the reading, he'd slugged down a quarter of a liter of vodka with friends. He squeegeed his forehead with the palm of his hand and flipped the sweat onto the stage with a gesture that said he was a worker's poet and this was honest worker's sweat. He ended his poem with his arms outspread, palms open, embracing all: "The taiga is of us. For us. Ours." He took a deep drag on his cigarette, closed his eyes and exhaled slowly.

Isaak Ginsburg applauded enthusiastically and said, "Wonderful! Wonderful!" *Bullshit! Bullshit!* Pavlichenko was a raging asshole. Ginsburg had a fleeting vision of himself smashing a surprised Pavlichenko in the face with his fist. Ginsburg turned to the jowly man on his left and said, "Powerful material, don't you think? Powerful. Pavlichenko knows how to read."

"It's a pleasure to hear him," the jowly man said.

Isaak Ginsburg said, "Incomparable." He followed the jowly man down the aisle and onto the stage to congratulate Pavlichenko on his performance. The jowly man walked like a huge, obese goose. Ginsburg remembered his grandmother's wonderful pâté.

Pavlichenko was glad Ginsburg had attended the reading. "Comrade Ginsburg! What do you think?"

"I think you were wonderful, comrade. Your best work, I think." Could anything be worse than having to listen to Pavlichenko? Ginsburg embraced Sergei Pavlichenko. "Congratulations," he said. "Beautiful work."

Pavlichenko, pleased, said, "You will stay to drink a little vodka, won't you, comrade? Selyutin's throwing a party."

Ginsburg said, "Ordinarily I would, but I've been working on an epic poem and it's coming for me. Nights are my best time, as you know. When it's coming, it's foolish for me not to get it on paper. You know how it is."

"I understand, Isaak. Believe me, I understand. Thank you for coming to the reading."

Isaak Ginsburg went to retrieve his coat from the cloakroom and froze. Up ahead, Felix Jin, coatless, waited by the entrance to the lobby.

When Ginsburg got near, Jin said, "Comrade Ginsburg! Good that you came. Are you going to Selyutin's gathering?"

"No, I think I'll go on home tonight, Comrade Jin."

"Me too," Jin said.

"I'm working on an epic poem commemorating the completion of the BAM." The BAM was a rail line in the Soviet Far East that looped north of the old Trans-Siberian tracks. It was intended to help develop the interior as well as provide tracks farther away from the Chinese border.

"Up all night, eh?"

Ginsburg said, "Yes, comrade."

"Writing poetry?"

"Writing poetry is hard work. Even reading it can be work. Did you see Pavlichenko sweat? That sweat is from his heart, believe me."

Jin said, "You don't seem to have come with anyone in particular, Comrade Ginsburg. Are you alone? Do you mind if I join you on the ride back into town?"

"Join me, certainly."

Ginsburg and Jin waited their turns at the cloakroom. They put on their heavy coats and *papakhas* and wrapped woolen scarves around their throats. They waited patiently for their turn through the heavy revolving door at the main entrance. There were policemen at the door to prevent the importation of knowledge.

Outside, snow twisted and whirled in the gusting wind. Ginsburg and Jin walked along a path that curved through a narrow parklike strip that bordered the main street in front of Moscow University. Ginsburg liked to walk among the wintry ghosts of white-barked birches. In the spring and summer huge fat-bodied Russian magpies watched the sidewalks from the birches. These magpies, the ones that had apparently inspired Pavlichenko, were big as crows or ravens. Behind the two men, the spires of the university loomed high, cathedral-like.

"A wonderful Russian experience to walk among birch on a snowy night," Ginsburg said.

"Yes, it is. Cleans the lungs."

"We come and we go, but the birch remain, and the snow returns every fall. Where would we be without the birch?"

Jin looked up at Ginsburg's face. "Did it seem to you that Pavlichenko might have engaged in parody as some kind of prank tonight?"

Ginsburg looked surprised. "Why, no. I'm sure he was sincere."

"When they defect, you know, the defectors tell the British and the Americans that they survived on irony, survived laughing at their countrymen."

"I can't believe that of Pavlichenko," Ginsburg said.

Jin nodded his head in agreement. "I can't either."

Ginsburg's heart fluttered and a sickening wave of anxiety coursed through his stomach. His face flushed momentarily. Ahead, in the huge expanse of an empty parking lot, he saw a crowd surging toward them. He was saved. "Look there!" he said. "The circus is letting out."

Hundreds of bundled Russians were moving rapidly in the direction of the metro stop, preparing for a wild scramble for seats on the underground trains.

Unless they hurried, Ginsburg and Jin had a wait ahead of them. Either way, they would have to ride packed into the metro car like oily, smoked sprat.

They joined a huge knot of people surging into the station, then waited while those ahead of them were sucked quickly downward by a metro escalator. The escalators on the Moscow metro were said to be the fastest in the world, a claim that went unchallenged by visitors who rode them. The deeper the escalator, the faster it seemed to hurtle. The escalator at University Station slung the line of people down, down, down. The platform was twenty-five yards below, a precaution against American rockets.

The wooden steps of the escalator whipped *zip, zip, zip* as they emerged from the top. Passengers descended at a dizzying rate, stomachs aloft, as on a swiftly descending Ferris wheel. At the bottom of the escalator the stairs disappeared *zip, zip, zip*, at the same startling speed.

A woman in a blue uniform watched at the bottom lest a child or confused older citizen get sucked, screaming, into one of the quarter-inch spaces that were grinning jaws on either side of the descending stairs.

Jin was quick and aggressive. He pushed his way to the front of the platform and they were able to board the first train back into town. They both stood, holding on to a stainless steel post, listening to children talk about bears that roller-skated, about the "American rodeo" that was part of the show. There had been bucking broncos and lassos. Ginsburg wondered if Russian cowboys could ride and rope better than American cowboys.

The train rumbled into the darkness of the tunnel and after a couple of stops emerged onto a bridge. The Moscow River below them was frozen and white. The V. I. Lenin Central Stadium, also under a mantle of snow, was to their left. It was dramatic and beautiful to ride over the Moscow River in a snowstorm. The heart of Moscow was up ahead.

The snow twisted and swirled above the city. The young couple next to Ginsburg and Jin had been most impressed by an acrobat who had been catapulted from a seesaw onto the top of ten men standing feet on shoulders. It had been a seemingly impossible feat. The young woman said Russian circuses were the best circuses in the world.

The metro entered a tunnel again. Ginsburg said,

"Perhaps you would like to come up to my apartment, Comrade Jin. Have a little vodka."

"Do you mean that?" Jin sounded surprised and pleased by the invitation.

"Certainly, comrade. If you like, I'll show you the poems I'm working on. They're some of my best, I think."

Jin knew Ginsburg was up to something. Ginsburg secretly hated Jin, had to. "Yes, that would be nice," Jin said amiably. "Maybe for a few minutes."

Isaak Ginsburg wondered if Colonel Jin knew that he had been seeing Natalia Kropotkina.

Twenty-Two

ANATOLI STALNOV HAD BEEN SUMMONED FROM NOVOSI-birsk to function as Ginsburg's officially approved mentor—an honor bearing with it a Moscow residence permit; the Soviet Union had put an eight-million cap on Moscow's population and so extruded unhappy exiles from the city at the same pace as it received delighted new residents.

No Muscovite mentioned Stalnov's professional exile in Novosibirsk. He once had been of no use and was sent away; he was now useful and so was returned. His duty was to screen invitations and requests extended to Isaak Ginsburg. The official reason for this romantic but absurd chore was that Ginsburg needed privacy for the arduous hours he put in at the typewriter.

In the second week of December, Anatoli Stalnov told Isaak Ginsburg the two of them had to talk. Saying no more, he led the way to the Moscow River. The awful Russian winter was upon the city. This was one of those evenings when Moscow took on an eerie calm, sitting alone out on the edge of Asia. Ginsburg and Stalnov, breathing frigid air that seared their lungs, strolled along an icy path beaten in the snow along the eastern bank. The northern lights unfolded overhead, celestial curtains of greens and yellows and reds.

"Moscow is a beautiful city," Stalnov said.

"You can smell the cold."

"It's like this all winter long in Novosibirsk," Stalnov said. His breath came in frosty puffs that hesitated an instant in the wind, like delicate crystal, then disappeared.

"The avenues look like canals iced in."

Stalnov said, "No traffic and the snow muffles everything else."

Did the snow muffle even the screams in Lubyanka Prison? "It's lovely," Ginsburg said.

Stalnov said, "We could be walking alone by a river in Siberia. Just us."

The two men walked, listening to the crunch of their boots on the frozen crusts of footprints. "Listen, Isaak, it hasn't been announced yet and won't be for a couple of weeks, but Comrade Zhukov has negotiated a resumption of the Geneva arms talks."

"Really?"

"You're part of the bargain, Issak Avraamovich. You'll read a commemorative poem at the signing of the resumption agreement, which will be held at Vladivostok during the first week of May."

Ginsburg was confused. "Vladivostok?"

"At the airport there. We want to remind the world that the last agreement we signed with the Americans—at Vladivostok—was never approved by the U. S. Senate. Zhukov will give Secretary of State Kaplan a bust of Lenin. Kaplan will give Zhukov a carved eagle. You'll read your poem. I tell you this so you'll have time to do your best work." Stalnov paused. "Anything less than your best would be an embarrassment to us both, comrade."

"Thank you. I won't let you down, believe me."

Stalnov checked his wristwatch. "I suppose we should be heading home." He led the way up the long trail to Red Square. At the top of the slope and on their left, the heavy, gloomy south wall of the Kremlin overlooked the river. Stalnov's star rose with Ginsburg's, but if Ginsburg turned out wrong, then Stalnov would pay.

Stalnov said, "It has been suggested that you ride a train across the Soviet Union so as to impress the foreign reporters with your love of country. You could read a poem somewhere in between, Irkutsk say. By the way, Isaak, I think it would be wise of you to consider carefully some of the people you meet in these gatherings. I'm thinking of the matter of ladies."

"Ladies?"

"You've been observed with Natalia Kropotkina. Natalia's an attractive woman, I know, and intelligent too."

Ginsburg looked surprised, but wasn't. He assumed that Anatoli Stalnov was working for the KGB.

"You should listen to me, Isaak. I don't want you to get into trouble, or her . . ." Stalnov's voice trailed off. "Isaak, you should know something about Leonid Kropotkin. He's insanely jealous of his wife. People know that here. You have to keep your distance."

Isaak Ginsburg had one of those wonderful moments of inspiration that had once gone into his poetry, an unexpected coming together of associations: the talk of presenting a bust of Lenin to Stuart Kaplan; Stalnov's suggestion of a trans-Siberian train ride; the mention of Natalia.

It was time to write Jaan Birk.

Isaak Ginsburg took the subway to the edge of the city and back. He rode to the southwest, got off, blended in with the crowds, and rode to Nogina Plaza, where he changed for a third and final run. He had gotten a lot of practice in the routine in the weeks since he had met Natalia; one of her artist friends had an apartment near the Kosmos Hotel and the Monument to the Conquerors of Outer Space.

This area was far north of Red Square—near the edge

of the city. The monument and the hotel were dwarfed by the nearby Ostankino television tower, 536 meters high, which looked like a bizarre metal Tinker Toy anchored by guy wires.

Ginsburg was happy to take whatever precautions were necessary for his meetings with Natalia.

When they were finished with their coming together and lay side by side, sweaty, enjoying one another's smell, Ginsburg said. "I talked to the conductress today, Lado Kabakhidze's daughter. She got in from a run from Novosibirsk yesterday afternoon."

Natalia sat up in bed. "Will she do it?"

Ginsburg was still surprised by the vehemence of Natalia's desire to steal the head. Defecting was one thing; stealing Lenin's head was quite another. In addition to her good looks and intelligence, Natalia Kropotkina was a gutsy woman. Ginsburg admired her nerve. "Lado's dead."

"What?"

"They extended his sentence again, Nina said. He died three weeks later. Of a heart attack, they told her." Ginsburg sighed at the memory of Lado Kabakhidze.

"I'm sorry to hear that, Isaak."

"Lado was my friend." Ginsburg fell silent, then said, "Nina's with us. For her father. She's Lado's daughter, all right. She'll take a letter to Jaan Birk. When we find out what Jaan needs, she'll get one to Kashva. If Kashva agrees to pass Birk's list on to Abu Ali, we'll see—that's all we can do. It's up to the Americans then. If the Americans say yes, I'll figure out a way to retrieve Birk's equipment. The hard question is, can you get the commission for the Vladivostok pin?"

"Listen, Isaak, Ivan Dmitrov wanted me to have the pin commemorating his Gorky Park statue, but I was screwed out of it by some damned bureaucrat on the committee. Dmitrov would have gotten a better-looking pin from me, and he knows it. So now he sculpts the bust Zhukov gives Kaplan. Believe me, he'll want me even more for this one.''

"More than ever?''

Natalia studied the tip of her finger. "Oh, I might have to talk sweet, but I think he'll come around.''

"Then you know him well enough?''

"I know him, and they won't turn him down twice.'' Natalia put her cigarette out in the ashtray on the floor by the bed. "Vladivostok in May sounds fun. They have a beach there, don't they?''

"Stalnov knows we've been seeing each other, so I suppose Jin does too.''

Natalia looked startled. "He doesn't know about our meetings here, does he?''

"I've been careful,'' Ginsburg said. "Say, Tashenka, I loved those sexy panties you were wearing today. Where did you get those anyway?''

Natalia Kropotkina smiled. "At Bloomingdale's in New York. When we get there, I'll wear them for you all the time if you want.'' Natalia reached over and slid her soft hand onto Isaak's thigh. "Why, just look at that thing! Standing right up there, and so soon after last time. Lucky for me your Captain Mikheyev was just having himself a little fun.''

Twenty-Three

JAMES BURLANE WAS THE COMPANY'S RANDY GENIUS AND *Bohemian spy—the man, it was said, who got things done. The gangling Burlane ambled on alone, a paperback in his hip pocket. He combed his hair with his fingers. He dug at his crotch if it itched. He laughed out loud if something struck him as funny, which was often.*

Burlane was long of face and long of nose, which turned slightly to one side. He was irreverent of authority, indifferent to fashion, and disdainful of possessions, saying he doubted if anyone on his deathbed ever remembered owning a Ford. Women found him attractive for reasons that were obscure and infuriating to serious men who wore neckties and drove washed BMWs.

More than one Company official—wondering about Burlane's background—had pulled his dossier for a quick peek. To their amazement, they learned that he was the son of a railroad worker and had grown up in the unlikely town of Umatilla, in the desert country of northeastern Oregon. Burlane had no power at the CIA; in fact, he scorned it. Everybody knew it would be stupid to put a man of his imagination in charge of anything.

Burlane cheerfully agreed. He didn't give a damn about power.

At the bottom of his dossier, a Company psychologist had noted: "Subject J. Burlane apparently regards the world as some kind of interesting zoo or menagerie. We see no reason to believe this mild neurosis should be incompatible with his present duties."

Burlane preferred penguins and lazy cats to pit bulls and Dobermans. He entered battle on behalf of the former. He was the Company's ace, and everybody knew it, which is why the director and deputy director of the CIA summoned him to consider Contact David's proposal.

Twenty-Four

T HE ENORMOUS RED WALL THAT DEFENDED THE KREMLIN, citadel of the Soviets, built on the banks of the Moscow River, was in fact an isosceles triangle with a blunt tip that faced the southwest. The northern wall of the triangle—which actually ran to the northeast, reckoning from the apex of the triangle—faced Volkhonka Avenue and the Square of the Fiftieth Anniversary of the October Revolution.

The base of the triangle faced Red Square and ran just slightly to the southeast—reckoning from the Square of the Fiftieth Anniversary of the October Revolution. The southern wall curved inward slightly. This was to accommodate a bend of the Moscow River.

In front of the Northern Wall there was a narrow garden with sidewalks—a promenade of sorts—where pilgrims and tourists strolled among lovely birches. There were five towers on this stretch of the wall, including the two at the corners; the tower in the center was replete with turrets and cupolas, and marked the main entrance to the Kremlin. Just behind the main entrance was the tallest of the onion-shaped domes of the Russian

Orthodox church that rose, golden, dazzling, on the inside of this most secular of secular capitals.

The promenade in front of the northern wall was bordered by a high black fence of heavy metal pickets. There was a gate at the eastern end of the park. Just inside this gate—facing the Square of the Fiftieth Anniversary of the October Revolution—lay the entombed body of the Soviet Union's Unknown Soldier.

Two soldiers wearing stainless-steel helmets and white gloves, with chromium bayonets on their rifles, guarded the eternal flame at the gravesite.

Just in front of the grave began a four-inch-wide white line that led to Lenin's tomb. The line went east, then turned an oblique right and entered Red Square.

Inside the square, the line made a second oblique right and ran parallel to the eastern stretch of the Kremlin wall.

There was a broad sidewalk along the base of the wall, then a row of small trees, then the mausoleum that contained the tomb of V. I. Lenin—and Joseph Stalin too, until he was evicted by followers of Nikita Khrushchev. There were concrete bleachers on either side of the mausoleum, where members of the Politburo and other Soviet officials watched the May Day demonstrations and various military parades.

The mausoleum, made of granite and porphyry—a hard, purplish-red stone containing small crystals of feldspar—was a terraced, four-sided pyramid some forty feet on each side. This pallid, purplish-red porphyry was as close as the Soviet architects could come to the symbolic socialist red. Although the mausoleum was built some forty feet in front of the Kremlin wall, when viewed from the front—from Red Square—it looked as though it projected directly from the wall itself.

Visitors filed into the mausoleum and past the body in a steady line from 11 A.M. to 1 P.M. daily—Tuesdays and Fridays excepted.

* * *

Jaan Birk used the first three days of his ten-day New Year's furlough studying the tomb. He waited patiently in line each time through. He timed each trip with the second hand of his watch, and after the fourth trip through knew exactly how long it took.

The line entered the main entrance of the mausoleum, turned left, and went down a dimly lit flight of stairs. There was a guard at the bottom where the corridor turned right. Then a second flight of stairs, shorter this time, with a guard at the bottom. The corridor went left again, down a longer flight of stairs. Another guard, a turn to the right, more stairs.

There was a guard.

More stairs. Steeper this time. To the right again.

And there was a guard, and heavy metal doors opened for visitors.

The room was small and dark.

The coffin was in the middle. It sat atop a raised rectangular pedestal so that Lenin himself lay roughly at eye level. Visitors entered from the southwest corner of the room, parallel with Lenin's shoulders, and circled against the walls to the northwest corner where they exited. This was a U-shaped tour. It was done quickly and silently, with no lingering: other citizens waited their turn.

There was a moat between the visitors and the coffin, far too great a distance for even a champion athlete to clear from a standing start. There was no water in the moat, but rather soldiers—five of them. Two stood on each side of the coffin, at Lenin's shoulders and feet. The fifth soldier stood above Lenin's head at the open end of the U-shaped promenade.

The coffin itself was enclosed in glass. There was a black blanket folded to Lenin's waist. One hand was slightly open, the other slightly closed. Lenin's head rested on a red pillow. The room was black save for a soft red light that bathed Lenin's face from above.

The guards, Birk noted, were stiff from standing at attention.

The Soviets were understandably careful to preserve their embalmed icon underneath the Kremlin wall. The troops housed at the base of Spasskaya Tower carried loaded AK-47s. The guards carried loaded weapons. When the inevitable alarm went off, more soldiers would appear from Spasskaya at once.

Jaan Birk considered the vast size of Red Square. He held out the palm of his left hand: Red Square. He put his right hand in front of his eyes. He couldn't see his left hand anymore. Birk considered that and opened a pack of cigarettes. He took a drag of hot air and eased the smoke onto his hand and grinned.

He remembered a yellow mongrel named Boris, and grinned even more. Birk thought of Viktor Konnen, the animal trainer who had reared him, and of his aunt, Greta, whom he loved dearly.

Birk decided to go to Tallinn on the Gulf of Finland. Perhaps, once he had been there, he would have a plan ready for Ginsburg.

In Tallinn, Viktor and Greta Konnen lived in retirement from the circus. Birk looked forward to juggling brown eggs tossed to him by Viktor. He looked forward to Greta's borscht. Greta put an extra splash of vinegar into her borscht, which Birk thought had to be the best in Estonia.

Jaan Birk sat backward, watching Leningrad Station, then Moscow, slide away from him. He rode backward because the railroad hadn't bothered to turn the day car around. Travelers going to the capital were somehow favored over those leaving. Sit forward entering, backward leaving; this saved labor, no doubt. Whether or not it was political, even the cynical Birk was uncertain. Anything was possible with Russians.

The train passed the Ostankino television tower on Birk's left, then a large labor camp downhill on the same side. The Kryukovo labor camp. Officially the camps did not exist. Nevertheless, the Soviets had attempted to block the train passengers' view of the camp by erecting a solid wooden fence on stilts. The bottom of the fence began twenty feet off the ground.

Almost all the isbas had painted shutters and many were painted all over. Birk assumed the peasants here had gotten extra rations of paint because their isbas were built alongside the main run from Moscow to Leningrad.

The far end of Birk's car was filled with uniformed soldiers. Enlisted men, they had crude haircuts and drank vodka from bottles in paper bags. They were drunk and getting drunker, loud and getting louder. Russians! Birk despised them.

Boris was not a fancy breed of dog. He was a cur, a yellowish-brown mongrel so nondescript and totally dog-like as to be almost an abstraction of a dog, suitable for an illustration in a children's book. He was part terrier possibly, part hound of some kind. He had a short coat, and his ears hung rather than perked. He had friendly brown eyes, and his tongue was given to good-natured flopping.

Boris had one distinction: he had been retired from the circus for political reasons. In what had started out to be a comradely joke among circus people, Victor Konnen had trained four dogs—a center forward, two wingers, and a goalie—to ice-skate and play hockey. The Soviet Union had a famous hockey team of ice-skating bears that played at state circuses. Konnen's dogs had beaten the bears nine to four in Novosibirsk, and destroyed them by an eye-popping eleven to two in Moscow.

Nine of these eleven goals were scored by Boris. He was too quick for the bears, who were intense and determined, but awkward on the ice. Both Boris and his Estonian master were summarily retired on the orders of an unnamed Kremlin official who was enraged at the debacle.

Viktor Konnen petted Boris's head. "Poor Boris." Boris had once been a lively dog, but he was bored now. He missed the circus life.

Birk couldn't wait until Greta got back from the communal kitchen with the borscht. When she did, it would be like old times.

"Sure. He's a friendly old guy. He likes a little affection. Isn't that right, Boris?"

Konnen massaged the back of Boris's neck. Boris gave a contented sigh. He just loved it when Konnen gave him a little massage. Boris had worked harder for Konnen than for the other trainers at the circus because Konnen liked him. Konnen respected him. Konnen saw to it that he got everything he wanted to eat. Konnen did special little things for him.

Birk fondled Boris's ear and thought surely he saw the dog smile.

"He hasn't been feeling well, I don't think."

Birk stroked Boris's ear. "Good old Boris." Boris looked extra contented. All the attention was wonderful.

"He's not old. For a dog he's middle-aged. It isn't age that slows him down. He's bored not having anything to do. He misses the circus."

Boris stretched out on the floor, receiving one hand each from Birk and Konnen. It was splendid. Ahhh!

Birk told Viktor Konnen what Birk and Ginsburg had in mind and why. He told Konnen how it was he proposed to get Lenin's head out of Red Square. Konnen was an Estonian too and hated Russians.

When he had finished, Konnen said, "I can do that. You'll have to get me the silent whistles. Boris should be able to hear one a quarter of a mile away."

"Boris will have to take his chances when it's over."

"We all die someday, Jaan. Some sooner than others."

"Some sooner than others," Birk agreed. "How long will it take you to train him?"

"Two or three weeks if I work at it every day. He's the kind of dog who's not afraid of anything, so the smoke shouldn't bother him. But I should run him through it with the smoke the last three times." Viktor Konnen knew his nephew and his dog were going to die soon anyway. Boris had spirit. If Boris could talk, Konnen was certain, he would volunteer just as the dying Jaan had volunteered. "I can practice in the taiga. I know of a place," Konnen said.

The door opened and Greta was back, pot of borscht in one hand, jar of vinegar in the other, and a smile on her face. She had a liter bottle of vodka tucked under one arm.

Twenty-Five

ON THE LAST DAY OF HIS NEW YEAR'S FURLOUGH, ON HIS return to Moscow from Tallinn, Jaan Birk gave Isaak Ginsburg his shopping list. They met in a snack shop on Gorky Street where a few pastries were sold, along with slices of bland cheese and small sausages. Patrons ate standing at narrow tables. The tables were chest high so they could be leaned on—elbow high if the customer was short, elbow low if he was tall. Ginsburg and Birk sipped tea that the counterwoman had ladled out of a large stainless-steel pot.

Ginsburg and Birk had to hunker slightly, elbows low. There were two women workers in the snack bar and three customers: an old man and two young women. Ginsburg and Birk were pensive as they watched the traffic on Gorky Street outside. The small Ladas on Gorky suddenly began pulling to the side of the road. People outside the snack bar stopped to watch.

A heavy, black formation of shiny Volgas appeared with a surreal quickness. The Volgas, said by tourists to look like 1955 Chryslers, had curtained windows and small red flags flying from staffs mounted on the fenders just above the headlights.

Three cars in the middle of the phalanx carried members of the ruling elite of the Communist party. They were on their way to the Kremlin. To the Politburo.

"Look at them go," Birk said. "Another day of hard work saving us from the Americans." Birk opened a blue-and-white pack of TU-134s, Bulgarian cigarettes. An Aeroflot TU-134 was on the front of the package. Both Ginsburg and Birk lit up, thinking.

"They say TU-134s are the best cigarettes in the world," Ginsburg said. Hot air. Ginsburg knew that. Everybody knew it. Inhale a Russian cigarette, and you got hot air. The current joke in Moscow was that the Soviet Union made the biggest microchips in the world.

"Wonderful cigarettes," Birk said. Birk knew that if he inhaled a French Gauloise, or an American Marlboro, he'd get a rush of nicotine. That's what cigarette smoking was all about; that's why people smoked cigarettes. They liked the nicotine. They got hooked on it. Birk had long ago wearied of hot air.

Birk would have preferred catching his cancer from cigarettes rather than a uranium pit. That, at least, would have been his choice. His risk. There was no doubt that it would have been more fun. Birk said, "I love the taste."

Ginsburg looked south down Gorky Street where the black Volgas had disappeared. "Well, Jaan, let's go for a stroll. I want to see your list."

Birk shrugged. "Let's go." And so they walked south on Gorky toward the Kremlin. Moscow's layout resembled the cross-section of a felled tree, with concentric rings intersected by spokes fanning out from the center. Gorky ran north to south, where it ended at the entrance of the red-bricked State Historical Museum. The other side of the museum was the northern end of Red Square.

The Kremlin and the districts adjacent to it were encircled by the Boulevard Ring and the Sadovoye Ring. A third ring, the Moscow Circular Road, marked the city limits. Gorky was one of the wide avenues or "prospekts"—Leninsky, Kutuzovsky, Mir, Leningradsky, and others—that radiated from the center of the city. These prospekts were far too wide for pedestrians to negotiate above ground, so there were subterranean sidewalks at the intersections of streets.

Isaak Ginsburg and Jaan Birk walked south on Gorky, past the Museum of the Revolution, past the Moscow City Soviet, past Central Telegraph, past the Hotel Intourist, to the wide Square of the Fiftieth Anniversary of the October Revolution just north of Red Square.

It took Ginsburg and Birk two underground hikes to emerge at the southern end of the Hotel Moscow, which itself was the eastern border of the Square of the Fiftieth Anniversary of the October Revolution. They walked south, the State Historical Museum on their right and the Central V. I. Lenin Museum on their left. Then they were into it, into the northeastern corner of Red Square.

They walked south in front of the huge GUM department store, which was the eastern edge of Red Square and the chief obstacle to their plan.

Ginsburg angled to his right, toward the center of the square. "Natalia wanted to come. She wanted to meet you, but she couldn't get away from her husband."

"I would have liked to have met her also. Please tell her that I'm doing my part for her father as well as myself. Tell her he'll be with us in spirit." He handed Ginsburg the list, which Ginsburg studied.

"Can you get them, do you think?"

"I hope so. If I can, I'll have them for you on March sixteenth, when I get back from a reading in Tbilisi. The question is, is that time enough?"

"It should be. Later, a dog will have to be delivered from Tallinn to Moscow."

Ginsburg looked at the list again. "A dog?"

"Can it be done?"

"It can be done." A dog?

"I'll send you an order of battle in which everybody's responsibilities will be clearly specified."

Ginsburg cleared his throat. "I want to tell you, Jaan, that if Natalia and I make it out and ever have a son, we will name him for you. He'll be yours as well as ours."

Jaan Birk embraced his friend. "We'll see what happens, Isaak."

Twenty-Six

NATALIA KROPOTKINA SLUNG HER JAPANESE CAMERA OVER her shoulder and locked the door to her Lada. She'd never been able to get within a yard of Ivan Dmitrov without him somehow pawing her. He'd insisted on showing her the working model of the monumental Oktyabrskaya Square statue, the Dmitrov masterwork begun twenty years earlier—Natalia was then just thirteen years old—and still unfinished. Natalia knew perfectly well that the socialist Michelangelo had something more interesting in mind than talking about the difficulties of completing the Oktyabrskaya monument. So did she.

The Kremlin had decided that if Comrade Grigori Zhukov gave a bust of Lenin to the American secretary of state at Vladivostok, then the statue ought to be something special. Thus the Soviets had instructed Ivan Dmitrov to sculpt a Lenin bust for the occasion— something special, just for the Americans. This bust—a thoughtful, contemplative Lenin for the American barbarians—was displayed at the Hotel Rossiya, and would remain there until Zhukov took it to Vladivostok. In the Rossiya, European visitors to Moscow could

132

appreciate the man of peace, whose journey to America would commemorate the reopening of the Geneva arms talks.

Natalia knew Dmitrov was worried that whoever designed the Vladivostok pin wouldn't get every nuance of his Lenin just right, precisely the way Dmitrov had rendered the bust—or worse, choose not to include Lenin on the Vladivostok pin at all. That was possible.

Dmitrov's Oktyabrskaya sculpture had a long and complicated history. Joseph Stalin's original proposal for a thousand-foot pyramid topped with an immense statue of Lenin had failed because of the cost involved. Another suggestion was to sculpt a huge Lenin to overlook Moscow from the Lenin Hills. That was rejected as being too far away from the center of the city. Following Nikita Khrushchev's visit to New York City in 1959, the Soviets set about to strip the old-world charm of Oktyabrskaya Square—at the eastern tip of Gorky Park—and replace it with a modern look. This was to provide an appropriately grand setting for the long-absent Lenin monument in the capital city.

Ivan Dmitrov, who, it was said, drew his first portrait of Lenin when he was six years old, had spent a lifetime given over to the glorification of communism through monumental sculpture. He was given the task of creating this, his masterwork.

The Oktyabrskaya statue would stand on elevated ground in the center of the square, almost within sight of the Ferris wheel in Gorky Park; to the north across the Moscow River lay the golden domes of the Kremlin. The chief architect of Moscow and one of the planners of the monument told *The New York Times* that this location—on the route taken by dignitaries from the airport to the Kremlin—was "an important, prestigious place."

There were those who thought that if Natalia Kropotkina had been allowed to develop as a sculptor, she would have been Ivan Dmitrov's equal. Natalia herself found it hard to imagine the Soviets giving a woman a chance at sculpting the grandiose Lenin that was Dmitrov's chief claim to immortality.

Dmitrov was supposed to be Natalia's colleague. The truth was, Dmitrov did not consider her any sort of colleague at all. Dmitrov sculpted celebrated monuments to Communist heroes; he was the Rodin of the USSR. Brezhnev had sat for him, so had Andropov and Konstantin Chernenko and Petr Spishkin. Natalia Kropotkina merely designed lapel pins.

So Ivan Dmitrov talked down to her, which she accepted without apparent resentment. The truth was, Dmitrov made her furious. On top of that, Dmitrov apparently thought his status as celebrity gave him the right to rest his hand on her rump whenever he felt like it. His hand roamed casually, with professional aplomb— as though he were contemplating curve and line for a statue of Aphrodite.

Ivan Dmitrov opened the door to his studio, tilted his face to one side, and grinned broadly, "Tasha! How good to see you!" He removed his thick-rimmed glasses and there—with busts of Karl Marx, Yuri Gagarin, and Fidel Castro looking on—gave her an embrace that lasted five or six counts more than a little bit too long.

"You're so kind, Comrade Dmitrov," Natalia said. She successfully broke from his grip and ran for the model of Dmitrov's monumental Lenin at the far end of the room. The model, four-feet-three-inches tall, sat atop a revolving pedestal beneath the skylight. "Oh, Ivan Yevgennivich, tell me all about it! I want to hear it from you. A treat! How is it coming?" She laid her camera and handbag on one of Dmitrov's workbenches.

"Let me take your coat." Dmitrov was a slow-talking man who took his Lenin seriously. He knew that Natalia Kropotkina felt bad about having had the Oktyabrskaya pin taken from her. "Do you like it?"

Natalia walked slowly around the model of the

Oktyabrskaya monument. The tail of Lenin's heavy coat furled dramatically in the wind; at Lenin's feet, a heroic group of comrades strode into the future. It was in fact, a thing of beauty in its way—somehow blending the imaginations of Diego Rivera, Norman Rockwell, Che Guevara, Shostakovich, and Yevgeni Yevtushenko. "I think it's beautiful, Ivan Yevgennivich. How much longer before it's finished?"

"A year, eighteen months possibly. Here, let me show you the model. My pleasure." Dmitrov put his glasses back on and took her confidently by the elbow. "The real statue will sit on a two-hundred-ton pedestal of Ukrainian granite. This model's on a revolving pedestal, you see, so I can see what it looks like from various angles. Here, let me show you." Dmitrov turned the statue slowly with his hand, then stopped it. "This is how it will look from the entrance of the subway exit." He turned it again. "This from Leninsky Prospekt. See?"

"Yes, the profiles are most dramatic, you're right."

Dmitrov was pleased. "Let me tell you about the smaller figures at Lenin's feet. I wanted them to dramatize the essential Lenin: striving toward the future of peaceful coexistence, a future without the exploitation of man by man." Dmitrov gave Natalia a little hug to punctuate the sentence, and continued his explanation. "The woman above them, you see, is the symbol of the victory. She's calling them all forward under the direction of Lenin. I finished her left shoulder last month. Then we have a peasant soldier here. A commissar. A young woman from the intelligentsia. You see, here, the newspaperboy has news of Lenin's revolutionary decrees. See, a warrior from the Caucasus here, and beside him a Kirghiz tribesman."

Here, Dmitrov's hand strayed to her hip, then on to the curve of her behind, where it remained. "We have representatives of oppressed people of Asia. All these are symbols of the individuality of nationalities living together in harmony in communism." He moved his hand slightly on Natalia Kropotkina's flank. A reassuring touch.

Dmitrov turned the pedestal. "Now, on the back here, facing Leninsky Prospekt, is the figure of a woman, symbolizing motherhood and womanhood. The child is the future, you see." Dmitrov's hand gripped Natalia's rump, sharing with her his commitment to the future.

"It's wonderful, Ivan Yevgennivich."

Dmitrov stepped back and admired Natalia's figure. He slipped his arm around her again. "The model I had for the victory woman had a fabulous body—much like your own figure as a matter of fact. Isn't she heroic? She was proud of herself, felt good about herself. She wasn't afraid to show me. I said, 'Galya, be dramatic. I want passion. Drama.' "

"Very dramatic," Natalia said.

"Tasha, have you ever modeled? Have you? You should, you know. You have a wonderful body. I suspect better than Galya's even. You know that, of course. You can't hide it. Men can't hide their imagination. It's natural to seek beauty, you know, to have it. I'm no different than other men. By the way, Natasha, I'm sorry you didn't get the commission for the Oktyabrskaya *znachok*. I recommended you for it."

Both Natalia and Dmitrov knew Natalia had lost the Oktyabrskaya pin because she hadn't protected her flanks in the party. In fact, she had lost it out of envy. There was always that risk when one seemed to outshine the group in the Soviet Union. Ivan Dmitrov had escaped that quicksand years earlier, but he was one of the exceptional and fortunate few.

She said, "Well, it's done. There's nothing we can do about it. But they are going to do a pin commemorating the Vladivostok signing, aren't they? There was an article in *Pravda* the other day."

Ivan Dmitrov had not escaped the quicksand without being able to perceive an exchange in the making. Dmitrov said, "Why, yes, they are going to commission a Vladivostok. I have a friend who's on the committee."

"Do they want something special or just another lump of pot metal? They'll put your Vladivostok Lenin on it, surely—you sculpted it specially for the Americans."

Dmitrov smiled. "I believe they have something unusual and dramatic in mind."

"The designer who gets the pin would have to go to Vladivostok to witness the signing, wouldn't she? If I did that pin, I could guarantee to put your bust on the front and do it right."

Dmitrov smiled. "Would you like a trip to Vladivostok, Natalia Serafimovna?"

"I don't mind travel. I like it, in fact. Especially trains. I'd like to go on the Trans-Siberian. They wouldn't have any objection to that, would they, Comrade Dmitrov? Maybe I could design a train *znachok*. I've always wanted to do a train *znachok*."

"I can't imagine they'd have any objections," Dmitrov said. "As a matter of fact, it would probably be impossible for you to get a spot on an airplane if you wanted one. Aeroflot will be overwhelmed with journalists and officials on their way to the signing." Dmitrov drew Natalia closer.

Natalia said, "You can be sure I understand the unusual and dramatic, Ivan Yevgennivich. I'd probably need to study the bust for many hours. That will be difficult in the Rossiya lobby."

"But you can borrow my copy—it's impossible to tell it from the original. And don't worry about the pin, Natalia. I'll talk to people."

"I probably won't be able to get the copy back until after Vladivostok. Would that be a problem for you, comrade?"

Comrade Dmitrov was getting an erection. "No, no, that's fine, Natalia. It's a copy. What do I need with the copy?"

"They couldn't very well overturn your recommendation twice in a row, could they?"

"You may rest assured they won't overturn it twice, Natalia Serafimovna." Ivan Dmitrov was eager to unwrap his prize.

Natalia Kropotkina felt Dmitrov's hand at the zipper of her skirt. She undid the two buttons in front and slipped the skirt down. Natalia hated this business, but she didn't have any choice. At least Dmitrov was excited by her and that was affection of sorts, she supposed. That was better than Leonid, who only wanted to beat her—but certainly nothing compared to the joy of being with Isaak; she hoped Isaak would never know what she had to do to guarantee the Vladivostok pin.

Natalia turned and raised her leg, showing Dmitrov a triangular patch of jet-black pubic hair through sexy American panties. She figured if Dmitrov wanted drama, drama he'd get. She arched her back and gave him the profile he had wanted. She took off her sweater, and turned as she removed her bra. If she had to perform, she was determined that it be a winning performance. Second place was no place.

Dmitrov led Natalia Kropotkina onto a bed in the next room where he sometimes took a nap after a hard day in the studio.

Natalia settled on the bed thinking of the cafés in Greenwich Village where she'd hung out with young artists. Sure, some of them, the most ambitious, made whores of themselves to get what they wanted. Others didn't have to. Others sculpted, painted, or wrote whatever they wanted to. Maybe they weren't rich, but they followed their imaginations.

Natalia decided that if she and Isaak got caught, they got caught.

She turned, giving Dmitrov a dramatic angle of her hip. Dmitrov, down to his socks and shorts, looked beside himself with anticipation. However much Comrade Kropotkina wanted to ride the Trans-Siberian Railroad with Issak Ginsburg, she had to resist the urge to vomit.

Twenty-Seven

None of the staff at the Perm Cancer Clinic knew what to think of the remarkable upsurge in morale among the twelve bald subjects in the leukemia experimental group. In early January, they seemed to perk up for no discernible reason.

Then, in March, came the odd request. The subjects' spokesman, Jaan Birk, asked if it might not be possible for them to join one of the periodic trips to Moscow to visit Red Square and the Kremlin. These bus trips were made possible by the Komsomol, the Communist Youth League, as a reward for deserving comrades.

The commandant of the Perm Cancer Clinic hesitated. It was one thing to inflict upon the patients boring, repetitious lectures about the Leninist dream. But this? Were they laughing at him? he wondered. There was no printed directive or regulation for something like this. On the other hand, the researchers monitoring the group said to let them have an occasional trip or furlough if they wanted; it was good for morale.

The commandant signed the form authorizing the trip. The baldies were going to get their plugs pulled in July anyway. What difference did it make?

*   *   *

As an investigator, Colonel Felix Jin was grateful for the mountain of forms, receipts, dockets, and ledgers that paralyzed the country. There were residence permits, travel permits, work permits. Receipts were piled upon receipts. There were cynical comrades who considered this love of documents a cultural disease, a form of Soviet arthritis. The purpose of the paper was not so much to accomplish anything—nobody nourished hopes of that—but rather to record error and deviance from already lethargic norms. Just to be sure that no comrade got away with anything, the Soviets saved just about everything.

Colonel Jin thought it was a good thing the USSR had plenty of trees for paper.

When a cultural administrator in a provincial city asked for a local appearance by a Moscow writer, the request was forwarded through the Moscow Writers Union. The request was recorded—a figurative gold star for initiative. The writer's excuse for saying no—few writers wanted to leave Moscow for even a day, unless it was to go to a Black Sea resort—was recorded as well. If the writer was a Jew, the request was forwarded to Jin. Jin was amused to see that Isaak Ginsburg, who had recently had a poem published about noble peasants thriving in the heart of Siberian winters, had himself wangled a reading in Tbilisi, capital of the Soviet Georgian Republic.

Book 2

BOOK 2

One

JAMES BURLANE SAT, OR RATHER SPRAWLED, ON HIS CHAIR looking as though he were waiting for a movie to start. Neely and Schott were behaving like they had on the final night of the Townes affair. That time, Burlane had effectively taken charge, much to the relief of the two men who reported to Congress and the President. Here they were again, licking their lips and clearing their throats, loving the power but not wanting to make hard decisions.

Peter Neely said, "I assure you this is an interesting one, Mr. Burlane. I don't think we've had anything like this since that business with Philby and Derek Townes. Would you like to tell him, Ara?"

Schott considered the problem of Contact David with his finger resting thoughtfully on the cleft of his chin. "This one's right up there, Jimmy."

"We need your advice, Mr. Burlane."

Schott said, "You remember Rennie Kriss, Jimmy? The guy who grew up in Australia. Well, we've been working him out of Turkey as an exporter of cottage-industry stuff. Kriss has offices in Istanbul and Ankara, but he spends most of his time posing as a buyer in

eastern Turkey near the Georgian and Armenian borders. We got him a British passport so he can cross the
Iranian border if he wants. He's supposed to help monitor the flow of heroin from Turkey, to watch black-
market activities in the area, and to help our people in
Iran.''

''Poor bastard.''

''Yes, well, here, let me show you.'' Schott slid back
the cover from a white screen at one end of Neely's
office and flipped the switch of a projector that had been
wheeled into the room for the briefing. The map on the
screen was of the Caucasus—that narrow area of the
Soviet Union west of the Caspian Sea, east of the Black
Sea, and south of the Caucasus Mountains. This area
included the Soviet republics of Abkhaz, Georgia, Armenia, and Azerbaijan. ''Kriss spends most of his
time here, in Turkey—Erzurum is the place—and it was
here a couple of years ago that he made contact with a
Georgian black marketeer who calls himself Abu Ali.''

''Black market in what?''

''Consumer items that are hard to get in the Soviet
Union—video-tape recorders, jazz tapes, blue jeans, electric shavers, whatever. The Georgians are notorious entrepreneurs. There are Georgian lemon barons, millionaires
from smuggling citrus to Moscow.''

''God, does Kriss go across that fucking border?''
Burlane dug contemplatively at his armpit. He did his
best to stay the hell away from the Soviet Union. He
couldn't understand guys like Kriss.

Schott said, ''Yes, he has on occasion. Late at night
always, and blindfolded. Abu Ali takes care of the
rendezvous and makes the guarantees. He usually takes
the buyer into Turkey. He arranges the border crossing.
He guarantees buyer and seller. The buyer gets what he
wants. The seller gets a fair price. Abu Ali takes his
forty percent and everybody's happy.''

''Has Kriss ever talked to Abu Ali in person?''

"No," Schott said. "They always deal through intermediaries."

"It's not like there's an interstate highway across the Turkish border. Ali's gotta be scrounging for the local cheese and free-lancing for himself. Kriss's gotta be off his hinge."

"Kriss knows that, Jimmy. Now then, Abu Ali recently gave Kriss a letter, ostensibly an inquiry as to sensitive goods available on the outside, prices and so on. On the inside, Kriss found a letter addressed to the American ambassador at Ankara. Well, the ambassador read the letter and found out it was really for us. It was a shopping list, that's true." Schott leaned forward intently. "Listen to this, Jim. The sender wants twelve silenced automatic pistols. He wants twelve digital wristwatches with stopwatch and alarm. He wants smoke grenades capable of laying a quick, heavy pall over an oversize soccer field. He wants enough smoke bombs to do that four times. He also wants a flare gun—one that can be concealed in a coat pocket—and eight flares, four green and four red. Yes, and two silent dog whistles. That and fifty thousand American dollars."

"Oh! A mere fifty K. Does he want benefits too? Free dental care? Paid vacation? Little cottage in Florida? All the vodka he can drink?"

Schott grinned. "No, Jimmy, no paid vacation."

"I don't suppose he said what we'd be getting for all this."

"Yes, he did. He said the money was to pay two middlemen—Abu Ali and one other. He said he would use the pistols and the rest of it to bring the Soviet Union to its knees." Ara Schott lit himself a cigarette.

"I see," Burlane said. "An overachiever."

"Yes, it's beginning to look that way," Schott said. "Would you like to tell us what you make of all this?"

James Burlane said, "The buyer wants four lots because he wants to practice three times. It'd take balls to practice with smoke bombs. He gets caught and he'll wind up as a slave laborer north of the Arctic Circle drinking boiled pine needles for vitamin C.'' Burlane licked his lips and made smacking sounds. "*Zek* tea. Mmmmmmm! He isn't asking for any specific model of automatic pistol. The Soviets only go on the market for something they can copy; that would mean a specific model. The same thing for the smoke bombs. In addition to that, the buyer's unfamiliar with what's available on foreign markets—or wants us to think he is.''

"That's possible."

"Or Abu Ali could be KGB. Maybe they're funning us a little, haw-hawing us. Bringing the Soviet Union to its knees. Would the CIA be able to resist a hook like that? Hey, the KGB pockets a neat fifty and a good time was had by all.''

"Does it sound like that to you?''

"No. Abu Ali could be going for the entire fifty for himself, but that'd queer his connection with Kriss.''

"In which case the dissident could be . . . ?''

"A loon. A dreamer. Vladimir Mitty. Nobody brings the fucking Rooskies to their knees with twelve pistols.''

Schott said, "That's what Kriss thinks.''

"If he was an Albanian or somebody, I'd say give him the stuff, no harm done, except what if he's planning on assassinating somebody? Premier Spishkin, say. Do you really want that?''

Peter Neely spoke up for the first time. "We most assuredly do not want that, Mr. Burlane. Absolutely not.''

"If his idea of bringing down the Soviet Union is to assassinate someone, he's dreaming. But if he is a loon and can't get what he wants from us, he'll get it somewhere else. You have to consider that.''

"Exactly,'' Schott said. "Either way we get blamed if someone gets shot.''

"I say we talk to him. That way, at least we can see who he is. He probably has to train his dog; that's what the whistles are for. If he's going to practice with the smoke bombs and flares, he'll need privacy out in the taiga somewhere. All that'll take a little time."

Ara Schott said, "If we think he's going to assassinate someone, we tip off the KGB."

"Exactly. If he has something more imaginative in mind, we sit back with popcorn and a six-pack. We'll give them nine-millimeter Marakovs. More fun if they get shot with their own pistols."

"Peter and I would like you to talk to him, Jimmy."

"Me? Yalta was the last time, Ara. You promised. No more Rooskies. I want to travel to Rangoon while I can still get it up. Mmmmmm, those brown-bodied little lovelies!" Burlane pretended to straighten his underwear.

Schott said, "You won't have to cross the border, Kriss says. Abu Ali will bring the buyer to you."

Peter Neely spoke up again. "The President wants us to keep a close watch on this kind of thing, Jimmy."

"Hey, there're other people. This is the storied Central Intelligence Agency. You've got marksmen, linguists, pole vaulters, whatever you want. Get one of them. Rendezvous with this guy and you risk having KGB agents ride down on you like wild Indians. I told you no after Yalta. Spiriting Kim Philby from Yalta! Jesus!" Burlane shook his head at the memory of that one. "I caught some kind of fungus in Istanbul that I've never been able to get rid of. Hey, did the President give me a medal? Did you even give me a raise? If I get pranged, will you erect a Tomb of the Unknown Burlane? I hate those fucking Russians as much as you, but give a guy a break, Ara."

Ara Schott said, "Jimmy, you have to listen to reason now. You have to look at it our way."

"You want to look at the fungus I picked up on my way to the Philby grab? Your main man, Mr. Get-Things-Done. Here, let me show you." Burlane started to unbuckle his trousers.

Peter Neely said, "That won't be necessary, Mr. Burlane." Neely believed in neatness and hard work.

He'd risen up the corporate ladder at IBM where neat, efficient managers and engineers dominated the computer market. Since his appointment as DCI, everyone at Langley, it seemed, was a little neater, a little more serious. Yet the truth was that Burlane, this gangly, grinning man with hair that spiraled up in a rooster tail in the back, was the best man they had. "You work out the details with Ara, Mr. Burlane. Do what you have to do."

Burlane gave a tug at his prominent, slightly crooked nose, and laughed. "Well, in that case." He blew Ara Schott an obscene, sucking kiss. He started to give Peter Neely one too, then, out of deference to authority, left the director alone. "I get another fungus, I'm gonna be pissed."

Peter Neely smiled a nervous smile, as though he were an embarrassed parent whose child had just disrobed in public. Neely said, "Just the other day I was telling the President that morale's never been higher."

Two

"WHAT THE FFF . . ." JAMES BURLANE SAT UP STARTLED, and peered out of the window into the blackness. The voice on the loudspeaker, which had started high and wavering, a tenor at the Met, plunged into a low vibrato that sounded like a man gargling or maybe gagging. The gargling rose, hovered, rasping—Louis Armstrong maybe—then went loony, manic—a frenzied Mick Jagger working up a sweat. Burlane sat up and looked out the window to see if he could locate the source of the a cappella jamming. He saw the mosque silhouetted against the blue-black sky. The muezzin went into a riff of crazy *woo-woos*, Cochise on the warpath, that reverberated down the narrow streets of Erzurum.

Burlane got up to take a leak. If he'd seen the Islamic cuckoo's nest the night before, he would have gone to another hotel. He had had to put up with Islam before. The Iranian holy men were the worst, Burlane thought. Righteous zealots. Ayahtollah Assholas. When the muezzin had finished with his dawn call to prayer, Burlane returned to the warmth of the bed, his bladder pleasantly emptied, and thought about the sweet peppermint tea he would have for breakfast.

149

Later, after he had checked out and retrieved his passport, Burlane had his peppermint tea with Turks on rickety chairs at rickety tables that sprawled out onto the yellow brick street. The Turks watched him out of the corners of their eyes. He was an obvious European. They knew about Europeans in Erzurum. Europeans in Erzurum were drug dealers, spies, or losers of one sort or another.

Burlane assumed he wouldn't be able to buy the *International Herald-Tribune* in Erzurum, so he had bought a *Conan the Barbarian* paperback at Kennedy— this because of the wonderful cover that depicted the musclebound Conan rescuing an eminently porkable lovely who was chained to a tree. *Get me in the mood for dealing with Russians*, he had thought. Now Burlane sipped the sweet tea and wondered about the loon who wrote the Conan books; Burlane tried to imagine himself sitting at a word processor all day pretending to be a barbarian.

Burlane lingered over his tea. At exactly ten o'clock he left and strolled down the narrow street that emptied into a bazaar assembled around a fountain that didn't work. Vendors in the market sold fruit, vegetables, and virtually any kind of trinket or doodad imaginable. Burlane bought a hashish pipe and walked along admiring it until a young man fell into step beside him.

"Hashi?" the young man said.

"How much?"

"Very cheap."

Burlane said, "I think I'll pass today." He put the pipe away and kept walking. He bought a fig and walked along eating until a second young man fell in beside him. This one was sixteen or seventeen years old with the beginnings of a mustache on his upper lip.

"Hashi?"

Burlane said, "How much?"

"Special deal today for long-legged men."

That completed the sequence. "Hah!" Burlane said.

The young man slipped him a hunk of hashish. Burlane followed him to a room that was bare save for a weathered carpet upon which the bearded Rennie Kriss squatted by the four neatly-stacked wooden boxes that contained Burlane's merchandise. Burlane did not ask how Kriss had gotten the boxes by Turkish customs at Ankara. That was none of Burlane's business.

Kriss said something to the young man in Turkish and the boy left them alone. "My boy says you weren't followed. He's a good boy. Smart."

"There was a fucking muezzin jamming outside my bedroom window this morning," Burlane said. Burlane made a wobbling, guttural sound in the back of his throat in imitation of the crier. "Why can't they just set an alarm like everybody else? All that yammering."

"They take turns, you know. I think they try to outdo one another." Kriss nudged the boxes with his knee. "Whoever wants this stuff has to have real hair, trying to pull a hit inside there." Kriss motioned his head north, in the direction of the Soviet Union. "Can you imagine?"

"If I had my druthers, I'd stay at home and watch a ball game."

"You won't have to cross the border. That's how Abu Ali earns his fee. You drive east toward Kars and the Russian border. About twenty miles out, something like that, the road will flatten out in some crappy-looking country, desolate. Go until you come to an abandoned mud hut by what looks like a dry lake. The hut'll be on your right, and there's an upside-down abandoned car outside that's been stripped of everything except the paint and the bullet holes in the fender. Park your car and wait. The buyer speaks English."

"What will happen?"

Kriss told him. Burlane repeated the routine word for word. "That's it. You got it," Kriss said.

Burlane rose and took the bag. "In lieu of flowers send donations to the Portland Trail Blazers."

Kriss laughed. "Abu Ali's interested in bucks, not corpses. You'll be okay."

Three

James Burlane rented a Ford Escort with a caved-in fender. He had to pump the brakes furiously to make them work and the steering wheel wobbled, but he had driven worse. It was a balmy day. He loaded his hash pipe and drove along nursing a glowing ball in the bowl, his arm hanging out of the window, which wouldn't roll up. Burlane thought about all the American men driving air-conditioned Hondas to work that morning, puffing sweet tobacco in pipes intended to make them look serious and thoughtful, successful—contemplative if not intellectual.

Rennie Kriss's directions were accurate enough, and by three o'clock James Burlane was sitting in the shadow of the mud hut waiting, a tall paper bag at his side. It was his job, given him by Peter Neely and Ara Schott, to talk to the Russian buyer and to make the decision, yea or nay. If Burlane thought the buyer was a genuine nutter, bent on assassination of a Soviet Leader, then Burlane was to waste him. If he had something else in mind, then Burlane could give him the goods—that was if Burlane felt like it.

Thus it was, finally, that not Neely, not the President,

not the Joint Chiefs of Staff, would make this decision. It was James Burlane's alone.

Two, then three cars passed without slowing. Then an old Renault slowed and Burlane double-checked the settings of the camera in the bag. The car stopped, and when a slender, dark-haired man got out of the Renault, Burlane tilted the paper bag as if he were taking a drink and flipped the switch that activated the shutter *clack, clack, clack* of the Nikon behind a two-hundred-millimeter lens. Burlane wasn't Ansel Adams; the pictures would be grainy, but that wasn't the point.

When the dark-haired man got out of the car, Burlane could tell by the look on his face that he was the buyer and that he was an amateur. Burlane opened the trunk of his Escort and swapped the bag with the camera for a bag with a bottle of Greek brandy that Kriss had included with the two boxes of pistols, smoke bombs, and flares.

"I was wondering which way it is to Erzurum? I'm going to the market," the dark-haired man said in good English.

James Burlane smiled. He'd seen this man before. Where? "Well, you're in luck," he said. Burlane handed the dark-haired man the bottle of brandy. Then he took a pistol out of his pocket and said, "I'm a professional and good at my work. If I don't believe your story, I just might kill you. Do you understand?"

"I understand."

"I think we should sit in the shade, then. I take it you have a few minutes to talk."

"I have a few minutes."

James Burlane followed the dark-haired man to the lengthening shadow of the mud hut. When they were both sitting, he said, "When I travel in the Middle East, I always smoke hashish. Do as the Romans do, I always say. Better than pickling your liver in alcohol the way you Russians do. Christ!" Burlane held the hash pipe and his silenced .22 with his right hand and loaded the pipe with his left hand.

The dark-haired man started to say something, then changed his mind.

"What is it you want to do with these pistols and stuff there, Dave? You don't mind me calling you Dave, do you? Our man christened you David after he read your little note. Bringing down Goliath and all that. What is your real name, by the way?"

Contact David smiled and handed Burlane a European edition of *Time* magazine.

Burlane laughed. "Supersuck! I read that story." He glanced at the article, which included Ginsburg's picture. There hadn't been such a fuss over a Soviet writer in the United States in years. Ginsburg was an especially bizarre case; he was the literary darling of Moscow, writing lyric poems about the beauty of peasants and the spirit of sacrifice. "You don't mind if I keep calling you Dave for now, do you?"

Ginsburg smiled. "Of course not. I've been sucking, as you put it, for a reason."

"You want to give me the reason?"

"At first, I did it because I wanted an opportunity for foreign travel. I wanted to defect. Then I met a man who had a better idea, and I did it so I could meet you here."

"Fifty thousand dollars is a few bucks there, Dave. I suppose we can spring for that easily enough, but it's the risk that gives us the trots. Do you want to assassinate somebody or what? Is there somebody who doesn't like your poetry? We have to know these things."

"No assassination."

"Good. There's no point in them. You shoot one asshole and another pops up in his place. After each of your premiers dies we have to go through a period of uncertainty, not knowing who is speaking with authority and what the new government intends to do. We won't help you shoot somebody for the hell of it."

"No assassination."

"Now, exactly what is this nonsense about bringing the Soviet Union to its knees?"

"If it works, we will do just that," Ginsburg said.

"We? Dave! Dave! You have to be more specific than that. We? Are you pregnant or do you have a turd in your pocket?"

"I'm working with someone. He . . . he says the fewer people know what we plan, the better. Including you, he says."

Burlane considered that; it was a proper answer. "You can understand our concern, can't you? We can't risk having any of this blamed on the United States. Those people have ICBMs and submarines with rockets parked off our coast."

"I can't imagine that the United States would be involved in any way."

"Other than my giving you this stuff—if I do—is there any way at all, even remotely, that the United States might be mixed up in it? I have to know that."

"No."

"Where did you learn your English?" Burlane glanced at the magazine article.

"University of Moscow."

Burlane motioned with his head. "Why didn't you work through the Israelis? Mossad would have helped you any way you wanted."

"My Tbilisi connection said he had had problems with Mossad in the past. He recommended your Rennie Kriss instead."

Burlane shook his head. "You know, you could have your freedom now. Just go with me. Forget the slingshot crap. You've made it across. Forget it. There's nothing you can do that'll really hurt those people. Nothing. I can get you to Israel or the United States, whichever."

"I . . . No."

"Hey, no reason to worry because your life's in my hands. I'm a reasonable man." Burlane gave the hash pipe to the dark-haired man who took a drag, doing as Burlane had done. Burlane said, "If I give you these boxes and you hit someone, I swear to Yahweh, I'll beat the KGB to you and shove ham sandwiches up your ass."

"I understand your concerns and I assure you, you have no worry, none at all. What I plan on doing is outrageous, yes, but I guarantee that other than yourself no Americans are involved, and the United States will be safely out of harm's way. You may regard the Soviets as an American problem, but they're *our* problem. I do this for reasons that are both personal and public. They're mine, Russian, and not just Jewish."

"What personal reasons?" Burlane understood personal reasons. If Ginsburg had maintained that he was doing this solely for altruistic reasons, Burlane would have shot him.

"They did something to me personally, and to the man I mentioned."

"They? There you go again." Burlane thought, *Christ, I'm sounding like Ronald Reagan.*

"The commandant in the camp mentioned in the magazine there. His name is Mikheyev. I took everything the Soviets did to me until then. That's when I decided to do something. The people helping me all have reasons of their own."

"What did Mikheyev do to you?"

"You wouldn't believe me if I told you." Ginsburg swallowed at the memory. "Americans have nothing to do with what I want to do. I don't especially admire or hate Americans. I haven't been allowed to learn a whole lot about them."

James Burlane took a hit on the hash pipe. "I'm typical. We Americans are violent as hell, just like they're always telling you. We walk around with hard-ons and guns blazing. I would have wasted you if I thought you were lying, just bored a hole through your heart or taken half your face." Burlane couldn't help but grin at that line.

"I just want my country back. I'm asking for your help. That's it and nothing more, I assure you."

"How did you get in touch with Abu Ali?"

"Through a black marketeer in Novosibirsk, a friend."

"Are you going to steal something?"

"Yes."

"From the Red Army?"

"No."

Burlane thought Ginsburg was telling the truth, at least most of the truth. He believed something terrible had happened to Ginsburg. He wanted to give the Russian a shot at whatever it was he had in mind. He liked the idea of a poet and his pals going out in a blaze of glory like Butch Cassidy and the Sundance Kid. "Aw, fuck, that's good enough for the assholes I hang out with," he said. He retrieved a diminutive Czechoslovakian tape recorder from his pocket. "If you want to communicate with me again, you should use this. Do you know what a one-time pad is?"

"No."

"Okay, Dave, I want you to listen now and understand this. The one-time pad was invented by an American cryptanalyst named Joseph O. Mauborgne in 1918. It requires each of us to have an identical key and it is good for one message, one time only. It is foolproof as long as each party keeps his copy of the key secure. What I did was sit down at a word processor and filled a page with numbers at random. Just punched away like a monkey. Here." Burlane gave the dark-haired man a sheet of paper covered with numbers.

"This is the key. I have one identical to it. I've given you forty-eight lines with eighty numbers in each line. You can send me one message with as many letters as the numbers on this page will let you. To send the message you need to assign numbers for letters. The easiest way is to go from *A* to *Z*. *A* is oh-one because it is the first of the alphabet; *T* is twenty because it's the twentieth letter. That's what we'll use. You write the numbers of your text under the numbers of the key. Do you understand so far? Here, let me show you." Burlane took his copy of the key and began writing numbers under the key. "See how that's done?"

"I see."

"Now you add the numbers of your message to the key above it. You send me the total. I subtract the key and come up with the numbers that tell me your message. Forget about punctuation, spaces, and all that. I'll figure it out."

"But what about the Soviet computers? Surely—"

"Fuck the Soviet computers. They can run this through their compuers as much as they want. The key is patternless. They can come up with words okay, but they'll be all possible words in all possible languages. This is used for messages that must be absolutely secret. The problem is that there has to be a new key for each message. Governments have to communicate quickly with agents and military units. It's logistically impractical for all but rare cases."

"Like this one."

"Like this one. Keep your key secret and burn it when you're finished with it. Pour water on the ashes and mix it up a little. You send your one message with this. Send it to me, J.B." He held up the small recorder again. "You figure your message out carefully—add the numbers of your text to the key above it—then turn this on to 'record.' An American female voice will say hello and give a name, then you simply list your numbers—run them together without a pause from beginning to end. Take your time; there's no need to hurry. Dial the American embassy in Moscow. When the other person answers, you turn this on to 'play.' The woman will say hello and identify herself, then the recorder will speed up and deliver the entire sequence of numbers in a matter of two or three seconds. The Soviets will be recording the call. Hang up and get out of there.''

Ginsburg considered that. ''I assume the Soviets are clever enough to slow down their tape of the call.''

''Sure they are. Let them have the numbers. We just don't want them to have time enough to trace the call. The tape will distort the numbers so the KGB won't have a voice print on you. When you're free, destroy the machine. The bottom of the Moscow River wouldn't be bad. Any more questions, Dave?''

''I'm grateful.''

''Do what you have to do, but keep the United States out of it.'' Burlane put away his pistol. He helped Ginsburg pack the wooden boxes in the trunk of the Renault. Then he went back to his car and retrieved a liter of Canadian whiskey and a flight bag loaded with Japanese digital watches, German cigarette lighters, and small automatic cameras. ''This stuff's for your friends,'' Burlane said.

Ginsburg raised the bottle and said, *''L'chayim,* friend.''

Burlane took a snort too. ''Mud in your eye, Dave.''

James Burlane couldn't help but laugh on the way back to Erzurum. The poet's chutzpah was too delicious. Wait until he told Neely and Schott about this one: the guy was literally right out of the pages of *Time* magazine!

The Company trio monitoring the activities of Isaak Ginsburg were having yet another breakfast meeting when James Burlane spotted the story in *The New York Times* about the May signing in Vladivostok of the agreement to resume the stalled Geneva arms talks. On page five there was a sidebar reporting a curious addition to the Vladivostok ceremony, insisted upon by the Soviets.

Isaak Ginsburg, the Soviet Union's famous Jewish poet, would read a commemorative poem at the signing.

Peter Neely barely masked his irritation at Burlane,

however much a genius, who was so rude as to read a newspaper when the DCI was talking to him. "So now what, Mr. Burlane?" Neely's voice almost seemed not to rise.

Schott too was becoming impatient. He echoed Neely: "So now what, Jimmy?"

Burlane looked up from the paper with an expansive grin. Then he gave way to a Burlane giggle. "Hey, Ginsburg is my kind of man. Yessireee! Would you look at this!" He handed Neely the *Times* and pointed to the paragraph that said it all.

Neely read the paper, and even he couldn't suppress a smile.

Schott read the story over Neely's shoulder. "A commemorative poem in Vladivostok?"

Burlane said, "Isaak Ginsburg. Our man! The problem with you guys is you think small." Burlane rubbed his hands together and giggled. "Sweet! Sweet!"

Burlane said, "Remember, I told Ginsburg that if he needed any help, he should let us know. I taught him how to use a one-time pad. If he sends a message to us through the American embassy, we'll know I'm right."

Ara Schott, "Do you think he'll call, Jimmy?"

"Sure. He'll call. He'll want to get whatever he's going to steal out of the Soviet Union."

Four

THE LADIES FROM PERM KNEW ABOUT THE RESEARCH BEING conducted at the cancer clinic and would have preferred other companions for their outing to Moscow, but it would have been pointless to complain. The Perm ladies did their best to accept their bald companions despite the fact that the men had gotten drunk on the bus. The research subjects were singing romantic, sad songs.

They had left Perm early Wednesday morning and had spent the night sleeping upright in their seats. The women did, that is. The bald men continued their drinking, until, one by one, they too had fallen asleep in the early hours of the morning. As they approached Moscow they started drinking again. When the bus entered the city, the bald men resumed their songs.

The bus crossed the Moscow River on the suspension bridge and turned right on Komsomolsky Prospekt, which was nearly empty of traffic. They passed a busload of football players and a mechanical sweeper scouring the gutters. Mechanical sweepers kept the streets clean in this part of the city; the Soviets did not want foreign visitors to contemplate women in babushkas sweeping streets with twig brooms.

The bus slowed and entered the Square of the Fiftieth Anniversary of the October Revolution. The bald men fell silent. Two men coughed. Birk was suddenly afflicted with a sleepy, sluggish feeling. He sat, becalmed in the final minutes, as the bus joined a queue of blue buses waiting to unload passengers. He watched the emptied buses join a line waiting to be parked in the neat formation of blue buses in the square. Birk wondered if Russian minds, like Russian buses, did not spend a lot of time idling.

Birk remembered his dead wife, Nadia. His lids were heavy at the memory.

The bus turned right, around the corner of the black iron fence, and came to a halt near a restraining rope strung between the tops of movable stanchions. Behind this rope, unsmiling young army officers, bearing electric megaphones, paced with serious eyes and an air of self-importance. The gray of the megaphones matched the gray of the officers' uniforms, and the gray of the overcast sky.

Jaan Birk felt a shiver of anticipation. He wondered if the Bolsheviks had felt like this when they turned the guns of the Aurora on the csar's Winter Palace in St. Petersburg.

Four eighteen-man squads of Kremlin guards were detailed to guard the Lenin mausoleum. These squads, rotated every eight hours, were trained to form a perimeter around the mausoleum in the event of a disturbance.

The two South units—South One and South Two— were responsible for blocking access to the open area along the banks of the Moscow River. The northern edge of the square, which led to the heart of the city, was defended by North One and North Two.

South One and North One were lead units, which meant they were the first soldiers onto the square in case of an emergency. South One was housed in the base of Spasskaya Tower, to the left rear of the mausoleum; and

North One in the base of Nikolskaya Tower, to the right rear of the mausoleum. South Two and North Two were quartered inside the Kremlin.

In the event of an alarm, the seventy-two soldiers were given eighteen seconds to surround the mausoleum. This included a thirteen-second hundred-meter sprint by lead soldiers carrying AK-47s. These soldiers were handpicked and disciplined—the best the Red Army had to offer.

Older Lieutenant Vladimir Petrovich Zaytsev, commander of South One, spent his time sketching on a small pad in the CO's diminutive, bare office.

While Zaytsev sketched, his men watched a Soviet Union vs. Bulgaria weight-lifting competition on television or played a card game called Fools in which, one by one, players left the game until only one was left, the loser. The fool. The winners laughed at the fool and made little devil's horns with their forefingers sticking out above their ears.

Because of the architecture of the mausoleum—the steps and corners—the Soviets were convinced it was physically impossible for anybody to do harm to Lenin's body and escape from the mausoleum alive, much less Red Square. It couldn't be done. Could not. Even sprinters from the Red Army track squad couldn't do it.

The first pilgrim out of the Perm bus was a tall bald man with a cap on his head, the first of twelve becapped bald men to leave the bus. He took one step forward and was waved to a halt by a soldier. He looked up at the corner of the Kremlin wall. An officer with a megaphone said, "Stay clear of the ropes."

The bald man did as he was told. He gripped the pistol in his coat pocket.

A second man joined the first and a third joined the second. The bald men banded together out of training, out of the need for support, out of a kind of vague fear.

They shivered both from the chill in the air and the realization that they were about to die.

Birk was the seventh of the bald men out of the bus. He stood with the others in the tailings of the white cloud that issued from the bus's throbbing exhaust. The ladies from Perm tightened the knots of their flowered scarves. Jaan Birk found himself remembering the soft down on his young wife's stomach. She had been an athlete, a gymnast, and had a hard, muscular body from years of training. But when she was on her back, smiling, her stomach slack, the downy hair on her body was soft beyond description.

A stout young woman, one of Natasha Kropotkina's Lenin pins on her lapel, read their names from a sheet of paper. The Perm women and the bald men answered when their names were called.

In addition to Jaan Birk, the bald men were:

Aleksei Ivanovich Avdeyev, thirty-one, originally sentenced to five years imprisonment for his belief in God. Avdeyev contracted his cancer cleaning the nozzles of atomic submarines at Paldiski Bay, Estonia, on the Gulf of Finland.

Konstantin Davidovich Arlovsky, twenty-seven, originally sentenced to an indeterminate sentence in a psychiatric hospital for "failing to appreciate reality" after he requested permission to emigrate to Israel. Arlovsky contracted his cancer mining uranium underground at Cholovka, in the Ukraine.

Yuri Yevgennevich Chernetsov, forty-three, originally sentenced to eight years imprisonment for his work for Amnesty International. Chernetsov contracted his cancer at Chelyabinsk-40, a nuclear warhead plant in the Urals.

Mikhail Aleksandrovich Denisenko, thirty-six, originally sentenced to ten years imprisonment for advocating Ukrainian independence. Denisenko developed cancer at the uranium enrichment facility at Mangyshlak, on the Caspian Sea.

Jaan Gennadevich Fedoseev, thirty-two, originally sentenced to five years imprisonment for baptizing his son. Fedoseev became ill working in the open pit mine at Kavalerovo, in the Soviet Far East.

Vladimir Anatolevich Kesamidze, twenty-five, originally sentenced to seven years imprisonment for advocating the maintenance of the Georgian language. Kesamidze developed cancer working in high-level radiation at the underground uranium mine at Asht, just north of the Afghanistan border.

Mark Iosevovich Ivashov, forty, originally sentenced to ten years imprisonment for teaching the Yiddish language. Ivashov developed his symptoms while working in a nuclear enrichment facility on Vaigach Island in the Arctic Ocean.

Nikolai Prochorevich Karpekov, thirty-seven, originally sentenced to six years in a strict regimen camp for "denigrating the Russian past" in an article on czarist secret police published in a British magazine. Karpekov contracted his cancer in the mine at Cholovka, in the Ukraine.

Boris Samuilovich Lieberman, thirty, originally sentenced to seven years in prison for asking permission to emigrate to Israel. Lieberman developed cancer while working in the uranium enrichment facility at Shamor Bay, opposite the northern end of Sakhalin Island.

Oleg Simeonovich Mayeseen, thirty-four, originally sentenced to ten years in a strict regime camp for asking permission to emigrate to Israel. Mayeseen developed cancer in a nuclear enrichment facility at Kyshtym in the Urals.

Ivan Vladimirovich Bychkov, twenty-nine, originally sentenced to four years in a strict regime camp for staging an unauthorized production of Samuel Beckett's "Waiting for Godot." Developed cancer in a uranium mine at Omutninsk near Leningrad.

The stout young woman who had checked their names said, "You will stay together and do as you are told until it is your turn to join the line to begin the walk to the mausoleum. Knives and other weapons are not allowed inside. Cameras are forbidden. You will stay on the white line. You will walk in pairs. You will walk rapidly. There are many people who would like to see the body today. You will not talk or linger once you are in the tomb. Is that understood?"

The question was not asked in the manner that encouraged response.

Several hundred people milled about the ropes outside the gate, trying to figure out where the line would be formed. How long would they have to wait? Would they get to see Lenin that day? People wanted to know. Rumors and guesses were cheap.

The Komsomol leader of the Perm group showed the officer a form that had been signed by the stout young woman, and the officer unsnapped the rope.

"Make sure you have them all," he said.

The leader checked their names on a piece of paper— they each answered as before—and the Perm visitors were taken to a slowly forming queue that led to the beginning of the official line to Lenin's tomb. The official line began at the center of the promenade in front of the Tomb of the Unknown Soldier.

When the Perm group formed their section of the line, the bald men pushed their way into the positions assigned to them ahead of time by Birk. Each man had a place. The women weren't given a chance to protest.

After a twenty minute wait, the line, moving two by two, moved through the gates at the end of the park. Jaan Birk's squad of bald men were on their way to Lenin's tomb.

Five

THE HUSHED, CONTEMPLATIVE PILGRIMS, WALKING STEAD-
ily along the white line, advanced two by two by two
by two into the vast space that was Red Square, the
official parade ground of the Soviet Empire. There was
room enough in Red Square to accommodate scores of
companies of goose-stepping soldiers, squadrons of tanks
and armored personnel carriers, dozens of sophisticated
rockets poised skyward on mobile launch pads—whatever
it took to properly commemorate the anniversaries of
socialist accomplishments.

The Soviets used portable rope barriers to keep Red
Square empty as visitors filed into the mausoleum and
out again. The bald men kept their eyes on the Lenin
mausoleum as they walked; it was forward and to their
right. The Kremlin wall rose behind the mausoleum.
There was a large tower to the left of the mausoleum—
Spasskaya Tower—topped by a red star, and one to the
right—Nikolskaya Tower—also with a star.

Jaan Birk had taken the outside of the double line—
the Red Square side—so that as the line snaked through
the mausoleum itself he would be closest to the guards
standing at Lenin's feet.

Birk rubbed his thumb against the 9mm Makarova in his coat pocket. The piece of meat felt cool and dry in its plastic bag. Birk's adrenaline surged. His body felt wired, alive. He could do anything, he believed. Anything. Steal Lenin's head from the tomb. Anything.

He moved the pad of his thumb up and down, up and down, on the barrel of the pistol. He put the palm of his hand against the cool of the meat.

The turn toward the mausoleum's entrance came as the pilgrims were almost directly in the middle of Red Square. Birk's breathing quickened and his mouth felt cottony as he approached the point that was directly in front of both the Red Square entrance of the State Historical Museum and Lenin's mausoleum. There, abruptly, the white line made a hard right and the pilgrims followed.

Birk walked straight toward the entrance. He glanced at the empty concrete bleachers on either side of the mausoleum where Kremlin officials sat to review ceremonial and commemorative parades in the square. Birk glanced up at the Kremlin wall behind the mausoleum. The red flag with the hammer and sickle flopped lazily on the mast atop the massive green-roofed dome inside the Kremlin.

Birk swallowed. Lenin's body was the most sacred of sacred relics in the Soviet Union. It was also a festering, vile pox in whose name the Russians ruled, Birk was convinced, without any vision except the maintenance of absolute, unyielding power.

The double file kept a brisk pace.

Each bald man from the Perm bus punched a control on his digital wristwatch as he crossed the threshold of the mausoleum and turned left to descend the first flight of stairs. The alarm on each of these watches was carefully set to match the wearer's place in line. Birk had had a time working out the schedule.

They stepped into the main entrance.

There was a left turn.

The bald men went down the stairs.

There was a right turn.

More stairs.

A last right brought the pilgrims into the chamber where the coffin lay bathed in red light.

The bald men looked ahead for their assigned guards. Lenin's face was serene under the red.

Birk came to the end of the tomb. He was at the foot of the embalmed god.

The alarm sounded simultaneously on the wrists of twelve bald men entering, leaving, and spaced throughout the mausoleum. The bald men drew their pistols and fired point-blank at their assigned soldiers. The soldiers had been standing at attention for forty minutes and were rigid as boards.

The soldiers saw pistols being pointed in their direction as slugs thumped *plup! plup! plup!* into their chests and torsos.

In less than four seconds, twelve soldiers lay dead or dying inside the mausoleum—a perfectly timed ambush.

Jaan Birk leaped into the space around the pedestal and pushed the coffin hard, sending it crashing onto the other side.

The glass top shattered. Birk was upon the body.

At the main entrance to the mausoleum, a bald man who had brought up the rear waited for the Perm Ladies and others to get clear, then shouted, "For Russia!" He sprinted toward the middle of Red Square, throwing smoke bombs as he ran.

Inside, Birk grabbed Lenin's head. There was no need for him to twist. The head was not fastened to the torso. Because it was dehydrated and hollow, the head was surprisingly light.

Older Lieutenant Zaytsev was sketching in the shoulder of a young girl when the alarm went off in the bottom of Spasskaya Tower.

The soldiers were on the move, running, falling into place.

Lieutenant Zaytsev was the first one out the door. "Go! Go! Go!" he yelled.

Within five seconds the soldiers of Zaytsev's South One squad were sprinting into Red Square, looping wide in the direction of St. Basil's Cathedral, then north. South Two followed Zaytsev's unit. North One emerged, sprinting, from the base of Nikolskaya Tower.

The point soldiers of the lead units, sprinters, raced to complete the encircling movement that arced toward the middle of GUM.

The only sound was the rapid *clump, clump, clump* of their boots as they triple-timed across the square.

The perimeter was not yet completed and there still were no police sirens when the soldiers saw the first figure running for the center of the square.

The figure was throwing objects.

"Fire!" Zaytsev shouted.

The objects burst into smoke as the chatter of AK-47s reverberated against the Kremlin wall and echoed off GUM.

The runner's body straightened. The upper half of his torso toppled onto the square, but a final smoke grenade tumbled from his hand onto the pavement in front of him and exploded. The smoke spilled onto the square, rolled forward toward GUM, rolled backward toward the mausoleum.

The soldiers had been trained to respond to terrorists and smoke bombs, but nobody really believed they would ever have anything to do. In Moscow? In Red Square?

Lieutenant Zaytsev said, "Hold your places. Shoot them when you see them."

Another figure emerged from the smoke, throwing. He died as the first man had. His final smoke grenade exploded at the very feet of Zaytsev's soldiers.

Zaytsev realized what was happening, understood the terrorists' strategy. Another of them must be running through the smoke to spread the perimeter. The terrorists were attempting to fill the space that was their enemy.

"Fall back!" he shouted. "Fall back!" That was what the contingency plan said to do.

There was another burst of machine gun fire. Another explosion. More smoke. A pall hung over Red Square. The open space that had been an impossible barrier thirty seconds earlier was suddenly eliminated.

The terrorists would try their rush next, Zaytsev knew. Correctly, he shouted, "They'll be coming. Back! Back! Back!"

The troopers knew the contingency plan as well as Zaytsev. They backpedaled, eyes on the murk, fingers on the triggers of their weapons. The seventy-two-soldier perimeter gave and stretched. The firing lanes widened, then narrowed again at the five entrances to Red Square.

The soldiers knew the rush was next. The terrorists would be upon them at nearly point-blank range.

Jaan Birk opened the mausoleum door wide enough to fire the flare pistol. When the flare had burst green over the white haze, Birk took out a silent whistle and began blowing.

Isaak Ginsburg saw the spectacular burst of green above the smoke. He fondled Boris's ears and released the eager dog.

Boris raced into the smoke. There had been meat at the other end when he had practiced with Viktor Konnen in the taiga.

Ginsburg squatted against the curving eastern base of St. Basil's Cathedral and waited. . . .

Six

OLDER LIEUTENANT ZAYTSEV STARED HARD INTO THE murk, looking for movement. His life depended on his being able to see the enemy first. Zaytsev held his AK-47 waist high, lest the enemy come from the smoke without warning. He checked his men, checked the murk again. It hung, scarcely thinning.

"Back! Back! Back!" He trotted backward, groping for the edge of the cloud.

One of his soldiers fired into the murk, but not before another bomb exploded, enveloping St. Basil's in thick smoke.

Zaytsev shouted, "Four! Four! Four! Four! Stand fast!" He raced along his line as his troops retreated quickly and set themselves into Perimeter Four, which was the rope barrier between St. Basil's and GUM. The firing lanes had closed.

Then it came, bursting high above the smoke: a green flare.

A signal. Intended for whom? Somebody beyond the smoke, obviously. Nobody could enter or leave the perimeter without being wasted by AK-47s. Still, Zaytsev's initial confidence that he had been trained to handle anything, could handle anything, softened slightly. The contingency plan said the rush was next. The rush hadn't come.

The lack of a rush was illogical, suicidal. It was madness. Zaytsev was worried. He didn't understand what his enemy was up to.

Lieutenant Zaytsev had so many responsibilities and worries that he didn't see the mongrel dog loping happily through the smoke dragging a bag behind it.

The Kremlin was surrounded by the wailing of police sirens. The police would form a perimeter well back, on the streets and avenues leading to Red Square. The encircling perimeter of Kremlin guards was secure. Nobody could take it from the rear; the police would see to that. If the perimeter failed for any reason, the police were there as a backup.

No one talked on the perimeter. The soldiers—alert, mouths dry, hearts pumping—reloaded their AK-47s.

Jaan Birk blew his silent dog whistle at the door of Lenin's mausoleum wondering if his plan would work. How could it not work? Boris had been through this routine literally dozens of times. How could it not work now? Birk was certain his Red Army instructors would have approved.

Then, suddenly, there was Boris standing in front of him. While Boris gobbled his meat, Birk put the head in the bag and tied it to Boris's collar, lest he get hurt and had to travel wounded. He put the heavy cotton drawstrings into Boris's teeth.

Birk reloaded the flare pistol. He kneeled and embraced the dog, then straightened and fired the red flare. He felt Boris tighten under his hand.

Then Boris was gone, disappearing into the smoke, following the sound of the whistle Jaan Birk could not hear. Birk shut the door and checked his watch. He opened the door slightly. He unscrewed the silencer and fired four blind shots into the murk in the general direction of the soldiers that were out there. Birk hoped he didn't hit anyone. He didn't want to hurt some poor soldier doing his duty.

Lieutenant Zaytsev couldn't conceive of what his enemy might be up to. First a green flare, now a red. To what point? Why? When Jaan Birk fired the shots, Lieutenant Zaytsev was loping along his perimeter, asking each of his men in turn, "Have you been breached? Have you been breached? Have you been breached?"

The answer, around Zaytsev's portion of the defensive half-circle, was *"Nyet. Nyet. Nyet."*

After Birk's shots, Red Square was eerily silent; a lazy pall of smoke hung low in the midday air. Higher up, the green and red flares drifted and thinned above the unfolding drama.

Zaytsev's walkie-talkie crackled. Colonel Igor Ivanovich Stargov said, "Situation, South One. Report."

The smoke didn't bother Boris. His master had taken him deep into the taiga where there was nobody to see the smoke.

Boris was having a good time. He could hear the whistle more clearly as he made his way back to the southeast corner of St. Basil's Cathedral. When he found the man with the whistle, he would be given more meat.

Boris was a smart dog and strong, but basic just the same. When he was hungry, he wanted to eat. He was still hungry. He couldn't wait for the meat.

On the walkie-talkie, Lieutenant Zaytsev said, "South One reporting. We are established at Perimeter Four. We have not been breached, repeat, have not been breached. Visibility zero." Zaytsev wanted to ask his commander why the rush had not come, but he said nothing.

Colonel Igor Stargov said, "Stand fast and await further instructions, South One. If they rush you, shoot them.'' Stargov paused. "Lieutenant, have your men shoot them in the legs. I want prisoners.''

"Yes, sir,'' Zaytsev said. When the colonel was off the air, Zaytsev toured his area of the perimeter again. "If they rush you, take their legs,'' he said. "If they rush you, take their legs.''

Zaytsev returned to his post at the Red Square side of St. Basil's, and allowed himself a sigh of relief. The flares had popped, and nothing had happened. The enemy had not tried to breach the perimeter; now he was trapped. The haze was still thick, but clearly Zaytsev's men had done their job. They had not been breached. All they had to do was wait for the smoke to thin. There would be medals when this was over, a promotion.

The smoke thinned more rapidly now. Zaytsev counted seven dead bomb throwers.

A half minute passed. Zaytsev wondered if there were any terrorists alive other than the man with the pistol. No sooner had he thought this than from the direction of the mausoleum two or three pistol shots were fired at the perimeter, a pointless gesture at that range.

Why hadn't the terrorists made their final rush when they still had cover from the smoke? Surely the terrorists would be better off taking their chances with the perimeter than facing captivity in Lubyanka Prison after having defiled Lenin's tomb. Zaytsev hesitated to imagine the tortures they would endure. Their timidity in rushing the perimeter was insane, mad. Now they were doomed.

The thinning smoke looked romantic. *Later,* Zaytsev thought, *I'll tell people I felt like an artillery captain in the Crimean War.* He would be on television on every conceivable Leninist anniversary until his dying day. Zaytsev smiled.

The outline of the mausoleum became clear. Zaytsev saw the front door open and shut quickly. There were more terrorists inside the building. *Why* hadn't they taken advantage of the smoke when they had it? Had they simply panicked and lost their nerve?

And why the flares?

One of the terrorists opened the door quickly and fired a shot at the perimeter, hurting nobody.

One of the soldiers on the northern rim of the perimeter returned the fire.

This was followed immediately by Colonel Stargov on the walkie-talkie. "Hold your fire! Hold your fire!"

Lieutenant Zaytsev was glad it wasn't one of his men who had returned the fire. He wondered if they might not have to storm the mausoleum. He was not permitted to issue an assault order on his own. He waited, listening to his walkie-talkie for instructions. . . .

Isaak Ginsburg blew on the silent whistle. Would Birk's plan really work? Could a dog really hear this whistle that he himself couldn't hear? Ginsburg was standing beside the curved base of St. Basil's, not fifteen yards behind Zaytsev. In fact, he could hear Zaytsev's conversations with his commander and knew that so far Birk's scheme was working.

Suddenly the cheerful Boris was standing at Ginsburg's feet looking up at him.

Ginsburg handed Boris his second hunk of raw meat and grabbed the bag. He didn't look at Lenin inside with his flattened nose and battered eyebrows. Ginsburg dumped the bag into a larger plastic shopping bag.

Ginsburg put his hand on Boris's neck. "Stay," he said. He strode off in the direction of the Hotel Rossiya, leaving Boris behind, wolfing down his meat, which was delicious, well worth the effort of dragging the bag through the smoke.

The mausoleum was clearly visible now. Lieutenant Zaytsev awaited word. Then Colonel Stargov spoke on the walkie-talkie: "Hold your present position, Lieutenant. Your instructions remain the same."

A minute later, with the mausoleum even more clearly

visible in the dissipating haze, Colonel Stargov appeared in person at Lieutenant Zaytsev's post.

It was Stargov who first saw Boris, sitting where he had been told to sit, with a happy look on his face, his tongue lolling.

Boris knew he had done a good job. He had followed the two whistles as he was supposed to do. He had devoured two wonderful chunks of meat, and now the show was over. It was his time to be praised and played with. Would these nice men pat him on the head and ruffle the fur behind his ears? That's what his master always did. He tried a wag of his tail.

"Lieutenant, how long has that dog been there?"

The door to the mausoleum opened and someone took some more wild shots at the perimeter.

Zaytsev turned back to St. Basil's. A dog! Zaytsev was amazed. "Why, I don't know, sir! We've been expecting a rush from the smoke."

Colonel Stargov had seen trained dogs before. This one looked for all the world as though it had been trained to stay. Stargov beckoned to Boris. "Come," he said.

That was the magic word. Even the magic gesture. The affectionate Boris came happily, tongue flopping, expecting some attention.

Colonel Stargov couldn't help but give the dog a friendly pat. The dog's tail went *flop, flop, flop*.

A green flare, a red flare, now a trained dog. What was going on? Colonel Stargov thought he'd seen everything in his days of commanding nigger guerrillas, but this one was a real puzzler. Stargov said, "We have decided to take our time, Lieutenant. We have decided on Potemkin Three."

"Yes, sir." Potemkin Three meant that South One and North One would surround the mausoleum while South Two and North Two stormed the interior. Zaytsev and his North One counterpart were being relieved of the primary responsibility. Zaytsev was relieved but didn't show it. Zaytsev pitied the prisoners. Colonel Stargov had served in Angola, Somalia, and Afghanistan. He was said to have bragged of hammering men's testicles to putty, of skinning women alive.

Boris thought Stargov was wonderful. He slurped happily at Stargov's hand.

Stargov was equally taken by Boris. Somebody had to take the dog, why not him? He said, "What do you say, boy? Would you like to come with me? Huh, boy? I've got a dacha on the Volga. You can romp around in the summer and chase squirrels."

Boris knew a friend when he saw one. His tail flopped furiously. He grinned a dog's grin, drooling slightly.

Seven

Isaak Ginsburg was not the only Russian or foreign visitor to retreat from the smoke and shooting at Red Square. The streets of central Moscow quickly emptied as people ran from the danger. Ginsburg himself walked, he didn't run to the Hotel Rossiya. He did not want to attract attention, although it was impossible for anyone to attract attention away from the shocking drama unfolding behind him.

Ginsburg slipped unnoticed into the hotel entrance facing the Moscow River and so away from the square. The hotel guests were gathered around the windows at the western side of the hotel, watching the smoke spilling around St. Basil's at the top of the slope.

Natalia Kropotkina waited.

She said quickly, "I've cut the patch out of the duct. It won't take but a minute."

Ginsburg handed the bag with Lenin's head to Natalia. "Work quickly, but be steady with the torch. They'll take this hotel apart board by board, brick by brick."

Isaak made his way to the bar where he had been when the shooting had begun; he'd been chatting with the bartender ten minutes earlier. Ginsburg said, "I

180

thought I could see better from higher up." He gestured, meaning one of the upper floors of the Rossiya.

The bartender said, "What did you see up there?"

"Nothing. Just smoke. Thought I might as well come back here and have another drink."

"What do you think's happening, Comrade Ginsburg?"

"Terrorists of some kind. I never thought I'd see that in the Soviet Union. Never." Ginsburg shook his head.

"A guy over there thinks somebody stormed Lenin's tomb. Can you imagine?"

Ginsburg shook his head no. "It's beyond me."

"CIA," the bartender said.

"That or Estonians. Americans are animals. Estonians are fanatics. Take your pick. I wouldn't want to be them." He thought of the strange American he had met in Turkey, and of Birk and his bald suicide squad in the mausoleum, holding the soldiers off to give him time to establish an alibi and Natalia Kropotkina time to weld.

The bartender poured himself and Ginsburg each a full three-quarters of a water glass of cold vodka. He said, "This'll be something to tell our kids."

Twenty minutes later Ginsburg was joined by Natalia Kropotkina.

The bartender said, "Ahh, Mrs. Kropotkina. A little interruption from your sketching, eh?"

"A double vodka, please," Natalia said.

The bartender said, "You'd better get your sketching done in the next few days, Mrs. Kropotkina. They're going to pack that bust for Zhukov to take with him to Vladivostok."

Outside, guards were being posted at the doors of the Rossiya.

In the heat of action, Colonel Igor Ivanovich Stargov had concentrated on the immediate military problem: establishing and maintaining a perimeter so as to prevent the escape of whoever it was who had stormed the mausoleum. It was only afterward, with the smoke thinned to nothing and the cold sun at one o'clock, that he had an opportunity to consider his burden of responsibility.

This was not any mausoleum; it contained the earthly remains of Lenin.

The command of the security forces at the Kremlin was largely an honorary assignment, but it was not taken lightly. In order to show their zeal, commanders of the Kremlin guard had a history of drilling their soldiers mercilessly so that in the event of an emergency, absolutely nothing could go wrong.

Igor Ivanovich could not make a wrong decision. He was not entitled to one mistake. He had to do everything right, and he knew it.

The mausoleum was now surrounded by an enormous semicircle of kneeling soldiers, ready to fire. A helicopter circled lazily overhead. Colonel Stargov approached the mausoleum from the rear and summoned the two older lieutenants who were commanders of North Two and South Two.

"We won't assault it. I don't want them accidentally shot. I want them alive. We'll use gas to knock them out. I'll go in first."

The two lieutenants were disappointed they weren't going to storm the mausoleum, but they did as they were told. They sent for the gas, which was kept in the Kremlin in the unlikely event that there should ever be some unpleasantness in Red Square. In five minutes they had gas grenades that could be fired from rifles.

Colonel Stargov donned a gas mask. He threw open the door, met no resistance, and fired a grenade down the stairs. The rifle bucked against his shoulder once, twice, three, four times as he reloaded grenades and fired. He then retreated to the square and removed his mask. He glanced at his wristwatch.

"They can close the doors if they want," Stargov said. "That'll get to them in a couple of minutes. It only takes a whiff. They won't even be able to see it." Stargov checked his watch again. After twenty minutes, oxygen in the air would neutralize the gas and it would be safe to enter without a mask. The men inside, however, would stay unconscious for another hour—more than enough time to take them over to Lubyanka. Stargov waited. He received a report: there was no unauthorized use of radio bands. All streets were blocked off, and the militia was awaiting further instructions.

No radio communication. Stargov considered the smoke. Considered the two flares. Considered the dog. So far the heroics belonged to Stargov and his men. But if something went wrong! Well, then, that was a different story. Stargov was amused that his seniors were keeping their distance from this one. Let Stargov have it. The bastards.

It was time to go inside.

"I want you all to remain up here, Lieutenant. I'll go down alone. I want no one, I repeat *no one* inside until I give a specific order." If the terrorists had somehow mutilated Lenin's body, there should be no witnesses. It would be easy enough to repair the corpse, Stargov knew. No problem.

Leaving his unit commanders guarding the main entrance, Colonel Stargov entered the mausoleum and pulled the wick out of a metal tube. If the wick was yellow, there was gas lingering in the air. When the yellow turned blue, the air was clear. The wick was blue, and Stargov took off his gas mask. He went down the stairs, stepping over the bodies of Lenin's honor guards. The door to the tomb was open. He stepped inside.

The small room was dark as it was before, but the soft red light shone on the pedestal where the coffin had lain. Stargov saw the terrorists, five of them, lying arm in arm against the wall, knocked out.

V. I. Lenin's body was at the bottom of the moat. The coffin was on its side. Stargov quickly knelt to check the body.

There was no head.

Lenin's head was gone.

Missing.

No head.

Stargov's blood turned sweet; his face warmed from a flush of adrenaline.

There was no head.

Lenin's head was missing.

Stargov looked around the tomb. Bodies, yes. Nothing else. He checked the stairs descending from the entrance. No head there.

He checked the stairs ascending to the exit. No head.

Stargov went back to the tomb. Perhaps he had overlooked it. How large was a human head, after all? He was just confused, was all. Excited. He searched the coffin again. Looked around the pedestal. It wasn't there. He walked over to the inert terrorists who lay open-mouthed, clutching their pistols.

Stargov first saw the pinkish-white splatters on the wall. Five of them. Then he pulled a bald head forward and saw the cavity in the back. Each of them had sat, an arm linked with a comrade's, and put a bullet through the top of his mouth and out the back of his head.

Colonel Stargov had fired knockout gas at dead men. And there was no head by the corpses.

Lenin's head was missing, gone.

Stolen from the tomb.

He picked up a stainless steel whistle in front of the dead men. He blew on the whistle. No sound.

Stargov suddenly understood why there had been a dog at the edge of the smoke. The dog had retrieved the head in the smoke. The flares were signals. Stargov put the whistle in his pocket.

Who could know where Lenin's head might be by now? Stargov knew his career was ended, possibly his life as well, but he had to do the best he could. He had to work fast, because the premier would be clamoring for an answer. The Politburo. Everybody. He knelt by the dead terrorists.

He pulled off their caps. They were bald, all five of them.

Four of them had stars of David painted on the tops of their bald domes.

He straightened the man in the middle, who had died slumped over. This man was bald like the others but did not have a star of David.

Instead he had an Estonian flag on his lap, together with a photograph of himself with his arm around a smiling young woman, and an ordinary sheet of typing paper folded once and containing one neatly typed paragraph:

We love our country, but not what it has become. The oppression of the czars has become our national way of life—this in the name of Lenin. We are loath to do it, but we will begin taping a protracted mutilation of Lenin's head in a month or less. We will mail copies of these tapes to television stations around the world unless you announce, publicly, that for one year, any resident of the USSR and its satellite countries in the Warsaw Pact, Cuba, or Vietnam may emigrate for any reason whatsoever. This is to include Jews, Estonians and other regional nationalities, political dissidents, artists, writers, scientists—anybody! This emigration will be supervised by Amnesty International and officials of the World Court at The Hague. If you announce your blessing of emigration before we begin, then we will return Lenin's head to you, one section each month, for you to reassemble in secret. At the end of the twelfth month we'll send you the last section, Lenin's teeth. Nobody will have to know we took the head in the first place. We do this to reclaim Comrade Lenin's honor. We are certain that if he knew of the atrocities committed in his name—worse than under the czars—he would not only approve of what we are doing, but he would do his best to help us.

Colonel Stargov read the paper three times through, considering the consequences of that single paragraph.

He put the paper in his pocket, took a deep breath, and walked up the stairs of the mausoleum to begin the horror of telling the Politburo what had happened. He told Zaytsev and the other commanders of the guard that the terrorists had committed suicide. Comrade Lenin's body was in perfect condition. The terrorists had damaged the inside of the tomb but had not harmed the body.

"Establish a tight perimeter around the mausoleum and shoot anybody who tries to enter. Nobody is to enter. Nobody. This descecration of Comrade Lenin's tomb is an ugly thing. Until my personal, explicit order to the contrary, the only visitors are to be accompanied by me or by Premier Spishkin.

Stargov issued orders that the area surrounding Red Square, which had been sealed off as part of the response to the attack, remain closed. In addition to closing Red Square, Stargov took the precaution of ordering the evacuation and closure of the State Historical Museum, the Central V. I. Lenin Museum, GUM, and St. Basil's Cathedral. He also ordered that guests be confined to their rooms in the National, Intourist, Moscow, Metropole, and Rossiya hotels.

That done, Stargov got into the black Volga waiting to spirit him to the inside of the Kremlin; the Communist leadership would be assembling to find out what had happened to Comrade Lenin's tomb. It was Stargov's bad luck to be the bearer of some very bad news indeed. Boris curled up at the feet of his new master, offering such comfort as he was able.

Eight

THE SOVIET UNION WAS JUST FOUR WEEKS AWAY FROM THE scheduled Vladivostok agreement to resume the arms talks at Geneva, and the American Secretary of State had even agreed to accept a bust of Lenin from Soviet Foreign Minister Grigori Mikhailovich Zhukov. It was a period of euphoria for the Politburo. The Soviets could hardly believe that the idiotic Americans would so humiliate themselves. And now this: an assault on Lenin's tomb!

There were those who said they hadn't seen senior Kremlin officials move so quickly since the Cuban missile crisis a quarter of a century earlier.

Those yearning for economic and foreign policy reforms were optimistic when Premier Petr Spishkin was chosen as the Party's general secretary. The old-guard of aged Stalinist warriors, hardened by the trials of the Great Patriotic War 1941–45, had refused to relinquish power, until one by one—Leonid Brezhnev, Yuri Andropov, and Konstantin Chernenko—they were dead. Spishkin looked good on television, but that was about it. Soviet bureaucrats, zealous in defense of their power, refused to yield.

Nine of the thirteen Politburo members were in Moscow that day, including Foreign Minister Zhukov and Spishkin's two principal rivals—Defense Minister Gennadi Stepanovich Vorobiev and the chief of the KGB, Valery Nikolaevich Karpov.

Spishkin's resolve was essential to the Russian reopening of the arms limitation talks with the Americans and everybody knew it. The Soviet economy was nearly exhausted from years of military competition with the United States. The Pentagon continued to demand and receive arms and rockets at a punishing pace. Then Ronald Reagan had proposed the prohibitively expensive "Star Wars" gambit aimed at screwing up Soviet rockets at launch.

Something had to be done.

The competition between Vorobiev and Karpov was now on hold pending the signing of the Vladivostok agreement.

Colonel Stargov entered the meeting at three o'clock.

The nine Russians had gathered in a small, windowless room, furnished with a lush red carpet, a large cherry table, and chairs covered with Armenian leather. There was a silver samovar in one corner where the comrades might make themselves a cup of tea.

Foreign Minister Zhukov, sensing that his agreement with the Americans somehow hung in the balance, watched with darkened eyes.

Premier Spishkin's hand was steady as he settled into his chair and lit a cigarette. "Colonel Stargov."

Stargov began by informing the Politburo of the security measures he had put in place. He then described, as best he could, the ambush inside the mausoleum, the directives and contingency plans in effect at the time, the actions of the terrorists, and the response of his officers and men. He detailed the smoke bombs, the flares, the dog, and the dead men inside. Then he dropped the shocker.

"The head is missing from Comrade Lenin's body,"

he said. "It is nowhere in the mausoleum, I assure you. It is gone, stolen." Stargov then read the typewritten paragraph that offered to swap Lenin's head for one year of open emigration from Warsaw Pact countries, Cuba and Vietnam. When he had finished, he read the paragraph again. Then he gave the piece of paper to Premier Spishkin.

Premier Petr Spishkin hesitated. He read the paper, his hand on his chin. He hadn't felt like this since he'd commanded a tank in Poland in 1944. "The head is missing! You're sure, Colonel?"

"I checked the mausoleum carefully. That includes the tomb itself, and both the entrance and exit stairs, the bleachers, and the trees between the mausoleum and the wall."

"It was smart of you to keep the square cleared, Colonel. Tell me, what do you think happened to the head?"

"I think the dog we found carried it out under cover of the smoke," Stargov said. He hoped they didn't confiscate the dog, whom he had already decided to name Vladimir. "I think he was sent in and out again."

"Under cover of the smoke," Vorobiev repeated. "This could be done, do you think, Colonel Stargov?"

"Yes, sir. I think the colored flares were used to send signals to someone handling the dog outside the smoke. They would guess that we jam radio signals immediately in a case like this. One of the dead men had what I take to be a silent dog whistle."

"And the men—who are they?"

"I don't know, sir. They ranged in age from their mid-twenties to early forties, I would say. They're all bald, as I said. They burned their papers before they killed themselves. We'll be able to trace them through their fingerprints, but that will take time. Four of them, they . . ." Stargov cleared his throat. "Four of them— they were inside the mausoleum—four of them had the Star of David painted on the tops of their bald heads."

Spishkin looked stunned. "Zionists!"

Stargov said, "The man with the note had an Estonian flag in his lap. And a small photograph of himself with his arm around a young woman."

"Jews and Estonians!" KGB chief Karpov was enraged.

Premier Spishkin said, "The decision we have to make, quickly, is whether or not to search for the head. The sooner we act, the better our chances for getting it back, whoever they are. On the other hand, we can hardly conduct an adequate search without telling our people what they're looking for."

Vorobiev said, "That's one course, immediate action. Close the city and turn it upside down. But if we fail . . ." Vorobiev saw no need to complete the thought. "I think that we should continue Colonel Stargov's story that the body is intact. We can always make another head."

Karpov said, "I can see to that and personally guarantee the maker remains forever silent. If an innocent finds the skull, we simply confiscate it and announce that it is bogus. We can turn GUM and the museums and hotels upside down looking for other conspirators. Colonel Stargov and I could head the search. If a head is found, we should be able to neutralize the finders."

Thus did the members of the Soviet Politburo quickly coalesce around a plan: they would announce that the tomb was desecrated, but Lenin's body was unscathed. The attack had been perpetrated by Romanians (the Politburo was currently angered at the introduction of private enterprise in the Romanian economy and had been thinking of invading Bucharest). Karpov would conduct an immediate, intensive search of the area surrounding Red Square looking for unspecified "evidence" left by the terrorists.

Vorobiev said, "If you need any help at all, Comrade Karpov . . ."

Premier Spishkin coughed and took a sip of tea.

"Which brings us to Colonel Stargov's note. I'm afraid that's your problem as well, Valery Nikolaevich. I want every KGB agent in the country put to work finding out who these people are. Find their co-conspirators, and we just might have a chance. Perhaps you can help there, Gennadi Stepanovich."

"Certainly," Vorobiev said.

"I don't think we can overestimate the importance of finding Comrade Lenin's skull." Spishkin passed the terrorists' sheet of paper down the table.

"We have some time. They have to get the head out of the country," Spishkin said. "I think it makes sense to put Comrade Karpov and Comrade Vorobiev in charge, to be assisted by Colonel Stargov. I think the rest of us should wait as patiently as we can, ready to help if called upon. Other than the conspirators, we in this room are the only ones who know Lenin's head is missing. If word gets out, the one responsible will be found out and shot. I don't think that's unfair. We cannot fail. Cannot."

The other members of the Politburo assented by their silence. It was just possible, if their plan failed, to put the entire blame on Spishkin, Vorobiev, and Karpov. If that happened, any one of them might have a chance to become premier, and they all craved power as others craved chocolate, alcohol, and sex.

Later that day, Foreign Minister Grigori Zhukov, who kept a personal journal for most of his adult life—smuggled to the West before his later imprisonment—entered his thoughts during that historic meeting:

"Nowhere in the mausoleum," Colonel Stargov told us. Lenin's head was missing. Words fail me. I cannot describe the terrified silence that followed. Yes, terrified rather than melancholy, because survival is the most powerful of human instincts. We all wondered: How much more could our scaffold bear? The Politburo was torn by dissension which had seemed to worsen over the years. The Eastern Europeans were pressuring us for more freedom. The arms race was consuming forty to fifty percent of our gross national product. The agricultural collectives, which had cost us millions of lives during the Stalin years, had never worked, and we couldn't feed ourselves. We were falling dangerously behind the West in high technology. Under Lenin's banner and in Lenin's name, we had persevered.

We had used Lenin as the Christians used Jesus. "Yes," we told them, "it is true you may do without now, but stay with us, believe, and we will deliver you to Comrade Lenin's promised land." If Marx was right that religion is the opiate of the masses, had we not used the same drug? After all these years of attempting to suppress Christians, stubborn believers persevered. We sent them to camps and psychiatric wards and still they persisted in their superstitions, still passed their Bibles from hand to hand. Was there really any qualitative difference between Christianity and the secular religion we built around Lenin? Had we not replaced Christian icons with our own?

There was a stubborn will to believe among the Russian peasants; we all knew that. Until we were vouchsafed the return of Lenin's head, we were vulnerable to a passion that the KGB might not be able to control.

We had always portrayed ourselves as mere caretakers of Lenin's vision. We did Ilyich's work for him. Now his head was gone. True, the head had been a joke to anybody of intelligence. We had insisted against common sense that we had miraculously preserved Lenin against the bacteria that level us all. Stalin had had the idea that the peasants would see an eternal body as proof of a messiah, and he had been right. The head was symbolic of our trust.

Now, after all our talk, we had managed to let bald-headed thieves steal Lenin's head. What if it were true, as we secretly suspected, that Russians loved Lenin but only suffered us because we gave them no choice? In the terrifying emotion of the moment would they, in loyalty to the desecrated Lenin, hold us responsible for all that had gone wrong? Would we be trusted with anything?

For more than sixty years we had conducted a secular version of the Moslem jihad, or holy war; now it was coming back on us. Surely not all my comrades would agree with this analysis, but we all knew our decisions tonight were fraught with uncommon danger. Even Vorobiev and Karpov, who were probably planning on assassinating or imprisoning one another, put aside their differences. When one spoke, the other, for once, listened. It would have been amusing had it not been so tragic. As I pen these words I can hardly believe it yet.

Nine

THE KREMLIN WATCHERS IN LANGLEY AND AT THE STATE Department didn't know what to make of the Politburo's reaction to the assault on Lenin's tomb. The watchers had really been through it in the last months of Brezhnev, Andropov, and Chernenko. But even the most veteran and perceptive of the experts had never seen anything like this. Kremlin spokesmen were releasing all manner of contradictory statements. Lights were on all night at the White House and the Executive Office Building.

Nobody knew if Premier Petr Spishkin still ran the Kremlin or not. There had been one rumor that Gennadi Vorobiev, the minister of defense, was in charge; another theory was that Valery Karpov was in charge.

The President and the secretary of state demanded that the Company tell them what the hell was going on in the Kremlin. The signing of the agreement to renew negotiations for arms limitation was to take place on May 5—twenty-three days away. Would it be aborted after all that hard work?

"We need answers, and we need them now, Peter," the President had said. "This is top priority, urgent."

The President didn't believe the arms talks would do any good, but he needed them so that his defense budget would survive intact. The generals and defense contractors were counting on him.

Schott and Burlane went to Peter Neely's office the day after the assault. Schott seemed slightly apologetic about having gotten the Company into such a mess. Burlane seemed unconcerned, if not actually amused.

Peter Neely's face tightened and the muscles of his jaw tensed. A goddamned poet! Who would have believed? Smoke bombs and flares in Red Square. Why did this have to happen on his watch? When Burlane had reported back from Turkey, the DCI had been convinced his man had done the correct thing. Now he wasn't so sure. Was he wrong to trust someone who was so different from himself as James Burlane? Neely looked first at Schott, then at Burlane.

"Well, now," Neely said. "What do we make of all this? Jesus Christ! Smoke bombs! Flares!" Neely's voice rose. The tension in the room hung like that brief lethal millisecond before lightning strikes. Neely slammed the *Washington Post* and *The New York Times* on his desk. He was furious.

Schott said, "Our Moscow people say there've been rumors of a dog. That would fit with Ginsburg's request for silent whistles."

Peter Neely didn't need the Company's Moscow people to tell him the obvious. Burlane had given Ginsburg green and red flares, hadn't he? And smoke bombs. He glared at Burlane. "Mr. Burlane?"

"He told me he was going to steal something. I believed him." Burlane grinned.

Schott said, "From Lenin's tomb? Jimmy, dammit, this is serious business! We're set to sign an agreement to resume the Geneva talks."

"They probably did find a dog," Burlane said. "I

can't imagine even Ginsburg would try to smuggle a dog out of there in that confusion.''

Schott said, "Peter, our people tell us the Soviets sealed off the blocks surrounding the Kremlin almost immediately. Only the people at the fringes who heard the shooting were able to get out. The Soviet press says Vorobiev and Karpov are leading the search personally, along with Colonel Igor Stargov, commander of the Kremlin security forces.''

"Looking for the rest of the Romanians, *Pravda* says.''

Burlane said, "Hey, it's ridiculous for those guys to search those hotels room by room themselves. If they're after clues, they've got professionals who know how to look for clues. They're looking for something else, I say.''

Peter Neely said, "Like what, Mr. Burlane, please?'' Neely had an edge to his voice, having seen that Burlane was wearing off-brown socks with his unpolished black shoes. This was the man who had given Ginsburg what he needed to attack the mausoleum. If the goddamned newspapers ever found out what they'd done, Neely'd have to roast the Company's best agent in public.

Burlane said, "The Kremlin damn well wants to find out whatever it was the dog carried out of the mausoleum under the cover of the smoke. It was easy enough to do, if you think about it. Someone carried one of the silent whistles into the mausoleum. Someone had one at the edge of Red Square. If the Soviets know about the dog, which they probably do, then Stargov will figure out what happened.''

"Exactly *what* was easy enough, Jimmy? We can hardly wait, Jimmy.'' Like Neely, Ara Schott was most comfortable with serious and orderly people.

"The Soviets say they'll open the mausoleum when it's repaired,'' Burlane said. "They have to show folks there is nothing wrong with Lenin's body, just like they said. Only the deal is, Lenin's head is missing and the new one's going to be a complete as opposed to a partial fabrication.''

"Be serious, Jim.''

"A dog could do it. Under cover of a bank of smoke, he could do it. I checked on that this morning. I didn't tell the animal people what I was talking about. You wouldn't even have to have that large a dog. Ginsburg got away with it, too, or they wouldn't be conducting this incredible search. The wristwatches were needed for timing. It was apparently perfectly executed, a quick surprise hit. Boom! A quick layer of smoke. The dog in. The dog out. The guys in the mausoleum don't make it, but Ginsburg—or the other guy—does.''

Schott said, "The Russians say it was a suicide squad. They could be telling the truth, I suppose. But where do you get warriors like that?''

Burlane looked thoughtful. "You've got a point there. Yes, probably a suicide squad. Ginsburg couldn't possibly risk having one of them live.'' Burlane slouched further down in his chair. "I don't know where he got them, but I'd make book he did it. This guy had a certain kind of lethal calm about him. He's a smart son of a bitch. I don't think he did anything by accident.''

Neely said, "Why not Lenin's hand? Wouldn't that be easier? And it'd have his fingerprints, wouldn't it? Or wouldn't they still be good?''

Burlane said, "Take Lenin's hand when you can have his head? Come on, now. That'd be like snatching a wristwatch when you can have the money belt. Ginsburg's got Lenin's teeth along with the skull, hasn't he? You can identify the skull by the teeth. At the risk of coming off like Sherlock, I think that's it. Ginsburg's clever, and he hates the fuckers. He figures out how to make the grab and pulls it off. He got the head past the search. Now he has to get it out of the country to do anything with it. How? Notice how he's anticipated success.''

At the end of the meeting, Peter Neely directed that any one-time pad received by the American embassy in Moscow addressed to J. B. be treated as Priority One. Peter Neely was to be beeped or called immediately in the event of a Priority One.

Ten

THE CALL CAME AT 3:24 A.M., WEDNESDAY, APRIL 14, two days after the assault on the mausoleum. Peter Neely turned from beneath his sleeping wife's leg and answered the phone.

A woman said, "Jackie?"

Neely said, "You have the wrong number," and hung up. Neely left his warm bed, put his clothes on, and drove his Mercedes to Langley—followed at a discreet distance by a black Trans-Am containing the two men who were there for his protection.

This was the message to J. B. in Langley, Virginia:

Have Lenin's head. Being followed. Riding the Trans-Siberian Express from Moscow to Vladivostok, 10 A.M. Moscow time, 28 April, with 1 May stopover for reading at Irkutsk. Traveling with accomplice Natalia Kropotkina. We seek one-year open emigration from USSR and Soviet bloc countries, Cuba, and Vietnam in return for the head. Can you ride this train also, J. B.? I have a need for your services that I will make clear at an appropriate time. We wish we could do this alone but we

cannot. If you are honorable men and value freedom as you say you do, you will do this. Isaak
Avraamovich Ginsburg.

Neely, stunned, reread the message. James Burlane
was right. Isaak Ginsburg had stolen the head from
Lenin's corpse with the help of the Central Intelligence
Agency. Ginsburg was going to ride the Trans-Siberian
to Vladivostok to read a commemorative poem at the
signing, and he wanted Burlane with him. Dammit!

Peter Neely now knew why the Kremlin had gone off
its nut. No wonder! If Petr Spishkin found out the
Company was involved in a scheme to steal Lenin's
head from the tomb, Spishkin would probably launch
the goddamned rockets.

In Moscow that day, Felix Jin and the other colonels
of the KGB's Jewish Department were called before
their chief, Valery Karpov. Comrade Karpov's comings
and goings were mysterious to all but a handful of his
subordinates, but everybody knew that he had virtually
gone without sleep in the two days that had passed since
the raid on Lenin's tomb. Karpov and Defense Minister
Gennadi Vorobiev had personally led the day-and-night
search of the area surrounding Red Square.

Karpov ordinarily kept himself aloof from mundane
labor, preferring instead the pleasures of conniving. His
desires were made known by memo, and failure to meet
them was dealt with harshly. Jin and his fellow officers
knew that for Karpov to call a personal meeting after
two sleepless days of hard work meant something very
serious indeed.

The assembled officers were those who monitored
lists of Jews considered to represent the greatest poten-
tial threat to the state. One colonel oversaw a list of
outspoken scientists and engineers. A second watched
Jews who attempted to contact the world outside the

Soviet Union. The third, Colonel Jin, followed the activities of writers.

Felix Jin had spent most of his adult life learning how to read opaque, ambiguous statements. An aptitude for separating the truth from outright lies was the secret of success for Russian bureaucrats, but Karpov's performance was so fraught with possibilities that Jin was stunned.

Karpov told the officers of the Jewish Department that the Romanian terrorists who trashed Lenin's tomb had connections to Zionists, and possibly to Estonians. That fact was to be kept secret.

Karpov then said there was reason to believe that one or more Zionists who were part of the plot had traveled to Perm within the previous year. That fact also was to be kept secret. Karpov did not specify the connection between Zionists and Perm.

Karpov told the colonels they were to personally review their respective lists for any Jew who had been to Perm in the last year. If any of the officers had such a Jew on his list, he was to personally supervise a total surveillance of that Jew.

"Comrade Colonels, we are looking for specific physical evidence. This is not in microdot or microfilm. To give you a rough idea, it is as large as this perhaps." Karpov held his palm out and weighed whatever it was he was looking for. "You'll know it when you find it. This is to be top secret among us. If you find it, immediately isolate everyone involved. They are to talk to no one." Karpov reviewed a note he had made to himself.

"I hope you have all followed the personal computer memorandum and have learned how to operate the portable American computers we stole for you. That's what we got them for, so we can work quickly and efficiently in an emergency. I assume you've all learned your"—he glanced at his card—"your 'software,' it says here."

Only Felix Jin said, "Yes, sir."

Karpov stared balefully at the other two officers. "What this means, comrades, is that you're going to have to use a KGB operator and shoot him for security when you're finished with this. You're to shoot him—or her—yourself. When this is finished, I want you to learn how to use those computers. Now, I have these." He held up a small box containing floppy disks.

"These contain the names and data from all the people that were interviewed in the Red Square area for the past two days. This includes individuals on the streets, in the subway, in the museums, GUM, and hotels." Karpov held up a second box of floppies. "These contain the names and identifying data of all visitors to Perm hotels in the previous year."

Colonel Felix Jin and his colleagues wondered just what evidence it was that was so sensitive that Comrade Karpov felt obliged to keep it secret. *Sure, comrades, find this thing on penalty of your careers, but I can't let you know what it is.*

The colonels walked out of the new KGB headquarters as though such bizarre instructions were commonplace. They couldn't complain or speculate lest word get back to Comrade Karpov.

Felix Jin, feeling good that he alone had followed Karpov's orders and learned how to work his brandnew Kaypro, happily took his disks to his office at Dzerzhinsky Square. To have scored like that in such an emergency was a political coup in KGB politics, and was good for Jin's career.

Jin slipped into the chair, turned on the machine, punched the reset button, and slipped his Perfect Writer disk in Drive A and the disk with the interview data in Drive B. The prompt came up, and Jin typed "MENU" and hit the return bar.

The menu appeared and Jin typed D, B, to see exactly what was on the disk. Nothing happened. He tried again. Jin was puzzled. He removed the disk in Drive B and slipped in one he'd been using to write reports. This time the disk directory appeared as requested.

Something was wrong with Karpov's disk. Jin called the new KGB headquarters and got through to Karpov. "They've sent me faulty disks, Comrade Karpov. I'll have to have good ones to do my job."

Karpov swore. "Good that you called me personally, Colonel. Send them back. I'll get you new ones."

Felix Jin did as he was told and waited, impatient to get on with the investigation. He smoked a cigarette, bewildered at the number of fuck-ups in the KGB.

A half hour later Karpov called back, an edge to his voice. He said, "I'm afraid I have some bad news for you, Felix."

"Yes, comrade?" Jin wondered what could possibly have happened.

"It seems there was a disagreement over what kind of computers we should buy. Some of your colleagues, Felix, said we should buy IBMs because they're more famous. Others said Kaypros are the better deal because they're cheaper and will do everything we need. In the end there was a compromise; we decided to buy IBMs for the officers here at Moscow Center and Kaypros for those of you still at Dzerzhinsky."

"What?" Another decision by committee. Jin had read the computer manuals and guessed what the screw-up was. He was furious.

"The codes used to operate those machines are different, Felix."

"I could have told you that, Comrade Karpov."

"I'm sorry, Felix. Who would have thought they don't use a common code? You can have somebody else shoot the operator if you'd like. It's not your fault and I understand that."

"I'd prefer to isolate the operator until this matter is finished." Jin remained calm with effort.

"Of course, Felix." Valery Karpov hung up.

The computer specialist, a personable young woman

named Vera, used an IBM PC. The computer singled out one name, which appeared in neat green letters:

Isaak Avraamovich Ginsburg.

Comrade Ginsburg had been in the Hotel Rossiya at the time of the assault on Lenin's tomb, and he had spent one night in Perm the previous August.

Jin sat back in his chair and considered the stunning connection.

He pulled Ginsburg's file. The stop at Perm had apparently been made en route to Moscow from Novosibirsk. Jin had the operator input all names mentioned by KGB agents who had been following the poet. These were people Ginsburg had known from school and in his days as an underground poet as well as his most recent past in Novosibirsk and Moscow. With growing excitement, Jin watched the operator key in the names. Jin instructed the operator to find out if any of these names were on Karpov's Red Square or Perm list.

One was: Natalia Serafimovna Kropotkina. Comrade Kropotkina, like Ginsburg, had been in the Hotel Rossiya at the time of the affair on Red Square.

Jin reread Ginsburg's dossier. There was evidence to suggest that Ginsburg was having an affair with Natalia Kropotkina, the *znachok* designer who was married to the foreign service officer, Leonid Kropotkin. Comrade Jin picked up the phone and ordered a full KGB report on Natalia Kropotkina.

It was only then that Jin saw a one-line reference to something that had no meaning before and which he had forgotten: from March 12 through March 15, Ginsburg had been to the Georgian Republic to read his poetry. Tbilisi was just fourteen hundred kilometers from Tel Aviv. This was interesting because Ginsburg's landlord in Novosibirsk, Georgi Kashva, was believed to have contacts with smugglers operating out of Georgia.

Eleven

JAMES BURLANE KNEW IT WAS COMING, THAT PREDICTABLE old dumbshit mental constipation of bureaucrats faced with danger. It was choke time. Be careful time. Protect your ass time. Burlane was different. Burlane had been a fan of the Green Bay Packers when he was a kid. He remembered two things clearly: Bart Starr, faced with third and short, throwing long to Boyd Dowler or Max McGee, and Starr, money on the line, turning automatically to Paul Hornung.

Lenin's head! This Isaak Ginsburg affair was real money time. Burlane was the Company's main man, dammit, the Paul Hornung of the Central Intelligence Agency. He wanted that ball.

Burlane said, "Listen, Mr. Neely, you cannot, just *cannot* leave that man hanging out there alone. He's asking for our help. He's not asking anything impossible. He's not saying they have to hold free elections or let people own property or anything like that."

Ara Schott said, "We have to be very, very careful, Jimmy."

"Bullshit!"

Schott was surprised by Burlane's vehemence. "You

205

have to consider the consequences of something like this, Jimmy.''

Burlane looked disgusted. ''So tell me about the consequences.''

''Well, for one thing,'' Neely said, ''how could we conceivably handle all those people, assuming the Russians would let them go? That may seem coarse to you, but it's something we have to consider.''

''You could pull a Franklin Roosevelt, I guess. Leave them there to get crapped on and thrown in camps. I don't know about you, but that does strike me as a trifle coarse.''

''Roosevelt had a war to fight, Mr. Burlane,'' Neely said.

Burlane did his best not to glare at the DCI. ''If we don't do this, to what end did we fight that war? Ask yourself that. We must do this. We must.''

Ara Schott said, ''The European economies are running twelve to eighteen percent unemployment as it is. How are they going to handle a flood of Poles and Czechs?''

''And Jews?'' Burlane put in.

''And Jews,'' Schott said. ''I'll be honest and tell you I'm not certain Israel would be too excited about this.''

Burlane shook his head.

Neely said, ''You've got education to think about, language problems.''

''Not to mention the risk of having the Soviets find out we helped Ginsburg out.'' Schott doodled on a piece of paper.

Burlane leaned forward, serious as he rarely appeared to be. ''As civilized men, we have a moral obligation here and we all know it. There are some things we do because they must be done. This is one of them.''

Ara Schott looked surprised. ''A what, Mr. Burlane? Moral obligation? Civilized men? This is the Central Intelligence Agency. We're responsible for the security of the United States and nothing more. You know that, man!''

"We have to help him. I say again, this is an opportunity that transcends politics. We do what we have to do and the devil take the hindmost. What follows, follows.''

"Just how would you propose to get on that particular train, Mr. Burlane?'' In order to protect his reputation as a civilized man and an executive who considered all possibilities, Neely felt he should hear Burlane out. Neely jotted a note on a classified pad on his desk.

"He's given us everything we need, a setup. He's their wonder-boy poet, the house Jew. The Soviets aren't just tolerating attention for Ginsburg, they're inviting it with this commemorative poem business. We choose an influential left-wing magazine of politics and the arts. We tell the editor that the President of the United States would like a few words with him. A little tête-à-tête over breakfast, say.''

Schott said, "And the President would do what?''

"The President would ask the editor to make an urgent request to the Soviets. The editor wants one of his magazine's cultural reporters to accompany Ginsburg on the ride to Vladivostok. Me.''

Neely took another note. "Have you forgotten, Mr. Burlane, that we solemnly promised a committee of the United States Senate that we would forever cease and desist using journalists as cover for our covert operations?''

"Screw the Senate! Thomas Jefferson bought the Louisiana Territory without asking Congress like he was supposed to. That was unconstitutional, but you didn't hear anybody complaining.''

Neely looked surprised. "I thought you didn't want anything to do with going inside the Soviet Union ever again.''

"Changed my mind. I ski. I shoot. I read. They say Nelson won the battle of Trafalgar because he let his

commanders do what they had to do in the heat of
battle. For God's sake, please, please let me do this.''

Three days later, the editor of the liberal political
magazine *New Democrat*—still glowing from the pleasure of having eggs Benedict and melon balls with the
President of the United States, an affable man who had
called the editor by his first name—gave the Company a
list of writers. These were men and women who had
written for his magazine in the past and who might very
well be hired to write a story about Isaak Ginsburg's trip
across the Soviet Union to the Vladivostok signing. The
editor did this despite having written in his magazine—
just two weeks earlier—that the affable President was an
ignorant, bigoted, right-wing ideologue, an incompetent
whose refusal to confront the deficit threatened the country with economic chaos.

Ara Schott and James Burlane wanted a writer whose
known personality and temperament were a rough match
for Burlane. Their ideal candidate, they agreed, would
be well enough known for the Soviets to assemble his
dossier quickly, but would have an unknown face. He
could not be a columnist or public personality.

James Burlane received the list of names on April 17.
He ran his finger down the list, and when he reached
Quint, James Allen, he burst out laughing.

Jim Quint—who grew up in western Montana—did
magazine work and, under the pseudonym of Nicholas
Orr, wrote a series of paperback adventures featuring a
hero with the unlikely name of Humper Staab, so called
because if he wasn't humping somebody, he was stabbing them. Two years earlier, a boxed feature accompanying a *Newsweek* magazine cover story on the Company
described the adventures of an unnamed superspy who
was, in fact, James Burlane. The joke at Langley,
Newsweek said, was that this superspy was the real-life
model for "Humper Staab." Alas, poor Quint was later
sued for libel by Humperdinck Staab, a minor OSS agent
in World War II. Burlane claimed to be disappointed.

Burlane, originally from eastern Oregon, responded easily and naturally to James, Jim, or Jimmy. Under the circumstances, this was as good a match as the Company could hope for.

Jim Quint agreed to get lost for a while. He wrote a quickie autobiography for James Burlane to memorize and bought himself a ticket to Jamaica; he said he'd once had a helluva time there.

The Russian embassy in Washington, eager to please the editors of the *New Democrat*, quickly approved Jim Quint's application for a visa; Quint's passport now contained Burlane's picture. Yes, Burlane could accompany Isaak Ginsburg on his trip across the USSR on the Trans-Siberian Express.

Felix Jin studied the incomplete first report on Natalia Kropotkina on April 18; this was preliminary to the definitive dossier that Jin had requested. Although sketchy, it was suggestive.

Natalia Kropotkina had been a leading candidate to design the pin honoring Ivan Dmitrov's monumenal Lenin statue but had not received the commission, allegedly because of her ambition for personal attention. Then Dmitrov himself had apparently intervened to recommend that Natalia design the pin commemorating the Vladivostok signing.

In order to design the Vladivostok pin, Natalia Kropotkina said, she had to witness the signing. Comrade Kropotkina had requested space, subsequently approved, on the same train as Isaak Ginsburg.

Jin requested the engineer's drawings of the East German cars used on the railroad. He also ordered a search of railroad records to find Ginsburg's compartment-mate or mates on his way from Novosibirsk to Moscow when he had stopped to spend a night at Perm. He called Tbilisi and asked for a report on Ginsburg's visit there.

The railroad drawings were flown in from East Berlin

on April 19. There were far higher priorities for stolen American computers than for railway passengers, so the search for Ginsburg's traveling companion would take longer, perhaps weeks. Tbilisi said there was nothing unusual about Ginsburg's visit except that he was missing for a nine-hour period on a Sunday, March 15—the day before his return to Moscow. Tbilisi believed the missing hours were benign. The agents responsible for the lapse in surveillance had been disciplined.

Jin studied the drawings of the railroad cars. There were ten two-person compartments on a soft-class car. There were toilets at each end. There was a small compartment for bed linen next to one toilet, followed by the conductress's compartment, which contained one seat that served as a bed at night. The remaining compartments had two seats, one on each wall. The space under each was divided into an open and a closed baggage area. The seats, which were hinged on the wall, folded up for access to the closed areas. There was a loft for luggage above the door and the ceiling of the aisle.

In order to isolate and control Ginsburg and Kropotkina—and to find whatever it was Karpov was looking for—Jin ordered that the couple be berthed in a railway car placed at the tail end of the Trans-Siberian Express. He ordered them assigned to Compartment One, next to the conductress. If they were screwing now, they would be screwing on the train. Jin reserved the next compartment for the technicians needed to tape conversations and videotape their sex life.

Twelve

FROM THE MOMENT JAMES BURLANE LAID EYES ON THE Intourist guide who was to accompany him on the Trans-Siberian Express, he knew she was a honeypot. Whether the KBG was on to him, he did not know. If it were, KGB officers would know from his dossier that he had a hyperactive sex drive, something the Company tolerated because of his skills as an agent. Whatever. If the KGB had assembled a file on Jim Quint, they'd have found that the writer from Bison, Montana, was likewise damned with too much testosterone.

The Soviets knew how to break a man. The blonde who waited for Burlane/Quint at the main desk in the lobby of the National Hotel had a body upon which clothes were obscene.

The Americans called these women honeypots because men, drawn to the nectar of sex, become stuck like wriggling flies, susceptible to KGB blackmail. The KGB called them swallows, as in pretty birds, although Company men alleged the term was used in a sexual context.

The honeypot had watched Burlane from the moment he reached the foot of the stairs. She had a folder tucked

under her arm; Burlane noticed that the folder flattened
the side of her enviable breast. "Mr. Jim Quint?
My name is Ludmilla Kormakova and I'll be your guide
on the way to Vladivostok."

Burlane shook her hand and said, "Pleased to meet
you, Ms. Kormakova." He thought, *Good Christ!* and
followed her outside to the waiting Volga taxi, his eyes
somewhere below her waist. The odds of his accidentally drawing an Intourist guide who looked like Ludmilla
were statistically negligible. Burlane threw his one bag
into the trunk and joined Ludmilla in the back seat,
where he was overwhelmed by the French perfume she
was wearing. He wanted to dive into her lap sniffing
like a hog after truffles.

As the taxi pulled into the traffic, Burlane's guide
said, "You must call me Ludmilla. You are doing
articles on the Trans-Siberian Railroad and Comrade
Ginsburg. I'm told the *New Democrat* is one of the
better American magazines. Very influential."

"Please call me Jim," Burlane said. Nobody had
accused the *New Democrat* of being influential since
Franklin Roosevelt's first term. "We try to be the conscience of progressives in America." The truth was that
the *New Democrat* was too New Deal-Old Democrat for
Burlane's taste. He hadn't read it on his own for years,
and had had to OD on recent issues to prepare for this
trip. Ludmilla's perfume made him giddy.

"We are, of course, making the longest train ride in
the world. We will be crossing almost one hundred
degrees of longitude in Europe and Asia. We will be
crossing seven time zones, although we will be observ-
ing Moscow time throughout."

Ludmilla made Burlane want to lick his lips. He was
thinking this when he realized he should be taking notes.
He scrambled for his notebook and began scribbling as
the Volga wheeled through sparse traffic. "Seven time
zones," he said. "That's really something."

Ludmilla paused so Burlane could record the number

of degrees longitude to be crossed. She said, "Yes. It is fifty-eight hundred and ten miles from Moscow to Vladivostok on the Sea of Japan. This trip will take us a full seven days, or one hundred seventy hours, on the train. There will be four days to Irkutsk, which is north of the Gobi Desert, and three more days to Vladivostok. Because of Comrade Ginsburg's reading in Irkutsk on May Day, we will be arriving on the morning of the eighth day."

"I see," Burlane said.

"It will be Moscow to Perm the first day, Perm to Omsk the second, Omsk to Krasnoyarsk the third, and Krasnoyarsk to Irkutsk the fourth. We will arrive in Irkutsk the morning of May first and leave that night. We will have a room in the Intourist Hotel in Irkutsk so that you might rest if you like. It is a long ride on the Trans-Siberian Express."

"And we'll be arriving in Vladivostok . . . ?"

"The morning of May fifth, Jim, because of the delay at Irkutsk. As to time on the move, it will be Irkutsk to Mogocha the fifth day, Mogocha to Khabarovsk the sixth, and Khabarovsk to Vladivostok the seventh. Ordinarily, foreigners are not allowed in Vladivostok, and must go instead to Nakhodka. Foreigners are allowed to stop at Novosibirsk, Irkutsk, and Khabarovsk. That trip is longer—fifty-nine hundred miles—a trip of almost eight days or one hundred ninety-two hours and thirty minutes. This is because travelers must stop over for one day in Khabarovsk."

"Why is that?" Burlane said.

"It is done that way, Jim."

Burlane retrieved his map of the Soviet Union and found Khabarovsk by way of showing his interest. "I see. Well. Here it is: Khabarovsk."

"The Paris of the Soviet Far East," Ludmilla said.

"On the Amur River."

"The Amur River has one of the highest volumes of water of any river in the world."

Burlane wondered if a legit journalist would give a damn. He decided the safest course was to come on red hot. He scribbled "Amur River, much water" in an illegible scrawl.

Ludmilla said, "If you took the train from New York to Los Angeles via New Orleans, you would cover just thirty-four hundred and twenty miles."

Burlane was starting to get an erection watching Ludmilla rattle off facts and numbers. He'd have to tell that to Schott if he made it out alive.

"And you have to understand that if you go west from Moscow, it's another four hundred and eighty miles to the Finnish border. Incidentally, Yaraslavsky Station is so named because Yaraslav on the Volga was the original terminal point of the rail line that eventually spanned our country."

Their driver pulled to a stop at the bizarre Victorian building that was Yaraslavsky Station. Ludmilla brushed against him as she retrieved her bag from the trunk of the Volga. Burlane knew that to keep his hands off her would be a sacrifice of a magnitude rarely endured by soldiers of the cold war.

James Burlane and his guide strode quickly through a huge room with a high ceiling from which hung ornate electrical chandeliers. Black granite columns braced the ceiling. Burlane walked with the loose, confident stride of a man who had been in a lot of train stations in the Third World and so was familiar with the resigned faces and rancid odor of poverty. As far as Burlane was concerned, the only difference between the residents of the Soviet Union and those of Timor or Mozambique was that the Russians had ICBMs, and travelers there didn't have to worry about getting ripped off because the state had a monopoly on violence along with everything else.

The travelers in Yaraslavsky Station were encamped like refugees from a war zone, sitting upon or beside all manner of cardboard boxes and bags wrapped in news-

paper and tied with string or hemp. Some smoked cigarettes; others took quick hits of vodka so as to remain
oblivious. The women guarded the food: bags of cabbage, small apples, loaves of coarse bread, balls of
butter wrapped in greasy paper, and bits and pieces of
fat and hunks of smelly sausage rolled in paper cones.

Burlane stepped over the mud-encrusted boots of a
soldier sprawled in an alcoholic stupor. A man with a
crude haircut observed him idly, wondering, Burlane
supposed, where he was from. Patches of white from
the man's skull showed through where the shears had
strayed too close. A small boy in a coat so heavy the
sleeves would not bend at the elbows stared at him.
Ludmilla was a Russian, easily identified as a privileged
Intourist guide. Burlane was different. He was not a
Russian.

The watchful travelers didn't know Burlane was an
American; he could have been Belgian or Spanish for all
they knew. It was enough that he was from someplace
that was not the USSR. In the Soviet Union a foreigner
was a possible source of a watch that worked or blue
jeans that didn't come apart at the seams, but other than
that he was something to be avoided.

Burlane followed Ludmilla down the platform to Train
No. 1, which left Moscow for Vladivostok at 10 A.M.
Train No. 1 was called the Rossiya—the Russia—and
was red with a yellow stripe down its sides. Burlane
counted twenty passenger cars—ten on either side of
two dining cars—plus an enormous East German engine
up front. They walked to the very end of the train,
where the car that contained their soft-class compartment waited.

It did not surprise Burlane—as he and Ludmilla moved
down the aisle in search of their compartment—to see
Isaak Ginsburg waiting to enter his compartment two
doors down. Ginsburg was with a dark-haired woman
who would have attracted Burlane's attention by virtue
of her figure, but the fact that she carried a bronze bust

of Lenin under her arm was a showstopper. Burlane found it difficult not to stare.

Burlane and Ginsburg glanced at one another in a quick moment of mutual sharing and responsibility. Burlane and Ginsburg had a pact. The trust was theirs, and the danger.

James Burlane and Ludmilla Kormakova stored their bags under the seats. Burlane, followed closely by Ludmilla, returned to the aisle to watch the activity on the platform; he had a long ride ahead of him, and there was no reason to sit down too soon. Just as he did not believe it was an accident that he had drawn an Intourist guide of Ludmilla's remarkable beauty, Burlane knew it was not the luck of the draw that he and Isaak Ginsburg were assigned a car at the extreme rear of the train.

Burlane assumed that the dark-haired woman was Natalia Kropotkina, the accomplice of Ginsburg's message. Burlane wondered why she would want to lug a heavy bust of Lenin across the Soviet Union.

As the train began its journey, the conductress came in to sweep the carpet. She was a small woman in her early thirties. Her duties included taking care of the huge stainless electric samovar just opposite her compartment. The samovar looked to Burlane like a coffee maker in an American cafeteria. The conductress made and delivered tea, swept the carpets, stocked the toilets with paper, and made sure the passengers in her car were back on board after each stop. She performed these duties so quietly and unobtrusively as to be chameleonlike.

The conductress said something to Ludmilla, and watched Burlane as Ludmilla translated.

"She says her name is Nina Kabakhidze, Jim. She is originally from the Autonomous Republic of Georgia, which has some of the most productive citrus groves in the Middle East. She is a senior conductress. She will be with us all the way to Vladivostok. If you need help, you are to ask her."

Burlane nodded his head in acknowledgment, then promptly forgot Nina Kabakhidze's name. Kabakhidze was hard to remember.

Ludmilla said, "We'll have all the hot water we need for our tea, Jim. I brought us some special tea. From GUM. The very finest tea in the world is available at GUM."

Thirteen

THEY WERE NO SOONER OUT OF YARASLAVSKY STATION than the conductress, wearing a dark gray skirt and a light gray blouse, served *chai*, Russian tea, to the passengers in her car, drawing piping hot water from the enormous samovar. Even Burlane had to admit that Russian tea and bread were some of the best he'd ever had, and the idea of having a generous samovar of hot water on each car was civilized.

"Your Russian tea is wonderful," he said. "And your bread too. I like that." The truth was he'd had better Russian tea than this.

Ludmilla said, "Our Russian bread is the best in the world, Jim. This is because it contains no additives and is baked according to national standards. The only bread that can compare with it is the bread of Canada, which costs almost twice as much."

Burlane hadn't meant to provoke a lecture. "It is good."

"It is very important in our socialist way of life that such things as tea and bread be the best and available to everybody at a price they can afford. Which do you like the best, Jim, the dark bread or the light bread?"

"The dark, I think. Maybe we should have some tea in our compartment." Burlane hoped to end the discussion of Russian bread. He went back into the compartment thinking that socialist travelers must be a thirsty group; the samovar looked like it held three or four gallons of water.

Later, Burlane stepped into the aisle to stretch his legs, and met Isaak Ginsburg. It was time, Burlane knew, for Jim Quint to introduce himself. "My name is Jim Quint, Mr. Ginsburg. I don't know if you've been told, but I'm an American journalist assigned to do a story about the trip across the Soviet Union and your poems at Irkutsk and Vladivostok." The dark-haired woman in Ginsburg's car was sketching; her bust of Lenin sat on the fold-down table below the compartment window.

"Yes, for the *New Democrat*," Ginsburg said.

Burlane said, "A poetry reading in Irkutsk on May Day. That ought to be wonderful stuff for my readers." His eyes asked: *Is Lenin's head on this railroad car? Is that why you wanted me on this train?*

Ginsburg's eyes replied yes to both questions. He said, "We Russians are passionate people, Mr. Quint. We love poetry and language. Poets are valued in the Soviet Union."

Burlane said, "Most Americans want to learn, they really do. The problem is that the owners of most magazines won't let them print the truth. The *New Democrat* has a special empathy for working people."

"The truth is all we Russians ask."

"I assure you, I'm not a propagandist. I write what I see, and the *New Democrat* will print what I write; it's that kind of magazine." Burlane wondered where in hell Ginsburg could stash a human head on a train with the KGB watching over his shoulder.

"I'm living proof there is no repression against Jews in the Soviet Union, Mr. Quint. Poets of quality are published. There are no obstacles to getting good work published.''

"Are you telling me you can write what you want? There is no censorship in the USSR?''

"None," Ginsburg said. "We're encouraged to write the truth. Contrary to what you're led to believe in the West, the Soviet Union is a wonderful place for a writer.''

"I assure you, I'm after the truth, not rehashed propaganda." Burlane was outwardly sincere, serious. He thought, *Bullshit too, bub!* He said, "I should be getting back to my compartment. My guide is waiting. Perhaps we could have a chat sometime before Irkutsk.'' The dark-haired woman had put down her pad and was listening to their conversation.

Isaak Ginsburg said, "Certainly." Ginsburg glanced at the woman. "Mr. Quint, I'd like you to meet Natalia Kropotkina. Natalia Serafimovna is one of the most famous designers of commemorative pins in the Soviet Union. You know what they are, don't you?" Ginsburg showed Burlane the small red pin on his lapel. "This is one of Natasha's most popular.''

Burlane looked at the pin. "Very nice." He shook Natalia's hand. He envied Ginsburg.

Ginsburg said, "She's been commissioned to do a pin commemorating the Vladivostok signing.''

"I see.''

Burlane inspected the pin on Ginsburg's lapel. "Very nice," he said. "I saw you sketching your bust of Lenin there.''

"This is a copy of the bust Comrade Zhukov will give to Stuart Kaplan—it's identical, in fact. I need to study it for my Vladivostok assignment; it'll help pass the time on the train.''

"Six thousand miles is a long way," Burlane said.

Ginsburg said, "Mrs. Kropotkina's husband, Leonid, is a foreign service officer. He's at The Hague this week. The Americans are being tried for war crimes in Central America.''

"Ahh, I see," Burlane said.

Natalia said, "Would you like to take a closer look at the bust, Mr. Quint? The sculptor, Ivan Dmitrov, is an acknowledged master.''

Burlane stepped into the compartment and squatted by the table to examine the bust, which was slightly larger than a real head. As far as he was concerned, Dmitrov's Lenin looked like all the others he had seen in the Soviet Union, but he suspected that Natalia Kropotkina was telling him something.

"It's lovely, lovely," Burlane said. "May I pick it up?''

"Why, of course." Natalia Kropotkina's English was even better than Ginsburg's.

Burlane held the bust in both hands. "It's heavy.''

"That's because it's bronze!" Natalia laughed easily.

He knew he should not talk too long with Ginsburg and Natalia. Too much talk invited error. "I'd better get back to my compartment," he said. "My guide will be wondering what happened to me.''

Burlane had hardly turned around when he was confronted by a group of Western European men gesturing, laughing, and talking in English with varying accents. One of them, a pot-bellied Englishman in a vested suit, spotted Burlane as a foreigner—and a likely English-speaker. "Hello, there. My name's Bob Steele.''

"Jim," Burlane said.

"Some ride, eh, Jim? My friends and I are journalists on our way to Vladivostok. They've got us all berthed in one car. I'm with *The Daily Telegraph* in London.''

"I see.''

"Quite a bunch, actually. We're having fun. Stocked in a good supply of vodka for the trip. We've got a couple of matched sets, British and Dutch, plus a German, a Frenchman, and a Dane. Drinkers and talkers.

Good group. Even our Intourist guide's a nice guy, a bit serious maybe, but he likes his vodka too.

"What is it you do, Jim?"

Burlane thought, *Oh shit!* He said, "Well, as a matter of fact, I'm a journalist too." He thought, *Drop it, Bob, will you?*

Bob Steele looked puzzled. "What are you covering?"

"I'm doing a story for the *New Democrat* on the poet Isaak Ginsburg. That's why they've got me in this car instead of with the rest of you."

Steele grinned. "Ahh. I see."

Burlane felt relieved; he seemed to have made it.

Then Steele said, "Say, what's your last name? Maybe I've read some of your stuff."

Burlane's heart sank, but he remained cheerful on the exterior. "Jim Quint."

Steele looked startled. "Jim Quint?"

Burlane laughed. "That's it, fresh out of Bison, Montana."

Steele glanced at his colleagues. He seemed not to know what to say next. Finally he said, "Pleased to have met you, Jim. It looks like my group's heading on back."

Burlane watched them leave the car. Bob Steele, the last one out, glanced back at Burlane. Steele obviously knew the real Jim Quint. Damn!

When James Burlane returned to the compartment he found it suffused with Ludmilla Kormakova's marvelous odor. Its effect on Burlane was nothing short of aphrodisiac. He was in for a long, long ride across the Soviet Union.

"There are ninety-three assigned stops between Moscow and Vladivostok," Ludmilla said as they settled in with their tea. Over the edge of her teacup, she looked into Burlane's eyes and gave him a warm smile.

Decent photography required light, not darkness. That first night Ludmilla Kormakova established precedent by leaving the reading light on above her bunk when she undressed. Burlane, in boxer shorts that featured tiny strawberries with little green leaves, lay back under his blanket and watched the show with much appreciation.

Ludmilla, naked, was fabulous—sleek of flank and brown of nipple. Her pubic hair, blue-black and shiny, stood in sharp contrast to the white of her thighs.

Ludmilla had remarkable nipples. When Burlane saw them, he wanted to attack them, chewing.

Ludmilla turned out the reading light and slipped into the berth opposite Burlane's and said, "I can't stand clothes when I sleep."

"A person's skin needs to breathe at night." Burlane wondered where she had been trained. At Verkhonoye? Probably. The KGB's Verkhonoye sex school was located between Kazan and the Urals in the Tatar Autonomous Soviet Socialist Republic. Stories of the outrageous training given swallows there were legendary at Langley. Burlane had often speculated about what he would do if he ever crossed paths with one. Now that had happened, and he could do nothing. He hoped she didn't think he was gay, or else she might be replaced by some jerk in tight pants.

James Burlane lay back, incapacitated by a throbbing erection that gripped his crotch like a pair of pliers. KGB bastards. Burlane was infuriated. His taut muscle did not relax, stayed tight, demanded action. Discipline, he told himself. Discipline. It wasn't until 1 A.M. that James Burlane was at last released from the Ludmilla-induced priapism and fell asleep to the clanging, banging lullaby of the Trans-Siberian Express.

Fourteen

JAMES BURLANE AWOKE THE NEXT MORNING WONDERING where the train was. He fished his wristwatch from the heel of his shoe: 7 A.M. of his second day on the train. Ludmilla Kormakova had prepared for his arising and was now sleeping, or pretending to sleep, with one breast casually exposed for Burlane's pleasure. The morning light suffused Ludmilla's wonderful prominence with an erotic alpenglow. Burlane considered this bounty for a moment, then raised the sliding green shade above the window.

The train passed some isolated peasant huts—a shanty here, a shack there, a pathetic hut, each one fenced. They came upon an impoverished hamlet, then taiga and birch, a shallow swamp of mud, a river, and another squalid village.

Burlane was contemplating the morning sun when Ludmilla said, "Good morning, Jim."

"Well, good morning, Ludmilla!" Burlane said heartily. Burlane was thankful that Quint's name was Jim. Burlane could react quickly to Jim. Burlane could never react to a Russian word or phrase. If he did, any pretense of cover was finished; the real Quint did not speak

Russian. Burlane was curious about what Siberia looked like, but he did not want to spend the rest of his life there. Burlane wondered if Ludmilla would give him an inadvertent little show when she got up.

The answer was yes. Given the one hundred and eighty degrees in which Ludmilla could have exposed her lower charms, she chose to aim her stern directly at Burlane as she bent to retrieve her clothes from under the bunk.

Burlane, still under the covers, stared in appreciation. It was hard not to be moved by the nutty juxtaposition of ball-stirring physical beauty with the banging and clattering of the Trans-Siberian Express.

"You Russians are physically very similar to Scandinavians aren't you?" Burlane said. "Lovely!" His peers would have said that James Burlane was one of a select few agents in the world capable of deadpanning that line knowing he was being videotaped by a KGB camera.

As Ludmilla slipped on her clothes, the train hit a storm front and the sky turned suddenly dark. "We will enter the Urals later today, Jim. The Urals divide Europe and Asia. The USSR is both the largest European and the largest Asian country. Shall we go to breakfast, do you think?"

The first day out, the indifferent waiter had brought them an elaborate menu listing chicken Kiev, sturgeon, baked desserts and other delicacies, as well as beluga, sevruga, and malossol caviars, aged cheeses, and fresh fruit. As the Russians on the train understood perfectly, the menu had nothing to do with what was available; it was for show only. For breakfast the chef offered fried eggs served in a metal dish and floating in tepid yellow oil, plus a thin slice of cheese; rice and boiled meat was the treat at lunch; mashed potatoes and borscht were served for supper.

Breakfast was different the second morning. The eggs were served with more oil, and the slice of cheese had been replaced by an emaciated weiner.

Another gloom descended after breakfast, and the sleet returned. Then the sleet turned to a dry snow that came down furiously. The snow stopped twenty minutes later, and they were into sun again with a bank of black clouds to one side of the train.

Ludmilla Kormakova drew hot water from the samovar for some tea. The Russian tea was served in clear glass cups held in silver-plated holders that had a handle. They were lovely cups. Ludmilla, in the manner of Russians everywhere, loaded her *chai* with several lumps of Cuban sugar.

Borscht was available for lunch. This version contained slices of sausages along with hunks of unidentifiable fat that floated in the reddish-purple grease on top. The reddish-purple borscht reminded Burlane of warm vegetable oil colored with Kool-Aid.

The train passed through more sleet, more snow, and into the sun again.

Late that afternoon, Burlane saw the Urals up ahead. There were places in the United States where the lowest Rockies rose like this, suddenly, up from the plains.

The Urals were low and rounded, much like the Appalachians, and forested largely by conifers that crowded out the ubiquitous birch of the taiga. The mountains looked to Burlane like the coast range of Oregon and Washington or the Rockies at their lowest. Rounded folds rose to higher ridges, the easternmost edge of Europe, beyond which a pale orange orb rose above the distant ridges.

Ludmilla curled up her legs, sipped her tea, and read an English-language edition of William Faulkner's *As I Lay Dying*.

Burlane nursed his tea and watched the Urals. An hour later the train was in a pass of sorts, high up, on a roadbed carved out of the mountains. Once, Burlane saw a derailed train at the bottom of a canyon. The train, far away and tiny, looked like a discarded toy.

Ludmilla looked up from her book and said, "I would

like to go to the United States sometime. Just to see what it's like.'' She turned a page. "I like John Steinbeck too—*The Grapes of Wrath.*''

"Have you read *Uncle Tom's Cabin?*'' Burlane asked.

"Oh, yes, Jim. That one was required in school. Jim, did you ever read *As I Lay Dying?*''

"A long time ago."

"One of Addie Bundren's sons accidentally bored a hole in her forehead while she was in her coffin. I can't figure out which one of the sons it was. I've read it and reread it. My English is not so good, I think."

Burlane said, "The mountains where the Bundrens lived are very much like the Urals. Do you like to camp?'' Burlane hated camping. Hated the sand and discomfort and bugs.

"Oh, I love to camp, Jim."

"I think I'm getting hungry again,'' Burlane said. In spite of the awful food, Burlane looked forward to mealtime because meals were a break from the monotony of sitting, staring at birch or more birch, sleeping, or standing in the aisle with the other inmates of the railway carriage, carefully ignoring Ginsburg.

When James Burlane and Ludmilla Kormakova entered the diner, Burlane saw they were watched by a black-haired, dapper man. The dapper man sat alone in the crowded car, sipping his tea with contentment while others waited for a seat. He wore brown slacks and a gray sweater. He had large brown eyes. He parted his black hair neatly on one side.

The foreign travelers ate in the second dining car. The travelers in the lead cars were entirely Russian and had the first dining car to themselves. The slightly built Russian man must have eaten in the other diner on the first day. Burlane wondered why he had switched dining cars.

After Burlane and Ludmilla had finished their dinner of mashed potatoes, two small pieces of boiled meat,

and a small salad of pickled vegetables, they sat sipping
Bulgar, a thick brown drink that tasted like yeasty cider,
and that Ludmilla said was made from fermented bread.
Then Ludmilla ordered a bottle of sweet, fortified red
wine from the Georgian Republic.

No sooner had Ludmilla poured herself half a water
glass of wine than she put her hand over the glass and
said, "I'm suddenly not feeling well, Jim. Do you think
you could finish this for me: You can join me in a few
minutes."

Burlane said, "You should never leave a writer alone
with a bottle of good wine." The wine was awful.

When Ludmilla was gone, the black-haired man rose
and walked to Burlane's table. He said, "My name is
Felix Jin. Do you suppose I could join you for a few
minutes? I see that you are a foreigner, and among other
things I collect foreign coins."

I'll bet, Burlane thought. He said, "My name is Jim
Quint. I'm an American." Burlane shook Jin's hand,
then started digging in his pockets for coins.

"I am a railway official, which is why I speak
English."

"A railway official?" Burlane gave Felix Jin a small
handful of change.

"I'm on my way to Nakhodka for a meeting, but I go
to Vladivostok first. And you?"

"I'm a journalist. The poet Isaak Ginsburg is in the
end car there, the same as me. I'm going to write an
article about him."

"I see. Very interesting. Isaak Ginsburg is very well
known in the Soviet Union. Is he well known in
America?"

"There've been some articles about him in the magazines. Americans want to know all about him."

"He is very good."

"I also write adventure novels, spy books. I have this
character named Humper Staab. If he's not humping a
lady, he's stabbing a bad guy. Americans like that kind

of stuff. Sex and violence." Burlane gave Felix Jin a goofy grin. "But this is strictly *New Democrat* work. I have to take a break from the fiction once in a while or it gets to me."

"And you are from where in America?"

"Bison, Montana. Mmmmmm. This is wonderful wine you folks have."

"Ahh, Montana. That's in the west, isn't it? Cowboys. The pretty lady with you is Russian, is she not?"

"She's my guide. She's with Intourist. A real professional, very helpful," Burlane said.

Suddenly Bob Steele was standing at Burlane's side. "Well, Jim Quint!"

Burlane put his foot on Steele's toe and pushed hard. "Bob, good to see you again."

Steele removed his foot. "You should come up and chat, Jim. We've got ourselves a couple of cribbage boards."

"Hey, thanks for asking. If I get bored later on, I just might do that." Burlane was affable. He hoped he'd broken Steele's fucking toe.

Bob Steele said good-bye and left the diner, trying not to limp.

After he had gone, Felix Jin said, "Mr. Steele and his friends are having a good time." He stood. "It was very pleasant meeting you, Mr. Quint. By the way, do you play chess?"

"I used to play a little years ago. I'm not any good."

"No matter. You'll find that your conductress will have a chess set for you to use. Chess is the national game of the Soviet Union. Perhaps we can play tomorrow. It will give us something to do." Jin left, heading toward the front of the train.

Ludmilla Kormakova had set Burlane up for a conversation with the charming Comrade Felix Jin. Comrade Jin was KGB. Burlane decided just for the fun of it to let the good comrade wait one more night before he let himself be taped *in flagrante delicto* with Ludmilla.

Fifteen

JAMES BURLANE'S WRETCHED LITTLE BLADDER STARTED complaining an hour after his hormones finally let him fall asleep. He awoke to a high-decibel din of booming and clacking, thundering and banging. Burlane wondered why it was he had had the misfortune to have been born with a little bladder and a big nose. People like Neely and Schott got to sleep all night and shave beneath okay noses in the morning.

How could anybody sleep in this din? Burlane sighed and let his eyes adjust to the darkness. Ludmilla had wrapped the blanket around her, cocoonlike, to keep warm. She was sound asleep, her blanketed form jerking and pitching to the lurching of the train. Burlane put his clothes on and, keeping his eye on Ludmilla, felt along the top of the sliding door of the compartment. Nothing.

Burlane felt along the bottom runner. Oops! There it was, a small switch screwed onto the center of the track. This told the next compartment when somebody opened or closed the door. The KGB had put them near the end of the train so it would be easier to monitor their movements. Burlane assumed one of the compartments would

230

be loaded with cameras to record Ludmilla's seduction of himself. That would no doubt be Compartment Two, between himself and Ginsburg and Natalia Kropotkina.

Burlane slipped his shoes off and got back into bed. His bladder would have to wait. There were some questions he had to consider:

Had Ludmilla been instructed to seduce a writer for the *New Democrat*, or was she stalking James Burlane, agent of the Central Intelligence Agency? The first was probably routine—get pictures for the possibility of blackmail in the future—but the second was malignant. If his cover had somehow been blown, did the KGB know about Isaak Ginsburg? Did the Soviets know Ginsburg had Lenin's head on this railroad car?

Burlane was sure Jin was the chief KGB officer on board. It was very possible that the KGB routinely followed the USSR's famous Jewish poet and were merely uncertain about Burlane—and curious. They would naturally expect spies to slip into Vladivostok for the signing; the city was ordinarily off limits to foreigners. Although the Company had publicly disavowed the use of journalists as cover, the KGB didn't believe that for a moment. Burlane probably wasn't the only journalist the KGB chose to offer a swallow that week.

Burlane slipped his silenced .22 pistol into his pocket—this lethal little weapon designed to Burlane's specifications by a Langley gunsmith. He rose quietly, put his shoes back on, slid the door open, and stepped into the aisle.

Burlane closed the door carefully and grabbed the handrail while he adjusted to the rhythm of the train. This was a hard, quick beat—one-two-three-four, one-two-three-four—like a rhythm set by gorillas pounding metal drums with sledgehammers. It was occasioned by wheels striking rail joints that were slightly askew from the spring thaw and by the hard pounding of traffic. Above the insistent beat was a rhythm brought about by the yanking and jerking of the metal couplers between the

cars. This was a rattling THUMP *boom-boom-boom,*
THUMP boom-boom-boom.

Burlane made his way to the conductress's end of the
car. He stopped beside the huge samovar, which radiated heat in the darkness, and considered the passing
taiga. He stepped into the john and was almost overcome by the odor of piss before he could find the light
switch. The floor was slimy with urine. The lid was up
on the toilet itself and Burlane relieved himself.

Burlane hit the center of the toilet okay. He wondered
why Russian men apparently let fly at random, not
giving a damn about the poor bastard who came next.
Maybe it was because Russian underwear didn't have
flies, so Russian men had to pull down the waistband or
aim it out the leg. Burlane stepped on the toilet's flush
lever and saw that the waste emptied directly onto the
tracks below.

Burlane stepped into the aisle again and said "Jesus
Christ!" out loud. He sucked in a welcome lungful of
fresh air. He supposed the smelly mess was the result of
too damned much vodka. If the soldiers with their fingers on the rocket buttons couldn't shoot any straighter
than Russian men could piss, the USSR was in deep,
deep trouble.

Colonel Felix Jin turned on the little color television
set to review the tapes of Ginsburg and Natalia's evening performance. It was one of the perks of his rank to
personally review sex tapes. These tapes gave the KGB
blackmail material. The library at Moscow Center had
tens of thousands of them.

Natalia Kropotkina was an especially attractive woman,
so Jin looked forward to the tape. He turned it on and
there was Natalia, modeling a G-string of translucent
white nylon for Ginsburg. Jin inadvertently sucked in
his breath when he saw her black pubic hair through the
nylon.

Ginsburg was on the berth on the camera side of the

compartment, and so out of sight of the camera. The effective result was a private performance for Jin as well as the poet; in seconds Jin had an erection. Natalia removed the wispy underpants. Jin made a small, inadvertent sound.

Natalia put on a pair of red bikini panties that had little strings on the hips. Felix Jin got out a bottle of vodka and poured himself a tall drink. He wondered where she got those things. In New York probably; he remembered that her diplomat husband had had a United Nations posting.

Natalia turned her back to Ginsburg and shifted her weight from one hip to the other, then untied a string.

Jin swallowed. The bikini fell. Jin poured himself another hit.

The next panties were black.

A receiver on the floor went *beep! beep! beep!* Jin slammed his hand on a small bar on top. The beeping stopped. "Yes?" Jin shouted angrily. He punched the hold button on the video.

"Quint has stepped into the hall, Comrade Jin. He is standing in the aisle by the samovar."

"The alarm functioned properly, I take it?" Jin found it hard to take his eyes off Natalia, frozen on the screen in her black panties. He reversed the tape as he talked to his subordinate.

"Yes, sir, it did."

"Beep me if the door to Ginsburg's compartment opens or if you hear any kind of tapping going on. Turn your instruments up." Jin had some more vodka. He punched the control on the recorder again, and Natalia Kropotkina began her strip all over again.

"Comrade Jin, the door to the lead toilet has opened."

"Call me when he's finished and back in bed, comrade." Jin went back to Natalia Kropotkina. Then he thought better of it, and turned the machine off. He began pacing in his compartment. He smoked another cigarette, wondering why other men always wound up with the Natalias of the world.

Five minutes later the beeping started again. He was still tense. "Yes, comrade?"

"He's back in bed, Comrade Jin. One strange thing happened. After he stepped out of the toilet he said, 'Jesus Christ.' "

" 'Jesus Christ'?"

"Yes, comrade."

"That's all?"

"Yes, comrade. 'Jesus Christ.' "

"Thank you, comrade. Your instructions remain the same. If anyone moves in that car, I'm to be notified immediately."

"Yes, Comrade Jin."

Felix Jin lay back down and adjusted his blankets to preserve the warmth. He listened for a while to the rattling and banging of the train. This was curious indeed. Jim Quint had said "Jesus Christ." Was that a Christian prayer of some kind? Was that all there was to it? Why would anybody pray after taking a leak? Pray for what? More than that, was it possible that the author of the Humper Staab books, a reported chaser of women, could be a Christian?

Americans were notorious hypocrites, Jin knew. The Protestants had ignored the rise of slavery in the United States and were currently the most diehard defenders of Pentagon budget requests. Jin was convinced any kind of aberrant behavior was possible from believers in deities; the Poles were a case in point. But what did Christians say in their prayers? Jin didn't know and couldn't remember from his courses on American social customs.

Jin had just reviewed the quickie KGB report on Jim Quint. The report hadn't mentioned Quint being a Christian, and it was difficult to believe he was one. Was Montana Christian country? No, Christian country was in the American South and the state of Utah. Would a

Christian write thrillers? Yes, if it made money. Jin had read stories about Christian ministers who made fortunes with their radio and television programs.

Jim Quint should be taught a lesson or two. Jin would pass word on to Ludmilla to turn on the charm. He wanted her to lure the good Christian into a performance that would really make him pray, although he doubted if Quint and Ludmilla could top Natalia's stunning fashion show.

Jin decided he ought to visit Ginsburg and Natalia the next day. He and Ginsburg knew one another, after all. He was curious about Natalia. It wasn't just that he admired her sexy underpants. He wanted to know why she chose to lug a heavy bronze bust across the Soviet Union. The truth was, all Lenin busts looked the same after a while and everybody knew it.

He should also get to know Jim Quint better, too.

Felix Jin decided he should review the Natalia Kropotkina tape one more time.

Sixteen

ON THE THIRD DAY OUT OF MOSCOW AND WITH THE TAIGA of Omsk somewhere behind them (the encyclopedic Ludmilla Kormakova was not sure if Omsk was east of Eden), James Burlane decided it was time to interview Isaak Ginsburg. Burlane assumed the interview would be recorded by the KGB—or even visited by the dapper little Russian who wanted to play chess.

Late that day—well east of Novosibirsk and with the sun setting behind the train—Burlane stepped into the aisle and rapped on Ginsburg's cabin.

Isaak Ginsburg opened the sliding door. "Yes?" he asked.

"Mr. Ginsburg, I wonder if I might ask for a few minutes of your time this evening. My readers will be curious about a lot of things."

"I see." Ginsburg glanced at Natalia.

"They'll want to know about your camp experience and your poetry." Burlane unfolded his notebook.

"Certainly," Ginsburg said. He seemed uncertain what to do next.

"We could do it in my compartment if you like."

Ginsburg said, "No, no. We can talk here. Won't you come in, Mr. Quint?"

It didn't take Robby Burns to tell James Burlane that the best-laid plans of mice and men aft gang agley. Burlane had no sooner stepped into the compartment than he heard Bob Steele yelling cheerfully after him, "Jim, old man! Quint!"

Burlane turned and leaned into the aisle. "Yes, Bob?"

"Say, if you're going to interview Comrade Ginsburg, I wonder if I might listen in? You can have all the directs. I'm doing Grigori the Terrible versus Noble Kaplan, but I can use a little color."

Burlane wondered how it would feel to grab Bob Steele by the throat and shake him a little.

Steele continued blithely on, "The *Telegraph* likes poets, proper stuff. Be a chap, Jim."

"If it would be okay with Mr. Ginsburg . . . ?"

Isaak Ginsburg said, "No reason why not."

Steele shook Ginsburg's hand. "Bob Steele of *The Daily Telegraph*. Rhyming's quite popular in London. 'There once was a man from Khartoum. He took a dyke up to his room. They spent the whole night, arguing who had the right . . .'" He grinned mischievously. He wasn't going to finish the limerick.

Burlane thought, *You son of a bitch*. He said, "Sit down, Bob."

Steele stared at Natalia, who wore a dress she had bought in New York. This dress—it was light gray—hung properly, which is to say clung lazily and sensuously, to the curves of Natalia's figure.

Steele stood transfixed, staring, his hand resting on his round belly.

Burlane grabbed him by the shoulder, squeezing as he did, and pulled him to the berth offered by Ginsburg. Steele licked his lips and fumbled for his notebook.

Burlane ignored Steele's attraction to Natalia. He said, "Mr. Ginsburg, my readers will be wanting to know about your experience in a labor camp—how you got there, how it changed you, and so on.''

Ginsburg said, "It was an education, Mr. Quint.'' He started to speak again but stopped to acknowledge the entrance of Colonel Felix Jin, who looked neat and dapper in a business suit.

Jin said, "I see you're having an interview, Mr. Quint.''

"It's kind of cramped, but you're welcome as far as I'm concerned. This is Felix Jin, Mr. Ginsburg. He's a railway official.'' Burlane thought, *Why not? Might as well invite the whole train into the compartment.*

Isaak Ginsburg said, "Comrade Jin and I have met before.''

Burlane thought, *I'll bet you have, Isaak.*

"I can stand,'' Jin said.

"I was telling Mr. Quint that my experience at the labor camp at Zima was an education for me, an awakening. I was an egoist when I went in. I wrote poetry for the wrong reasons. A man has no true peace unless he puts the group before himself. The group matters, not individuals.''

"The group?'' Jin asked.

"The larger whole, comrade.''

Burlane nudged Steele, who was beginning to embarrass him in his admiration for Natalia Kropotkina.

Jin said, "What do you think, Mr. Steele?''

Steele looked distracted. He struggled to remember the conversation. "Soup? Large bowl. Perhaps later.''

Oh, shit! Burlane thought. He said, "Pay attention, Bob, or you won't get any color.''

Both Jin and Natalia grinned. Isaak Ginsburg pretended Steele had said nothing unusual. Burlane thought he'd better let the interview peter out. He said, "I understand you're designing a pin to commemorate the signing, Mrs. Kropotkina.''

"Why, yes, I am,'' Natalia said.

Steele was moved to animation by the turn of the

conversation. He found Natalia Kropotkina more interesting than a bleeding rhymer. Sod the Russians. "Yes, I'd like to know about that," he said.

Natalia put her hand on the bust of Lenin on the table in front of the window. "I'll very likely feature this bust, a copy of the one our Comrade Zhukov will give your Secretary of State Kaplan. This is by Ivan Dmitrov, who is doing a monumental Lenin in Moscow. Lovely, is it not, Comrade Jin?"

"Dmitrov is a skilled sculptor," Jin said.

"Very skilled," Natalia said. "There are vastly different problems dealing with a bust this size, and the head of a monument."

"Or with one of your commemorative pins," Burlane said.

Natalia laughed. "Thank you, Mr. Quint. But it takes a great deal of courage to tackle a monument. A monument is dramatic and the stakes are high."

Jin said, "And the details, Mrs. Kropotkina? I was wondering where the details matter the most, in the small or the large—the commemorative pin or the monumental statue?"

Natalia laughed. "They're most important in a bust this size, life-size. In a monument, you're dealing with broad planes and dramatic light. In a pin, the figures are too small for details." She put her thumb under the *znachok* on the collar of her dress and pushed it out for Jin to see. "The cuts are few and subtle, yet this is clearly Lenin, as you can see." She looked at Burlane with her green eyes.

Burlane said, "It gets so cold back in Montana that a guy with a real full bladder can piss at a moose and bring it down with icicles. Does it get that bad in this country?"

Jin said, "Where was it you said you were from in Montana, Mr. Quint?"

"Bison," Burlane said. "Bison, Montana."

When they were back in the hall, Bob Steele said,

" 'And they spent the whole night, arguing who had the right, to do what, with which, and to whom.' " He giggled, and leered over his shoulder at Ludmilla, who waited for Burlane in their compartment. "Lucky you, Jim. They're giving you the treatment. We get a flatulent male."

"Ludmilla's real laughs."

"You have to remember they're taping everything. Still . . ." Steele looked at Ludmilla again. "If you ever get tired of fucking, you can come on up to our car and drink a little vodka." He sounded wistful. "We stocked up when we left Moscow so we could get loaded every night. When in Rome, do as the Romans and all that. Relieves the boredom." Then he perked up: "Say, that Comrade Kropotkina's something, isn't she? How'd you like to attack that dress? Pull it right on off. Wasn't that something?"

"Lucky Ginsburg," Burlane said. Beyond a doubt, somehow, Bob Steele was going to get in his way and cause a whole lot of grief. There wasn't a whole lot Burlane could do about this. He had learned the footprint rule as a rookie, an axiom of his clandestine calling: the best-laid plans of mice and men are almost always covered with the footprints of well-meaning assholes.

Bob Steele said, "Pecker up, Jim," and wandered up the aisle toward his own car.

Writers were well known for being loons; craziness was their muse. They were drunks and cockhounds. This was expected of them. The author of the Humper Staab novels would hardly be constantly shy or retiring when presented with a swallow like Ludmilla Kormakova. In order to establish his bona fides as Jim Quint, Burlane knew he would have to give a convincing show of eccentricity. A businessman or a family man might be shy or retiring, but not Quint.

It was time to protect Jim's good name.

Burlane wondered if Ludmilla Kormakova would give

him a dissertation on the magnificent length and breadth of Soviet penises. Did Soviet women tilt the Richter scale when they had an orgasm?

Burlane was certain he'd learn all that and more in the night ahead. He stepped inside the compartment.

Seventeen

James Burlane slid the door shut. At the click of the latch, his pants began to bulge; he couldn't help it. Burlane wondered what a swallow thought about at a time like this. The weather? How to keep her pussy in the best light for the cameras? What? Did Ludmilla think only of statistics, even now? One more capitalist male seduced and photographed for future blackmail.

Burlane dropped his hand to his belt buckle.

Before he got to the brass button of his Levi's, Ludmilla Kormakova had her sweater off.

The suspected Christian advanced toward Ludmilla. He lurched as the train entered a curve. His engorged member shivered like a Douglas fir in a stiff wind. The KGB swallow stretched out on the narrow berth for his pleasure, her eyes closed.

Burlane turned his swollen unit in the direction of Ludmilla Kormakova's Slavic face. The unit, excited, twitched in anticipation. Burlane slipped it into the softness of Ludmilla's mouth where it shuddered gratefully at the lovely warmth.

Ludmilla's mouth churned, a wonderful washing machine. She paused and looked up, catching Burlane's eyes straight on. "Do American men like this?" she asked.

"Oh, that's quite charming," Burlane said. He wondered if he could hold off for the kind of show he wanted to give the comrade photographers in the next compartment.

"Just you and me, Jim."

"Just you and me, Ludmilla."

James Burlane thought Ludmilla smelled wonderful. Her body was extra warm. Her hands and mouth moved lightly over his body pausing here and there, teasing.

Burlane wondered if it might not be possible, during the fun, to aim his behind at one of the KGB lenses close up, so that the Russian on the other side might get to see a vision of himself as in a mirror unadorned by anything except the truth. Burlane could give the Russian a little wink with his buns.

Burlane accepted Ludmilla as a challenge. Did he have it in him to keep up with a KGB sparrow, taking into account his biological handicap in the matter of endurance?

Ludmilla seemed willing to subject herself to anything to make the exhibition more outrageous. Burlane found it hard not to smile when the flushed and sweaty Ludmilla produced bonds and suggested that she be spread-eagled on the floor of the train, which had hit a hard stretch of rail and was jerking wildly to and fro, hammering and banging, hammering and banging. Burlane, brandishing a stuporous but functional third erection of the night, complied with apparent gusto, although he was in fact exhausted and wanted to go to sleep.

Ludmilla Kormakova was unwilling to show mercy until Burlane's game but tuckered unit hung like old glory on a rainy morning—limp, unable to stir. Burlane was pleased by his performance. He had provided Jim Quint with a suitably eccentric persona. In fact, he had given the author of the Humper Staab paperbacks a sexual appetite worthy of Harold Robbins or Danielle Steele—Henry Miller even. Quint's fictional Humper Staab would have been hard pressed to keep up.

A few minutes before dawn, exhausted, smelling of Ludmilla, giddy with the memory of her mouth and crotch, James Burlane fell asleep to a *whack, bang! whack, bang!* stretch of tracks.

Eighteen

LATE THE NEXT AFTERNOON, JAMES BURLANE LOOKED UP
to see Felix Jin standing at their door. He had a bottle
of Stolichnaya vodka in one hand and a chess set in the
other. "Would you like to play a game, Mr. Quint? It
helps pass the time."

"Sure," Burlane said. "Won't you come in? You
can play in here."

"Well, thank you," Jin said. He sat on one end of
Burlane's small berth and Burlane sat at the other.
Ludmilla went to make herself a cup of tea, then re-
turned to watch the game from her berth.

Felix Jin drew white and moved first, leading with his
king's pawn.

Burlane blocked him with a pawn.

The nature of the game was established almost immediately. Jin moved quickly to control the center of the
board and thus dominate the game. Then he built up the
strength and power of his pieces. He did this with ease
and efficiency. He was patient. He did not waste moves.
He was technically far the better player and soon had
both position and strength on Burlane.

Jin poured the vodka. He matched Burlane glass for glass. When a glass was empty, Jin refilled it.

"How long have you been a writer, Mr. Quint?"

"Oh, about sixteen years." That was the correct answer. Burlane wondered how specific a file on Jim Quint the Soviets had been able to gather.

"I see." Jin moved a knight. "Did you learn your skills in college, or do writers and journalists serve some sort of apprenticeship in the United States?"

Burlane considered the board. "I was a history major at the University of Montana." Quint had been. Burlane moved. He was impressed by the brutal efficiency of Jin's game. Burlane moved the best he could, striking here, retreating there. He had the saving ability to be able to anticipate Jin's build-up. When Jin took a piece, Burlane was able to retaliate. Burlane did not yield without striking in return.

Felix Jin was calm. He believed Russians could do anything if they put their minds to it and amassed their resources. They had done this in space, athletics, the ballet, the military, the intelligence business. In the first three of these efforts they had, respectively, demonstrated their superior minds, bodies, and culture. In the Red Army and KGB they had demonstrated their power and determination.

James Burlane seemed unperturbable. He didn't make mistakes, even as Jin's development slowly enveloped his king. He moved a rook onto a square that commanded both a critical rank and a critical file and refused to move it. Jin offered him a couple of cripples. Burlane refused to budge.

Jin threatened the rook.

Burlane shifted it slightly but retained its advantage.

Jin decided to go around the rook. Jin had superior power; it could be done. Jin circled the rook and bore down on Burlane's king.

Burlane defended his king, but his position was weakened with each move.

Jin was one move away from mate . . .

. . . when James Burlane casually pushed his rook the length of the board and grinned at Ludmilla.

Jin looked stunned. "Why, that's mate!" All of Jin's careful development of power and position had been in vain. His jaw fell. He'd been beaten. How could that have happened?

Isaak Ginsburg was restless. He lay on his bunk wide awake, unable to sleep. He turned onto his right side, then his left, then onto his back, even onto his stomach, which he ordinarily never did. He wanted to see Zima. What if he should miss Zima? What if he should let it go by? Ginsburg could not sleep. He spent the night counting off the stops.

There were small reading lights mounted above the berths, but they were on the window side. By putting his pillow at the other end, Ginsburg could see the leafless tops of the birch at least. After a while he gave up trying to rest and propped his head up. The green fabric roll-up shade on the window of his compartment was stuck in the up position, so he could watch all night long if he wished.

Natalia slept on the other berth, the moonlight shining off her black hair.

Ginsburg could see the front of the train up ahead in the moonlight that lit the Soviet Union from Severnya Zemlya in the north to the Gobi Desert in the south. It was a Russian moon; the hollow eyes and wide face were clearly Slavic, Ginsburg saw. The night was ablaze with stars and there was a circle around the moon. Beside the train, white-barked birches were ghostlike going by, going by, going by.

Boom whacka boom whacka boom! Boom whacka boom whacka boom! Ginsburg lurched against the wall of the compartment as the train hit a rough stretch of track.

The run from Kansk to Tayshet was an eternity of

scattered, stunted trees. There was more of the same, if that were possible, from Tayshet to Nizhneudinsk. They reentered the taiga at Tulan on the Iya River. Ginsburg looked at his watch. It was four in the morning; Ginsburg had been staring at the moonlit landscape for six hours. In a half hour there would be a stop at Kuytun, then two hours later, Zima, on the Oka River.

Ginsburg stood up. He would watch the taiga from the aisle and get some exercise; the station and the lumber camp were both on the aisle side of the train. The big diesels up front were pulling twenty passenger cars and nobody had bothered to line up the cars so the aisles were on the same side. The aisle was on the south side of one car, the north side of the next.

He slipped into his shoes and stepped into the aisle.

Where Felix Jin waited, smoking a cigarette. ''Pleasant night, Comrade Ginsburg.'' Jin looked at his watch. ''Or should I have said morning?''

''I shouldn't have drunk all that vodka with Natalia Serafimovna. Makes me pee all night.'' The train hit a rough spot as Ginsburg headed for the toilet, and he had to brace his hand against the window. He killed some time in the toilet, cursing Felix Jin.

When Ginsburg got back, Jin took a drag on his cigarette and said, ''I knew you'd want to see when we went past.''

''Zima?''

''What else, a man spends two years in a place like that. He has something happen to him like happened to you. He wants to see what it looks like.''

''I want to see, yes,'' Ginsburg admitted. There seemed no point in lying. ''I used to lie awake at night listening to the trains pass.''

''You want to see what the camp looks like from the train. I would, too.''

The engine was momentarily visible in the moonlight, then disappeared around a curve, pulling the necklace of red cars deeper into the maw of the taiga.

Jin said, "Looks like a mechanical dragon, doesn't it, with the yellow stripe and all."

A red denizen of Russia, Ginsburg thought, forged by the hammer, carrying tractors to fields where peasants still harvested by sickle. That and soldiers to watch the restless Chinese. He said, "Roaring dragon."

Felix Jin unfolded the small seat under the window and sat, his shoulder against the glass. He looked up ahead, at the front of the train. "So many birch, Ginsburg. Hour after hour after hour we travel. The birch never seem to stop. Have you ever wondered how many there are? As many birch as Russians who died in the Great Patriotic War, do you suppose?"

"The birch are survivors," Ginsburg said.

"As were the residents of Leningrad. We have a hard life in the Soviet Union, Ginsburg. We know the cold. Napoleon did his best to conquer us. The Germans tried twice. We stood fast each time. We know hardship. We work together."

The train entered another wide curve. The track did not run flat out, straight and true, as do the Union Pacific and Burlington Northern on their way across the prairies and farmlands of North America. The Trans-Siberian meandered through the taiga en route to isolated towns on the banks of cold, slow rivers.

Jin said, "I grew up in Irkutsk, you know. But of course you would have no way of knowing that. My paternal great-grandfather was Mongolian, which is how I came by my surname."

"You told me."

"Being a Jin can be a burden, as you can imagine." As they were approaching the stop at Kuytun, Jin said, "After that business in Red Square, the KGB checked the hotel records in Perm. They wondered who might have been visiting the cancer clinic, you know. I see you spent a night there on your way to Moscow from Novosibirsk."

"I was working on an epic poem about the spirit of

transformation. There is a dramatic valley of isbas to the east of Perm overlooked by a ridge of progressive communal apartments.''

"I read the poem in *Novy Mir*. Very clever. By the way, Ivan Shepelev, the man who rode with you from Moscow, remembered you clearly. He said you were carrying a bag that was so heavy the straps dug into your shoulders. What was in that bag, Comrade Ginsburg?''

"Some Ukrainian wine for literary colleagues in Perm, comrade.''

The train slowed for the five-minute stop at Kuytun. The platform was nearly empty. Some men whose breath came in frosty puffs unloaded some boxes from one of the cars down the line. A woman gave instructions over a loudspeaker. Ginsburg wondered if Olga would be working the night shift at Zima.

Ginsburg remembered talking to Lado Kabakhidze in their cell at Zima. Neither Ginsburg nor Kabakhidze had any responsibility while they were imprisoned in the camp. They did as they were told. Their only goal was to survive. They worked as little as they could get away with. They chiseled, hoarded, swapped, or stole what they could. Some of them snitched on their friends to please the guards.

Life was hard. The *zeks* made do.

The train left Kuytun.

The system at the Zima lumber camp was so designed as to encourage and reward the worst behavior both by prisoners and their guards, thus insuring Captain Mikheyev's authority and power. Ginsburg wanted to tell Felix Jin that in those essentials, Zima was the Soviet Union in miniature, a prison inside a prison. Ginsburg wanted to tell Jin that all he was trying to do was give the Russian people the Lenin they had been promised and denied. They had been promised their humanity. They had received Jins and Mikheyevs.

If Lado Kabakhidze were still alive, Ginsburg knew,

he would be proud of his daughter, Nina. Nina was fighting back.

Outside, the Siberian landscape rushed by.

Felix Jin said, "I was wondering why Mrs. Kropotkina is lugging that heavy Lenin bust across the Soviet Union."

Ginsburg looked surprised. "She's to do a Vladivostok commemorative pin. That's the copy of Ivan Dmitrov's bust."

"Does she really need that? For a little pin?" Jin was not convinced.

"She is proud of doing good work. When she does a *znachok*, she wants to do it exactly right," Ginsburg said.

"I see."

In time the Trans-Siberian Express was upon Zima and pulled into the dimly lit station. A lone man bundled in a heavy coat stood on the platform. Felix Jin smoked and said nothing. The dispatcher's office summoned carman Rosnoveyev to the brakeman's shack. A woman's amplified voice echoed among the buildings.

Olga. Nothing had changed.

If his plan worked, if Ginsburg got Lenin's head out of the Soviet Union and somehow escaped himself, he would find a way to smuggle a pretty Western dress to Olga. He didn't want to meet Olga especially, didn't care to know what she looked like. He liked her the way she was, an abstraction and so without flaws, a reminder of the Russian warmth and compassion that endured in spite of all the hard times and suffering.

The train began moving, began rolling. The whacking and banging gained momentum. The station gave way to the sprawl of peasants' isbas. The camp was at the edge of the wretched shacks; the cutting whorl of the barbed wire looped atop the outer wooden fence was clearly visible in the Siberian moonlight.

Jin lit another cigarette. "There it is, Comrade Ginsburg."

"Yes, there it is." Zima. Ginsburg thought:

The Möbius strip of barbed wire
Had two sides that were one,
Had no beginning, no end.
Circled all of Russia.
Truth cut.
Truth went
Snip-snip,
Snip-snip,
Snip-snip,
At the bloody snarl
That seemed to have no end.

Nineteen

A BLONDE WITHOUT A HINT OF SMILE LINES WAS TO TAKE them from the Irkutsk Intourist Hotel to the May Day demonstrations in Lenin Square. James Burlane had joined Bob Steele and the other journalists, and they were chatting among themselves when the blonde, who had been eavesdropping, said, "A parade? Who told you that?" Then, with tourists looking on in amusement, if not amazement, the journalists were singled out for special attention:

"You are to understand that this is not a parade," she said. "These are spontaneous public demonstrations. The citizens of Irkutsk themselves do this to show their support for workers of the world. Is that understood? Is that clear? We have a parade in November to celebrate the Revolution."

"I see," Steele said on behalf of the contingent of journalists.

"There will be no tanks or rockets today. Come back in November for that."

Steele, amused, dutifully noted: "Demonstrations, not a parade." He had been given to understand that the May Day celebrants would follow one another through the streets of Irkutsk, which was his definition of a parade.

The guide turned and pushed her way through the heavy glass doors of the hotel, and began walking north— downstream as the Angara flowed—followed by the journalists, then the tourists. The Englishman from the London *Times* gave Bob Steele a nudge with his elbow. "Stout show, Bob!"

Burlane noted that Felix Jin had chosen not to attend the demonstrations.

They walked along the sidewalk; the Angara was on their left. It was a swift, broad river. The roofs of the deteriorating shacks and decaying warehouses and leaf- less trees etched the skyline on the ridge beyond the river. The journalists and tourists walked into a steady, cold wind.

There seemed to be militiamen and soldiers and road- blocks everywhere, but the contingent from the Irkutsk Intourist Hotel was allowed by without a fuss.

The tourists were taken to a roped-off area on the sidewalk at one end of the large Lenin Square. The Intourist guide took the journalists, Isaak Ginsburg, and Natalia Kropotkina to the bleachers where local and regional officials were gathered.

The journalists waited in the bleachers. There was a Russian Orthodox church to their left, and an impressive fountain straight ahead. When they sat, Bob Steele man- aged to plant himself beside Burlane.

"So how's your story coming, Jim?"

"Ginsburg's a wonderful poet, he really is. You have to give it to him." Burlane's face told Steele nothing.

Steele winked at Burlane. "Remember the time I took you down to Soho and we got pissed on scotch and watched chaps with earrings and green hair?"

Burlane wished Steele wasn't quite so eager to partic- ipate in his Jim Quint cover. Unfortunately, Steele was both human and a newspaperman. Burlane knew he wasn't about to drop his curiosity. Burlane could hardly blame him; in Steele's shoes, Burlane would want to know also. Burlane said, "You drank scotch, Bob. I smoked a joint."

When the group of visitors and foreign journalists left the hotel—Ginsburg, Natalia Kropotkina, and Jim Quint among them—Felix Jin knew it was time. He checked his wristwatch. He would have at least an hour, even if they decided to return early from the demonstrations. That was unlikely, Jin knew. Ginsburg would be reading a commemorative poem from the people's dais and so would have to sit with the officials until the very end. The same was true of Quint, who would be obliged to stay with the press corps.

Colonel Jin dialed a number on the room phone and said, "Now, please." He hung up and took an elevator to the fifth floor, where four men waited with heavy leather briefcases. Jin and two of the men went into Isaak and Natalia's room. The other two went to Jim Quint's room.

Jin settled into a chair and smoked a cigarette while the two men began the search of Isaak and Natalia's room. He said, "If they're smuggling something and you don't find it, we'll send you to mine gold at Kolmya."

The two KGB technical men set to work with Jin's admonition ringing in their ears.

Jin smoked and watched the search, wondering again if Natalia Kropotkina really needed to drag that heavy bronze bust all the way to Vladivostok and back. He snubbed out one cigarette and lit another as a tech man examined colored pencils under a microscope that he had unpacked from his briefcase. Another man, using a slender wire, checked the interior of tubes of watercolor. They checked the soles of shoes. They checked the seams of clothing with an electromagnet plugged into the wall.

The technician who found Natalia Kropotkina's collection of sexy underwear held up a pair of transparent red panties. He grinned. "Artistic decadence!"

Jin and the other technician laughed.

Colonel Jin called for tea and lit a third cigarette. Jin began to sweat. He stood and paced. He sat when the tea arrived. "We'll save this for last," he said. He put the heavy Ivan Dmitrov sculpture in his lap. The larger-than-life size of the bust increased its impressiveness correspondingly. Jin looked at his wristwatch. "Better hurry, comrades," he said.

Jin decided that when he left, he'd send the technicians on ahead and pocket Natalia's sexy underwear for the computer specialist in seclusion. Vera would appreciate panties like that. Natalia Kropotkina was married to a foreign service officer; she could always get more.

Finally Jin could stand the suspense no longer. "Would you give me one of your hammers, please? Thank you." The bottom of the bust was fitted into a wooden base. Jin turned the bust upside down and held it with his arm. He began tapping at the wood. The base popped off.

Nothing!

Jin slumped in his chair. He'd allowed himself to become convinced the heavy bust was the answer to the mystery. Jin picked up the telephone and dialed a number. He said, "I will remind you again that I want the transcript of the Quint-Steele conversation as soon as it's ready. I want to know everything they said."

Twenty

THE LOCAL PARTY CHIEF, IVAN ZLOKAZOV, ARRIVED AT last, and officials began a series of speeches. They were pleased, they said, that Irkutsk was in the world spotlight that day; they were pleased that so many foreign journalists were there to witness the demonstrations. They were especially pleased to have as their guest Isaak Ginsburg, who would be reading a commemorative poem in Vladivostok. The peace-loving people of Irkurtsk were proud to stand side by side with the working people of the world.

While the spontaneous demonstration was being organized stage left, down a boulevard that led into the square, Zlokazov, a small man in a bulky blue coat loaded with colorful ribbons and medals, began a small dissertation on the wonders of Lake Baikal obviously intended for the visiting journalists.

Zlokazov began by stating that Lake Baikal, the deepest lake in the world, contained one sixth of the world's supply of fresh water, and had more fresh water than any other lake in the world, including all of the American Great Lakes combined. This was the third or fourth time Burlane had heard that statement, or variations of

257

it. Burlane wondered what foreigners were supposed to
make of it. Were the Soviets going to poison everybody's water and demand that thirsty people pledge their
allegiance to Lenin? Were the Soviets now able to halt
the rain? Who gave a damn?

Comrade Zlokazov talked about the special meaning
Lake Baikal had to the people of Irkutsk. There were
1200 species of animals in the lake that were found
nowhere else in the world. Lake Baikal contained the
world's only fresh-water seal. The sturgeon in Lake
Baikal grew to be 500 pounds. Lake Baikal contained
the unique gwyniad, *Coregonus omul,* a white relative
of the salmon. Zlokazov told of the lake's 280 varieties
of shrimplike crustaceans, of strange worms, of the
millions of flightless, waterborne insects called *rucheiniki.*
The *rucheiniki* remained in the larval state for two or
three years before they embarked on their two- to three-
hour life span—that is, assuming they weren't eaten by
an *omul* their first minute out. He told about *bikerit,* a
kind of inflammable wax that floated on the water.
Zlokazov said there was a fish in the lake so transparent
that one could read *Pravda* through its slender body.
Lake Baikal contained four kinds of emerald-colored
sponges. The finest sables in Siberia roamed its shores.

Bob Steele mumbled, "So what's the bloody point,
comrade?"

The man from the London *Times* said, "The sod's
giving us a biology lecture." He put down his ball-point
pen.

Zlokazov told about pop-eyed fish with eyes like
giant bugs that lived between seven hundred and sixteen
hundred feet below the surface of Lake Baikal where the
temperature was a comforting thirty-eight degrees Fahrenheit. The females gave birth to two thousand live
offspring. When all these fish eventually died, they sank
to the bottom of Lake Baikal, adding to the silt that was
five thousand feet deep in places. Zlakozov paused for
the kicker to the story of the deep-living, pop-eyed fish.

"This silt has allowed socialist scientists to calculate that Lake Baikal was formed twenty-five million years ago in the Tertiary Period, making it the oldest lake in the world."

Comrade Zlokazov finally wound down:

"The workers of Irkutsk have a special mission to preserve this most beautiful and unique lake in the world. We hold that trust dear."

This recitation of facts—humbling both the Galápagos Islands and the Great Lakes—was intended to give the foreign journalists a biggest-and-best Irkutsk peg for their stories. The assembled Russian guests applauded warmly, if not overenthusiastically; the bizarre facts of Lake Baikal were always recited when foreigners were present.

Ginsburg was now escorted to the microphone and introduced as "a modern Russian master."

James Burlane scribbled notes with professional aplomb.

At the speaker's dais, Ginsburg stood before the microphone to address the empty square before him; the residents of Irkutsk were either assembling for the demonstration, or humble spectators gathered along Karl Marx Prospekt a half mile away. Ginsburg's reading was for the comrades and their guests in the bleachers.

Isaak Ginsburg recited a long, passionate poem about Lake Baikal. When Ginsburg had finished, and the applause had abated, the unsmiling Intourist guide handed each writer a copy of the text—translated into English, French, and German—together with explanations of various allusions.

Finally the band began playing stirring music. Nine young people entered the square carrying enormous photographs of local party officials and an even larger photograph of V. I. Lenin.

This was followed by a series of young people in bright costumes of primary colors: yellow, red, green, blue. They held color-coordinated flags, cards, plastic

balls, or hula hoops. Once assembled before the bleachers, they did synchronized routines with the flags, cards,
balls, or hula hoops. They waved their arms and kicked
their legs high and did calisthenics in choreographed
unison.

"I like the spontaneity," Steele said.

Burlane said, "It's the spirit of community."

The young men did enthusiastic push-ups, squat-jumps,
and jumping-jacks to music played over the loudspeaker.
They ran in place, kicking their legs high, moving as
one. A man on the loudspeaker told about their schools,
how old they were, and how pleased they were to
demonstrate their solidarity with the working people of
the world.

Comrade Zlokazov and those assembled in the bleachers applauded politely.

When each group finished its routine it continued
around the square and left, heading for Karl Marx Avenue, a half mile away, where the local residents waited
to see some of the color.

After nearly an hour, a mass of Irkutsk citizens brought
up the rear. They were dressed in red, most of them,
and waved enormous red flags and banners that proclaimed peace. The silken flags and banners furled dramatically in the cold wind.

Burlane said, "A nice break from riding the train, eh,
Bob?"

"This is precisely the kind of stuff I was after. I was
impressed by the spontaneity."

"I was impressed by the drama," Burlane said.

After they were released from the demonstrations,
Isaak Ginsburg and Natalia Kropotkina joined the citizens of Irkutsk on the parklike promenade beside the
Angara River. The cold wind that had cut through Irkutsk
earlier had subsided; the sun was warming, and the local
residents, having the day off, were out for a stroll. The

promenade was nicely landscaped, but the trees had not yet begun to leaf out.

Ginsburg and Natalia passed three couples out together, drunk; the men carried the vodka in paper bags. Two of the young women were drunker than the rest. The couples talked loudly, the young women giggling nonstop. They staggered, laughing, tripping, bumping into one another. One of the young men, Ginsburg thought, looked ill and lagged behind momentarily, apparently to calm alcohol-induced nausea.

Ginsburg and Natalia, accompanied by the screeching of sea gulls that floated over the river, walked down one of the concrete stairways that led to the rocky shore. These stairs were spaced about every hundred yards along the promenade. To their left, upstream of the Intourist Hotel, a mob of people waited in line for an open-topped boat that took short tours on the river.

Below them, halfway to the tour boat landing, a small boy squatted by the side of the river. He was imitating the screech of sea gulls. Ginsburg and Natalia sat at the base of the stairs, not wanting to disturb him. He was no more than ten or twelve years old and cupped his hands around his mouth as he made the call.

A white gull, aloft above the water, gave a poignant cry in return.

The boy called. The Angara rushed swiftly by, deep and frigid.

The gull answered, the water far below it.

"Maybe he'll be a naturalist," Natalia said of the boy.

"Maybe he'll have a gull act in the circus," Ginsburg said. No Soviet circus was complete without a dove act. These were always performed by pretty girls, who pulled white doves out of hats, bags, boxes, whatever, and threw them into the air. These doves, joined by more birds pitched into the air from the wings, nearly always settled on the pretty girls' shoulders and extended arms while sweet music played and the accompanying narration over the loudspeaker talked about peace and the peace-loving Soviet Union.

Natalia looked up at the retaining wall at the edge of the promenade. The man they had noticed earlier was sitting on the wall looking down on them.

Ginsburg and Natalia returned to the promenade and continued downstream, followed by the man who had watched them from above. They were about to take another flight of stairs to the shore, when another drunk stumbled up onto the sidewalk from the river. He lurched this way and that. His face was a horror. He had pitched forward onto the shore and the right side of his face was bloody, a shredded mass of raw flesh. The blood was mixed with dirt and gravel. His right eye was closed. He had not been mugged or beaten. He had simply tripped. He grinned crookedly, using only the good side of his mouth.

A group of five May Day celebrants, themselves inebriated, parted to avoid the lurching drunk. Other than stepping lightly aside, they seemed not to have noticed him. It was as though he were invisible and the blood and raw flesh didn't exist. Only one young man looked back. He took a bottle of vodka from his jacket and took a long, hard drink.

Twenty-One

THE TEMPERATURE PLUNGED QUICKLY AFTER DARK, AND by the time they were taken to the Irkutsk station at nine o'clock, it was downright cold. As before, Burlane and Ludmilla, and Ginsburg and Natalia were placed in the end car. Like the train they had ridden from Moscow, this version of the Trans-Siberian Express was also called the Rossiya. When Burlane and his guide entered their compartment, Burlane saw the familiar camera hole in the wall. It was the same car.

After he and Ludmilla had settled into their compartment, Burlane checked his map and saw that Irkutsk was located 50 miles northwest of the southern tip of Lake Baikal—the Angara being a north-flowing Siberian river. The lake itself—from 25 to 50 miles wide and 350 miles long—ran from southwest to northeast. Burlane wanted to watch the passing of Lake Baikal, but it was more than an hour before the train reached the southern tip of the lake.

When the train turned east and the pine forests of the Khamar Daban Ridge rose steeply outside the compartment, Burlane knew they had reached the shore of Lake Baikal.

"Are you going to look at the lake, Jim?" Ludmilla asked.

"I think so. Give me a chance to stretch my legs." Burlane stepped into the aisle and there, below him, was the frozen surface of Lake Baikal, a great calm under the moonlight. Burlane stood, turning his map toward the light, while Ludmilla sat on one of the fold-down seats.

The train went in and out of a tunnel, one of a series of tunnels through the steep ridges that bordered the lake. These tunnels were guarded at both ends by barbed wire and soldiers with machine guns—standard security, Burlane knew, for Soviet tunnels.

"Lake Baikal is the deepest lake in the world," Ludmilla said as they looked at the expanse of ice in the moonlight.

Burlane wondered if he was condemned to a repetition of the impressive facts of Lake Baikal. He was.

Ludmilla said, "This lake holds one fifth of the world's supply of fresh water. That has been established. It is the oldest lake in the world."

"The speaker at the demonstration today told us it was one sixth."

"Yes, Jim, one sixth. He was right."

"He told us all about the wonderful biology of the lake," Burlane said.

"The white-fleshed *omul* lives here. It is a relative of the salmon. One of the most delicious fish in the world. Lake Baikal has four kinds of emerald-colored sponges and the world's only fresh-water seal," she said.

Ludmilla's recitation of Soviet onlys and bests was pushing Burlane to the edge. "Do you understand the English word lobotomy?" he asked.

Ludmilla considered the question. "No, I don't believe I do, Jim. English vocabulary is very hard to learn. Is it a kind of drink?"

"Makes you sleepy, they say," Burlane said.

"In Khabarovsk there is a kind of vodka that has ginseng in it. It—what is the American expression?—

yes, it will put lead in your pencil, Jim.'' Ludmilla brushed her breast lightly against Burlane's arm, then again. The second time she let it linger.

This casual gesture and others like it, at first provocative in the extreme, had become annoying as the birch trees and hours and firsts and biggests passed. Burlane had thought Texas bragging was a bore. Texans were modest, retiring, in comparison with the Russians. If Ludmilla would include more claims like the aphrodisiac Khabarovsk vodka, her patter might be tolerable.

For example, Burlane, who had studied the history of the railroad for his assignment, knew that Lake Baikal was the last link finished in the trans-Siberian run. In 1904, with Russian forces under siege by the Japanese at Port Arthur in Manchuria, the czar's engineers laid extra-wide ties across the ice and tried to get an engine across. The resulting hole in the ice was five feet wide and fourteen miles long. Burlane smiled at the idea of the Russians cursing in frustration as their train sank slowly under the ice.

The train left Lake Baikal in the early hours of the morning and entered into a forest of fir, pine, and larch. The passing of the wonderful lake brought with it two bounties: the end of Ludmilla's regurgitation of Baikal facts and the end of the taiga. The day turned out to be the most beautiful stretch of the six-thousand-mile trip.

As they passed Petrovsk-Zabaykal'skiy, Burlane asked the ever ready Ludmilla about the telephone poles sitting atop metal stakes driven into the ground. He assumed it had to do with permafrost, and he was right.

Ludmilla looked serious indeed. ''This is because of permafrost, Jim. When there is permafrost we cannot bury a telephone pole in the ground. In winter, the top of the ground freezes down to the permafrost and increases in volume at the same time. The surface lifts, Jim, ten centimeters, sometimes twenty. A pole would lift with the ground and a what-do-you-call-it would form beneath it.''

"A cavity."

"That's the word, Jim. Cavity. In the summer, when the ground thaws, the pole can't settle because dirt will have filled the cavity. After a few years the pole would pop out of the ground."

"You have problems with roads and railway tracks, I assume."

"Yes, Jim. The bed is soft in the springtime. It gives."

And so it did. The intensity of the whacking, banging, and jerking of the Trans-Siberian increased as it plunged farther into Siberia.

The train reached Chita shortly after noon and followed along the Shilka River, a tributary of the Amur. The river was a dramatic steamy haze, beneath which great blocks of ice crunched and bumped their way downstream—to the northeast—moving more quickly at the center than at the shores. Low hills on the sides of the river were topped by Korean pines turned white from a hoary frost. Everything was white: the sparse grass, fence posts, raised telephone posts. A warming morning sun shone from a pale blue sky. Burlane squinted at the wonderful white of the lovely valley.

Even the hoary frost of the Shilka River got boring. Burlane took naps and tried not to think about the fried eggs. Burlane was sick of eggs, sick of the hot little metal thingies they came in, sick of the yolks looking up at him, sick of the tepid yellow oil. He wondered how the Russians tolerated all that oil. The borscht had come more and more to resemble dishwater. How could the Soviets endure eating everything canned or pickled? Burlane thought of the vegetable section of an American supermarket. He longed for fresh fruit and vegetables. He thought of pears. Burlane loved pears.

Late in the afternoon, the train slowed for a bend and came suddenly upon yet another desolate town that did not qualify for mention on all maps, much less rate a stop on the run from Moscow to Vladivostok. The rough-cut, unpainted isbas each had its fence, its pile of birch firewood, its diminutive garden plot. Thin wisps of smoke trailed up from the metal chimneys.

Then, suddenly, Him, Lenin, on the side of a building. The red background of the portrait shimmered, luminous, bloodlike, a rose of communism against the dreary ochres and umbers of mud and winter swamps and leafless trees and weathered shacks.

Burlane didn't feel like giving the KGB another memorable performance with the perfect socialist woman. As the evening wore on, Burlane wondered what he should do. At last it came to him. "My newspaper friend, Bob Steele, has invited me to drink vodka with him and his journalist friends tonight. I think I'll take them up on it."

"Oh, Jim, I got us some vodka today. We have plenty of vodka right here." Ludmilla lifted her hinged berth and dug a bottle from the luggage stored below. "Stolichnaya vodka is the most famous in the world. The Soviet Union makes the best vodka in the world, also the most millions of liters, did you know that? We have more kinds as well. Some of them are named for animals. We have what you would call grouse vodka. We even have a bison vodka, Jim. We have brown vodka and yellow vodka. There is a proper kind of vodka to drink with each kind of wild mushroom."

Burlane had heard Russians were bonkers about wild mushrooms. He didn't want to trigger a dissertation about fungi in the Soviet Union. He said, "I wouldn't want to disappoint Bob. I told him I'd join them tonight."

Although James Burlane knew his conversations with Ludmilla Kormakova were taped, he was still surprised to find Felix Jin waiting in Bob Steele's compartment along with Steele and a tall, blond man with thick eyeglasses and a bemused look on his long face.

Steele was pleased to see Burlane. "Are you joining us tonight, Jim? Good. Good. Mr. Jin dropped by for a chat and I invited him to join us. The others are up front somewhere. I think they met some women.''

"Having their pictures taken perhaps," said the man with the eyeglasses. He grinned at Jin.

Steele said, "This is Wim Brouwer, Jim. Wim likes to kid. He's with *de Telegraaf* in Amsterdam.''

"Pleased to meet you, Wim." Burlane shook hands and accepted a glass of vodka from Bob Steele.

Steele said, "Mr. Jin, you told us you work for the railroad, but you didn't say what you do."

"Do tell us you're not with SMERSH, comrade," said Brouwer.

Felix Jin laughed. "You've been reading too much James Bond, Mr. Brouwer. Although it is true that I am a detective, of sorts. I work with contraband smuggling on trains. We have a very low rate of crime in the Soviet Union, as you know, but we have an occasional problem the same as everyone else."

Brouwer said, "The Soviet crime rate is far lower than Europe's, our guide told us."

"So it is reported," Jin said.

"Is somebody smuggling something on this train?" Steele asked.

Jin said, "As a matter of fact, there is."

"A mystery!" Burlane said.

"On the Trans-Siberian Express!" Wim Brouwer poured himself some more vodka.

"Indeed," Jin said.

Bob Steele refilled Jin's glass and his own. "What is it you're looking for, Mr. Jin?"

Jin looked embarrassed. "I shouldn't have mentioned it in the first place."

"Surely you won't care if we speculate," Steele said.

Wim Brouwer rubbed his large hands together. "Good idea, Bob."

"As you like," Jin said.

Steele said, "Let's start with Wim, then. What are

you smuggling, Wim? You look guilty to me. Look at those glasses and the size of your hands."

"My shaving cream can is filled with cocaine. I say Mr. Jin is after drug smugglers. Is that what you're after, meneer?"

Jin smiled. "We rarely encounter drug smugglers in the Soviet Union."

"All you Amsterdamers are druggers. Jim Quint? Your turn, Mr. Author." Steele pinned Burlane with his eyes and grinned mischievously. "Surely you can come up with something good."

"Look at him sweat." Brouwer was having fun. He said, "Everybody knows Americans are guilty as hell. Just look at him."

Burlane put his finger on his lip and considered the question. "I'm smuggling microfilms of the Russian SS-twenty rocket. They're hidden inside hollow buttons on my shirts. Humper Staab has a shirt with buttons like that."

"You shouldn't read your own books, Mr. Quint," Jin said. "And how about yourself, Mr. Steele? Do you have a confession?"

Bob Steele said, "You know that bust of Lenin Mrs. Kropotkina is carrying with her? I'll bet you thought that was cast bronze. Well, it isn't. It's pure Russian gold. I'll be doing much in-out with Natalia after we get the bust out of the country."

Wim Brouwer said, "Meneer Quint doesn't have to rely on fantasy, judging from the looks of his Intourist guide. You must have contacts we don't, meneer."

"I was fortunate. Ludmilla's quite professional," Burlane said. He grinned at Jin.

"She seems to be," Jin said.

Brouwer said, "Looks like talent to me."

"Quite a little performer, I'll bet," said Bob Steele.

When his head threatened to spin a half hour later, James Burlane decided it was time to go to bed. He said his good-byes and started down the aisle, holding on to the rail for help. Behind him, he heard Felix Jin, who was in his cups, ask, in his heavily accented English, "Why is not a woman like a man?"

Bob Steele and Wim Brouwer were still laughing when Burlane closed the door that led to the next car. His trip was a success; he was so loaded from his night with the boys that he wouldn't be able to perform for Comrade Number Cruncher.

Twenty-Two

THE NEXT MORNING, LUDMILLA KORMAKOVA ENTERED her sixth day of reciting unknown facts of Siberia. As far as the hungover Burlane could see, Ludmilla was encyclopedic; she had lost no momentum. Her commentary continued without mercy: X thousands of sable pelts were produced annually in this region; Y millions of cubic yards of coal were mined in that area. The Soviets weighed gold by metric tons. They milled lumber by the trillions of board-meters.

There seemed to be a prestigious research laboratory every mile of the trip. Burlane was told the advances made by the Zabaykal'skiy Combined Scientific Research Institute in Chita, as well as the Forest Economy Laboratory of the Siberian Department of the Academy of Sciences.

"Oh, well, that's very interesting," Burlane said, looking out at wretched shacks that would have embarrassed a dog in Appalachia.

"Darasun is famed for its mineral springs, Jim. It is said to be one of the best treatments in the world for abdominal, intestinal, and cardiovascular ailments. This

271

water has been exported to China and Korea since ancient times.''

Burlane made a note. "Oh, heavens!" He learned about gold in Vershino-Darasunskoye, about fluoric spar in the village of Usugli, about molybdenum ore deposits at Busheley. Except for gold, Burlane had no idea what these minerals were.

"Despite this great wealth, there are some drawbacks to Siberia, Jim. In winter the temperature can drop to minus sixty of your American degrees Fahrenheit. When you exhale, the air crackles because your breath turns into ice crystals that explode with a snapping sound. In the summer the sun turns wood to charcoal and burns off grasslands." Ludmilla paused in her commentary. "Yes, here we are passing the village of Skovorodino, Jim. This was named in memory of A. N. Skovorodin, who was the first president of the village council of workers' deputies."

At the impoverished sprawl of shacks called Blagoveshchensk, Ludmilla said, "Here we have medical, agricultural, and pedagogic institutions." Ludmilla consulted a small booklet. "There is a polytechnical and an agricultural college, a financial-technical college, a teachers college, and a college of civil engineering. We have the Far Eastern Branch of the Siberian Department of the Academy of Sciences, the Blagoveshchensk Latitude Laboratory of the Principal Astronomic Observatory of the Academy of Sciences, and the Far Eastern Zonal Veterinary Institute."

That such a wretched hole should have such grand institutions seemed pathetic and ludicrous to Burlane. He nodded gravely and took notes on the confusing jumble of Russian words.

"You see the bog outside. This is a *bolotnaya tryassina,* Jim. This means marshy swamp. The grass and shrubs form a thick, elastic carpet. You can walk on this and it won't break through; it gives, then comes back again, so that it's like walking on green waves."

"I bet that's a first. To be honest, I never did believe that business about the Red Sea," Burlane said. "If you don't mind, Ludmilla, I think I should go to bed early tonight. I have a headache."

Burlane saved his smile until he had turned under his blanket and was facing away from Ludmilla. He wondered if he might not have nightmares of copulating with a woman who turned out to be a computer. He did not dream that. Worse, he dreamed of a naked blonde on a scarlet bed. Her smile was for Burlane alone. She beckoned with a languid hand. She called, softly:

"First! Biggest! Longest! Tallest! Widest! Oldest! Best! Only! World famous! Acclaimed! Fastest! Most accurate! Most unusual! Finest! Most beautiful!"

Burlane awoke with a start, sweating.

The train was stopped at a station.

A woman was giving workers their instructions over a loudspeaker. The sound of her loudspeaker voice with Russian *v*'s and *z*'s echoed off a building.

In a few hours it would be daylight again, then only one night before Vladivostok. Colonel Felix Jin sipped his tea and considered the hunks of ice in the Amur River floating under moonlight, floating northeast toward the Sea of Okhotsk and the Pacific Ocean. He took another sip. He was down to the dregs. Jin gave the buzzer two quick stabs, a signal to his aide that he would like another cup.

Moments later there was a respectful knock on the compartment door; Colonel Jin rose to accept the tea. He settled back with it as the train entered a small forest of Korean pine. Jin unfolded the East German drawings of the soft-class car and for what seemed like the thousandth time considered the interior design.

Isaak Ginsburg's compartment had been disassembled and put back together at the May Day stop in Irkutsk. KGB technicians had done the same with the compartment occupied by whoever it was who was calling himself Jim Quint. The technicians found nothing. They had disassembled and reassembled the conductress's compartment. Nothing. In fact, Jin had ordered railway workers to disassemble the underside of the car and the roof, looking for . . .

What? Jin held out the palm of his hand and weighed the imaginary object just as Valery Karpov had done that day.

If Jin retrieved whatever had been removed from the tomb, well then. . . . Felix Jin had always wanted a nice dacha on the Volga where he could fish in July, forage for wild mushrooms in September, possibly, or hunt deer in October. Jin had always wanted to travel in the West to see what it was like. That too was possible with success. On the other hand, if he failed—even if he didn't know what he was looking for—Jin was doomed.

Colonel Jin would not lose this contest as he had lost the chess match with Jim Quint. Jin had position and strength: the train and everybody in it were his. As a matter of fact, Jin had Ginsburg in check. Ginsburg was trapped. At Vladivostok, he would be vulnerable. He would have to try to escape with whatever it was he was concealing.

Jin folded the East German drawings and turned his attention to the transcripts of the conversations between Isaak Ginsburg and Natalia Kropotkina and between Jim Quint and Ludmilla Kormakova. He finished his tea.

Felix Jin put down his eyeglasses and massaged his eyes. He looked at the ice on the Amur. He put his glasses on and read some more. He ordered more tea. He read some more. The tea came. He sipped it and rang for his aide.

Jin said, "Pavel, how long has the conductress been boiling this water? It tastes like yak piss."

Twenty-Three

THE NEXT MORNING BURLANE LINGERED UNDER HIS BLANket pretending to sleep so as not to endure Ludmilla's jabber. At eleven o'clock he could stand it no longer and got up. The train was passing yet another Siberian swamp. Shallow lakes had formed on both sides of the railbed as the spring thaw tried to work its way through the ice beneath the ground.

Burlane said, "We need a change of pace. I'd like to buy our lunch from one of those peddlers on the station platforms. Will you help me?"

Ludmilla hesitated. "Wouldn't you rather eat in the dining car? It's much nicer."

"The Russians buy their food on the platforms. My editor wouldn't want me to be any different from the people."

Ludmilla got up and took a walk. She came back later and continued her book. Then she said, "Make sure you don't miss the train, Jim. Some of these stops are quite short." Ludmilla lifted her feet as the conductress vacuumed the carpet on the floor of the compartment.

Burlane was surprised Ludmilla did not insist on accompanying him onto the platform when the train stopped.

He scrambled down the aisle where the conductress held up five fingers, telling him five minutes. He was too slow for the quick Russians who were grouped around several peasant women wearing dark blue babushkas. The women, among the few entrepreneurs openly tolerated in the Soviet Union, were selling loaves of bread, small jars of jam, boiled potatoes, and pickled cabbage. Burlane could not use his Russian, and so couldn't compete with the other travelers. He checked on the two small shops on the platform. One sold Russian publications. The other had food, including cold fried fish.

Burlane, intent on some fried fish, got into line. Maybe there was time.

Behind him a man addressed him in Russian, "Perhaps I could help you?" The man waited, then repeated the question in English.

Burlane—who had understood the question in Russian—turned, surprised, and said, "Why, yes, thank you. I'm interested in a couple of those fish there, but I'm at a bit of a disadvantage."

The man said, "Comrade Kormakova thought you might need some help." He ordered Burlane's fish for him, conducting the transaction with a stolid, unemotional face. He'd tried to trap Burlane and had failed.

James Burlane resisted the urge to give the Russian the finger and strode back to the car door where the conductress waited, waving her flock back with her hand.

The Trans-Siberian Express entered another wide curve and straightened out for the run to the next town and the next artery of the massive system of rivers that flowed northward to the Kara Sea and the Laptev Sea just below the Arctic Ocean. Burlane got his map out and studied the amazing river system.

In Europe—where the rivers flowed south to the Black Sea or the Caspian Sea—there was Yaroslavl' on the Volga, Shar'ya on the Vetluga, Kirov on the Vratka, and Perm on the Kama. The rivers flowed to the north on the Asian side of the Urals. The names of the cities and the rivers from which they drew their sustenance were as euphonious as those in Europe:

There was Yahutorovsk on the Tobol, Omsk on the Irtysh, Novosibirsk on the Ob', Krasnoyarsk on the Yenisey, Nizhneudinsk on the Chuna, Tulun on the Iya, Zima on the Oka, Irkutsk on the Angara, Ulan-Ude on the Selenga, Chita on the Shilka, Tygda on the Zeya, Harbin on the Songhua, and Khabarovsk on the Amur.

These were not puny or tiny rivers lost on an endless continent; Burlane had found that out. They were neither large creeks nor small streams wistfully called rivers by people who don't know any better. They were heavy, stolid rivers—rivers that demanded fat lines and heavy type on atlases and maps. They collected runoff from an incredible landmass. They were not picturesque rivers: there were no canyons or vistas or waterfalls. They were broad continental rivers like the Mississippi or the Missouri. They were working men's rivers with the utilitarian cut of working men's coarse cottons and woolens.

The rivers wound their way through the taiga until they came to the tundra and slipped quietly under the polar ice cap. When winter ice gave way in May, the slate-gray rivers moved through a taiga muddy from the thaw. Peasants with eyes the color of the water fished the rivers in the summer.

Ludmilla said, "Jim, in a few hours we will be entering the Jewish Autonomous Republic. In 1928 the Presidium of the Central Executive Committee of the USSR decided to turn this unoccupied territory over to settlement by Jewish workers. Settlers from the Ukraine and Byelorussia reached the Far East in July. They stopped here in the warm pine forests and established the village of Waldheim."

Burlane knew the settlement was forced by Joseph Stalin at the point of a bayonet and was a favorite recruiting ground for slaves to work the Kolyma gold mines, where three million slaves died between 1936 and 1950. "This is predominantly Jewish, then," Burlane said, knowing that less than seven percent of the population was still Jewish.

"Oh, yes, Jim. This would be the Jewish Autonomous region. It is too bad it will be dark and you will not get to see it."

At Khabarovsk the train turned south for the run to Vladivostok on the Sea of Japan. This was the last night on the train. At 11 P.M. the buzzer sounded in Felix Jin's compartment. Jin was wide awake. He could not sleep. "Yes?" he said.

"Ginsburg went to the toilet, comrade."

"So?"

"Comrade Jin, when Ginsburg returned to his compartment the sound to our microphone stopped for twenty minutes. The lens to our camera was also blocked."

"Slow down, Pavel. First things first. How long did it take him to go to the toilet?"

"No longer than usual. A few minutes. Do you want the numbers?"

"No need," Jin said. "Did you check the toilet after he left?"

"I didn't have a chance, comrade. The conductress got up to lock the toilet for the stop at Dolnerechensk. She unlocked it after Dolnerechensk and put another roll of toilet paper inside."

"And the other compartments?"

"No activity. The doors remained closed."

"Did you get the markers?" A white stake marked every meter of the ten thousand meters from Moscow to Vladivostok. Jin had ordered the windows locked on the end car. Since it was possible to dump something onto the tracks through the toilet, Jin had ordered the nearest meter marked every time Ginsburg, Kropotkina, or Jim Quint went to the toilet.

"Yes, comrade. I radioed the marker number. That stretch of tracks will be searched within a few minutes."

Jin sighed. "Tell me about the missing twenty minutes."

"Either Ginsburg or Natalia Kropotkina was leaning against our lens during that time. Or it could have been taped. We can't be sure which. We got our picture and our sound back at the same time, and they were drinking vodka and wondering if they couldn't see the Chinese border from the train."

"Is there any possibility that the break was accidental?"

"That's always possible. The microphone could have developed a short with all this jerking and lurching, comrade. But the accidental loss of both the microphone *and* camera is unlikely."

"What do you think they did in there?"

"I think they found our mike and lens opening and wanted to call off the nightly show. By the way, Comrade Jin, the journalists are at it again in Steele's compartment. They're really throwing one tonight, celebrating their last night on the train together. I don't know how they do it. Capitalists are such drunks."

"We were right to separate them from Ginsburg and Quint. That would have been too much activity."

"All that vodka!"

Jin said, "I want a guard posted outside Ginsburg's door; if either Ginsburg or Natalia get up again, follow them to the toilet."

"Yes, comrade."

"Go inside the toilet with them. Watch them pee. Follow them back to their compartment. Stay right behind them."

"Yes."

Felix Jin suddenly thought of something. "Stand by, Pavel. There's something I want to check." Jin hung up and began pawing through the transcripts of the various conversations his agents had recorded. Yes, there it was:

On the first day out, the British journalist, Bob Steele,

had introduced himself to Jim Quint; Steele had said he was pleased to meet Quint. A couple of days later, when Steele and Quint were waiting for the May Day demonstrations to begin at Irkutsk, Steele had mentioned drinking with Quint in London. The Intourist guide had reported it.

Colonel Jin called his subordinate. "If Jim Quint leaves his compartment tonight, kill him, please, and store his body somewhere out of sight. Also, I will remind you that Ginsburg and Natalia Kropotkina are to be strip searched before they are allowed off the train in the morning. See that their luggage is X-rayed. There will be equipment waiting at the station."

Having one's word obeyed and one's needs taken care of was one of the perquisites of rank in the KGB. Felix Jin was tired and wanted to sleep. He needed to be fresh in the morning. He said, "I'm going to bed now, Pavel. I need to rest. I'm not to be disturbed until morning. Is that understood?"

Ludmilla Kormakova, bored with useless bits of Siberiana, gave up on Burlane at midnight and went to bed. That was a couple of hours later than Burlane would have liked, but he was alone at last to watch the taiga in the moonlight they'd had for the entire trip. Burlane chose to sleep fully clothed that last night. At one in the morning a hint of pain flickered through his inefficient bladder. He put on his shoes and stepped into the aisle.

There was a guard in front of Ginsburg's compartment, so Burlane turned left to use the toilet at the forward end of the car. He would have preferred the toilet at the conductress's end because it was cleaner.

The guard followed Burlane down the aisle.

There was another man waiting in front of the toilet.

Burlane slipped his hand into his pocket and slid the safety off his silenced .22. This was Paul Hornung time:

Money time.

Truth time.

The man by the toilet had a silenced pistol in his hand.

The door opened behind the man with the pistol.

Bob Steele.

The Russian started to turn. . . .

James Burlane pulled his pistol and snapped four quick shots at the Russian's torso and dived, rolling, toward his target. Burlane came up snapping shots at the man behind him.

When the second Russian accepted Burlane's .22 slugs in his heart—*plup! plup! plup! plup!*—he was on his knee, holding the wrist of his gun hand for support, aiming. Those steps were required by the KGB manual. He had executed them almost simultaneously. This too was as he had been trained.

Next, he was to have pulled the trigger.

"Dumb Slavs," Burlane muttered. Although the racket of the train had muffled the reports of his silenced .22, the odds were none to worse that he would ever again get to drive to Annapolis for beer and soft-shell crabs. He turned to the shocked Steele, who was holding on to the door handle and staring at the bodies.

Burlane grabbed the feet of the corpse nearest to him and began dragging him toward the corpse at Steele's feet. "Dammit, Bob, help me out!"

"Is this the way to the diner?" Steele said.

"Grab his feet, Bob."

"We'd been drinking vodka and I went to bed with the spins. Poor Wim passed out, I think."

Burlane glared at Steele. "First, my friend, the diner is the other direction; you're going the wrong way. Second, this is the Soviet Union, not British Rail; there's nobody there at this time of night."

Bob Steele tentatively nudged the dead Russian with his foot. "Bloody sods. What do they do for aspirin?"

"They're Russians. There's nothing in there to ache. I said, grab his legs."

Steele did as he was told. "I was wondering how they drink like that. Jim Quint is an old friend of mine."

Burlane opened the door of the train and pushed the first dead Russian into the cold night.

Steele offered Burlane the arm of the second corpse. "Who are you?"

Burlane pulled the body into position and shoved it off the train with his foot. He turned and looked Steele in the eye and whispered, "I'm an ugly American."

Steele swallowed. "What do we do now?"

"We go back to our respective compartments and hope we get out of this country alive. If you're religious, pray." Burlane stepped into the toilet to finish what he'd started out to do. This was the first time anybody had tried to kill him for wanting to take a leak. When he came out, Bob Steele was wiping vomit off his mouth with the back of his arm.

"Too damned much vodka," Steele said.

James Burlane returned to his compartment. He reloaded his pistol and sat facing the door. If he could make it to dawn, he had a chance; it would be unseemly for the KGB to murder a foreign journalist on the day of the Vladivostok signing.

If they came before dawn, Burlane would take as many with him as he could and save the last shot for himself. He thought about his brother in Denver. His brother would be in bed with his wife at this hour of night. In the morning he would shower, eat a decent breakfast, and drive to work listening to the traffic report on the radio.

James Burlane waited with great moons of sweat spreading from his armpits. He remembered his first kiss. He'd been fourteen years old at the time and it was like being very softly electrocuted. He remembered being an end on the high school football team in Umatilla, Oregon, and running out for a pass at a place called Fossil. The game was played on dirt in a rodeo arena, and the dim lights were all at one end of the field. The pass arced up in the yellow, spiraling, heading Jimmy Burlane's way. Then it entered the darkness and Jimmy couldn't see it . . .

Coming his way . . .

Running as hard as he could but not being able to see it . . .

Then striding into the mud wallow in front of the goal line where an underground waterpipe had burst . . .

Couldn't see the ball. . . .

A kiss and an invisible football were what James Burlane remembered as he waited, considering the darkness.

Twenty-Four

LUDMILLA KORMAKOVA AWOKE CHEERFULLY THE NEXT morning and went into the aisle for hot water. "There's nothing like hot Russian tea in the morning, Jim," she said. "I am to tell you it is forbidden to take pictures in Vladivostok. Mmmmm. The tea is nice."

"It's delicious. Thank you. It tastes extra good this morning."

"The conductress took on fresh water in Khabarovsk. They have one of the world's best drinking waters in Khabarovsk, Jim. It is very soft. There are no minerals. This peninsula is named for the nineteeth-century Russian navigator, Nikolai Mouraviov-Amursky. Vladivostok is built around a series of bays that are surrounded by a series of steep volcanic mounds."

Burlane saw a tower on a high hill above the city.

"Do you see a tower, Jim?"

"Yes, I do."

"That is a one-hundred-eighty-meter television tower. It sits on the highest volcanic mound on the peninsula. That would be called the Eagle's Nest, Jim. These are resort suburbs we are passing here. They are Sad-Gorod, Okeanskaya, and Sedanka. The seawater is very salty

284

here; a warm current flows counterclockwise from the Sea of Japan. The climate is mild, and there are mud baths and beaches in addition to the forests. This is a favorite holiday spot for Soviet citizens in Siberia and the Far East.''

Burlane refused to jot this down in his notebook. He was tiring of the charade. All he saw was another ugly Soviet industrial town, only different in that these unpainted, deteriorating buildings had been erected in a shabby helter-skelter on narrow terraces and along steep streets that ascended the hills from the water. Here and there a modern high-rise building rose from the rubble like a mushroom on a pile of dung. A harborfront of docks, shipyards, and workshops seemed to run for miles on a shoreline that twisted in and out of the series of bays. It was positively unreal. Burlane had never seen anything like it; all the unloading cranes on the planet seemed to have been assembled on Vladivostok's harborfront. How many were there? One hundred? Two hundred? Easily that many, Burlane felt. The bays were populated by tankers, freighters, and seagoing tugs suffering from various degrees of rust.

Ludmilla said, ''This is the busiest port in the Soviet Union, Jim. It is one of the busiest in the world. More than half a million people live here.''

Burlane thought, *It's also the only ice-free Soviet naval base in the Pacific, luv.* The sleek vessels of the Russian Navy were on maneuvers in the Sea of Japan, out of range of spies among the journalists and officials in Vladivostok for the signing. ''It certainly does look busy.''

''The large bay in the center there is Zolotoy Rog Cove. We will be taking Lenin Prospekt to the signings, Jim.'' Here Ludmilla consulted a small booklet. ''Yes, on Lenin Prospekt is the Palace of Culture, the Drama Theater, the Far Eastern Polytechnic Institute, the Institute of Fishing Culture, and the Theater of the Young Spectator. This is a regional scientific and cultural center.''

I bet the bread here is the best in the world, too, Burlane thought. He said, "It's nice to see such a robust city." James Burlane smiled to himself. He hadn't given up hope; there was still a chance. But he was an American spy, and for an American spy to disappear on the shores of Zolotoy Rog was like a cowboy dying with his boots on.

Later, out in the aisle to stretch his legs, he met Isaak Ginsburg.

"Wonderful weather, don't you think?" Ginsburg said. He shook Burlane's hand and left a small note there.

"It's positively balmy. For some reason, I'd expected more ice and snow, this being Siberia and all." Burlane glanced at the note:

I did not want to give you details in case you got caught. So far, so good. The head is safe. Natalia and I wish to defect to the West. Can you help us? We will have the conductress, Nina Kabakhidze, with us at the airport signing. She has been indispensable; we cannot leave her to the Soviets. I cannot tell you how grateful I am for all that you have done.

James Burlane put the note in his mouth and masticated it, cudlike; he was as content as a Guernsey cow at milking time.

Twenty-Five

$\mathbb{J}$AMES BURLANE WAS RELIEVED TO JOIN THE STILL SHAKEN Bob Steele and his hungover colleagues for a tour of Vladivostok before the signing. The writers were stuffed into a large van, with Ludmilla Kormakova doing the honors of reciting local facts and numbers, biggests and bests.

The journalists were taken on a four-mile drive along Lenin Prospekt, which flanked Zolotoy Rog. They were shown a soccer stadium and a sandy beach. Ludmilla described the beach as "the most beautiful in the Soviet Far East," although it looked damned cold and bleak to Burlane. Did Russians on vacation in Vladivostok sun themselves in wet suits? Burlane wondered. Terraced gardens, overlooks, and residential blocks descended from the avenue to the water.

The journalists endured explanations of monuments for Sergei Lazo, a hero of the Revolution, for Admiral G. Nevelskiy, and for merchant seamen who died in the Great Patriotic War of 1941–45, and for the sailing vessel *Manchur* that had brought the first settlers to the area in 1840. A model of the *Manchur* sat atop a column upon which Vladivostok was written vertically. Beneath that was a marble tablet with more Russian.

"On here is repeated the words of V. I. Lenin," Ludmilla said solemnly. "This says, 'Vladivostok is far away, but it is our city.' "

"In the United States we say that about Cleveland," Burlane said.

"Is Cleveland a beautiful city too, Jim?"

"Cleveland is a grand place."

Bob Steele said, "In England we say that about Liverpool, although some argue."

After that the journalists were driven to yet another monument—also for Soviet soldiers dead in the Revolution—this one erected at the central city square. The Soviets had flown in veterans of the Great Patriotic War of 1941–45 to be interviewed by *Tass* reporters and photographed for Soviet television.

"These men are being interviewed because May ninth is the anniversary of the USSR's victory in the Great Patriotic War. We call this Victory Day," Ludmilla said, although May 9 was four days away.

Burlane and the others got off the van. The journalists weren't certain what they were supposed to do with all this—European readers didn't care about Russian war stories—but allowed themselves to be herded from one hero to the next.

The veterans had so many medals on their jackets—chain-mail vests of patriotic armor—that they clanked when they walked. They were aged knights, arthritic, some of them, but still fighting the glorious fight. Here and there a rheumy-eyed veteran used a cane or was guided patiently by the elbow. They walked stiffly, clanking. The heroes were living reminders of the sacrifices of the Great Patriotic War.

Ludmilla said, "We honor these men so that such an awful tragedy might never happen again."

The veterans spoke straight into microphones thrust toward their sincere, old-men's faces. Soviet television cameras recorded every word, every gesture. If their memories had become fuzzy with time, nobody cared. If the stories of deprivation and valor became a little more dramatic over the years, that was beside the point. One particular hero—a former colonel, to judge by his decorations—reminded Burlane of a venerated old bird.

The heads of the colonel's solemn flock nodded in sorrow that such terrible things could have happened.

Ludmilla provided a running translation of what the colonel was saying. "He says the Red Army has to remain second to none."

The heads of the colonel-bird's rapt listeners bob-bobbed yes-yes in agreement.

"The colonel says the awful tragedy of invasion will never happen again. We negotiate in good faith, but we stand in the world second to no one."

Heads waggled no-no. No more invasions. No second best.

The colonel recalled the details of battles fought more than forty years ago. Ludmilla said, "He says the spirit of sacrifice has to continue. The younger generation has to carry on, has to be unselfish for the good of all. The old soldiers will be dead one day; then it is up to us, the younger generation."

At this, there was a vigorous nodding of heads.

Ludmilla said, "He says that in the end we can never trust treaties. We can never turn our future over to a piece of paper, never. We have to remember these stories and tell them to our children and our children's children."

Another hero: a former sergeant with a broad, sad face.

"He's telling what it was like to eat bugs in a German prison camp. He says all prisoners had a moral duty to do everything they could to inflict the maximum harm on the people's enemies and to escape at the earliest opportunity."

"They do have that duty. I agree," Burlane said.

Bob Steele raised an eyebrow. "They do indeed. Say, Jim, you won't forget to pop over next time you're in London. I'll take you to my club."

Felix Jin was still furious when he arrived at the Vladivostok airport at 2:30 P.M. Jin had given Pavel two simple instructions: first, if Jim Quint left his compartment in the night, he was to be wasted; and second, Colonel Jin needed his rest and was not to be disturbed for the rest of the night.

Pavel, having lost his two best agents to Jim Quint—by then an obvious American spy—remained calm and obeyed order number two.

Followed the second order to the fucking letter! The damned fool! Not a word until Jin got out of bed just outside Vladivostok. Jin knew Pavel had done this to postpone admitting that his men had gone two-on-one against Jim Quint, and wound up dead. Jin lit a cigarette and puffed quickly, inhaling deeply. Sometimes he felt sorry for his people.

On top of that, the X-rays of the luggage and the strip search of Ginsburg and Kropotkina had revealed nothing but a pair of green lace panties. Nothing at all.

Jin got out of the Volga lighting yet another cigarette. He glanced at his wristwatch. Thirty minutes before the ceremony. Had it just happened that Ginsburg's trip to relieve himself and the blackout came just before the stop at Dolnerechensk, where the conductress was required to lock the toilet? Jin's mind raced like an Afghani in a tank sight. The toilet. The aisle. The compartment. The aisle. The conductress's cabin. The samovar.

The toilet.

The samovar.

The samovar!

Jin leaped back into the car and ordered his driver to take him to the train station. "You will drive this car as fast as you can, comrade."

The driver, who loved to hurtle through Vladivostok, was pleased to comply.

Colonel Jin lit a cigarette and held fast to the armrest. He checked his watch again.

Several travelers on the end car had commented on the improvement in the tea this morning.

Jin checked his watch: 2:35 P.M.

The samovars on the Trans-Siberian held a lot of water. Jin himself had taken the top off the samovar in the end car—just in case—but he had just glanced in.

Isaak Ginsburg could very well have fished something out of the samovar and stashed it in the toilet for the conductress to pick up a few minutes later—or could have put something into the samovar after he left the toilet.

Had Ginsburg and Natalia blocked the camera and cut the microphone to divert suspicion from the conductress?

Had the conductress made a pickup when she left off the toilet paper after Dolnerechensk?

Jin sprinted into the railroad station shouting demands. Accompanied by a railroad official, he cantered down the siding.

He got to the end car and scrambled up the steps.

Inside, Jin pushed the samovar over and leaped back to avoid the hot water. Yes, he was right. There it was.

Using his handkerchief as a pot holder, Felix Jin looked inside. Someone had put a false bottom into the samovar. The false bottom contained a single small metal loop in the exact center so the bottom, and whatever was hidden under it, could be removed by a long wire with a hook on the end. This was good work on somebody's part. At a casual glance, the bottom looked normal. The six neat holes that allowed water into the bottom chamber were drilled along the near edge and so were invisible to anyone not tall enough to look straight down.

Isaak Ginsburg had smuggled something across the USSR in the bottom of a samovar!

Without a word, Colonel Jin, checking his wrist-watch, leaped off the train and began galloping back to his Volga. The ceremony would begin in twelve minutes.

Felix Jin jumped into the back of the Volga, yelling, "Airport! Airport! Airport! Speed! Speed! Speed!"

Whatever had been smuggled in the space in the bottom of the samovar had to have been fairly substantial. But what?

Colonel Felix Jin thought an unthinkable thought, one that he most definitely could not phone ahead lest his conclusion be accurate and it was too late.

He shouted, "More speed, driver, or I'll have you shot! Drive this car hard!"

The driver thrust the accelerator to the floorboard.

Twenty-Six

A HALF HOUR BEFORE THE SIGNING, JAMES BURLANE and the journalists who had ridden the Trans-Siberian Express were taken to the airport to join the more numerous journalists who had taken Aeroflot flights from Moscow or entered via Tokyo from the south. There were more than a hundred print journalists, but the stars of the show were the television people.

The writers, including Burlane and Bob Steele, were roped off to one side of the concrete apron so they wouldn't get in the way of the people who needed to check the light, proper angles, and electrical connections. The Soviets favored television because photo opportunities could be controlled; writers often thought for themselves. The print journalists, pariahs, could do nothing but clutch their pathetic notebooks and mumble oaths in various languages.

A third, smaller group, also roped off, included various diplomatic aides of the two countries, plus Isaak Ginsburg, who carried a large, loaded shopping bag, Natalia Kropotkina, and the conductress, Nina Kabakhidze. Burlane did not see Felix Jin.

A battery of microphones was arranged on the apron

at the Vladivostok airport. The agreed-upon document setting forth rules for the arms talks, bound in the specially tanned hide of Russian reindeer, awaited on a small table, along with a carved wooden eagle and Ivan Dmitrov's bust of Lenin.

In order that all the participants might understand their place, there were security guards everywhere. The print journalists and the Soviet and American aides were honored with the most guards. Only the television people were given any freedom to move about, but they too were guarded by solemn-faced soldiers in immaculate gray uniforms with red trim. Burlane noticed that they had been given decent haircuts for the occasion.

The party had obviously stressed the importance of the guards maintaining an appearance of civility and decency before the world's press. There were no crass megaphones in evidence; there was no pushing people around. The despicable American secretary of state was to come, sign the document, and leave with his tail tucked between his legs like the cur he was.

Stuart Kaplan, a slender, neat man with jet-black hair and square jaw, waited patiently with his aides for Foreign Minister Zhukov to arrive. The agreed-upon, published script called for both men to arrive at the same time, but it was obvious that Zhukov had chosen to make Kaplan wait.

"It looks like they're going to make your man wait," Bob Steele said.

"They piss on people for the same reason we drink coffee or smoke cigarettes. Gives 'em a little kick."

"The only reason they insisted on Vladivostok was to remind everybody that your Senate refused to ratify the agreement Gerald Ford signed here."

Burlane shrugged. "Everybody knows they're assholes."

Kaplan looked elegant, a consummate statesman in his pin-striped blue suit. Kaplan smiled. He chatted pleasantly with his assistants. He did not look at his wristwatch.

The television cameramen, bored, took shots of Kaplan waiting patiently. The Soviets who were helping the cameramen looked pleased. Russian technicians—under orders from above—scurried to make sure the foreign cameramen got good shots of Kaplan being humiliated.

Steele said, "The pathetic bugger looks like Oliver Twist standing there with his cup in his hand."

"Pricks," Burlane said of the Russians.

At twenty minutes past three, a convoy of eight or ten black Volgas escorted by motorcycles could be seen in the distance. The Volgas had red flags flying on the front fenders.

Grigori Zhukov emerged from his Volga and began walking toward the designated spot for the handshake, a small circle painted in front of the table. The two men were to stand in this circle; this was to assist television cameramen.

The conversation between Kaplan and Zhukov was amplified by loudspeaker. Zhukov's Russian was translated into English by a man with a British accent.

Stuart Kaplan, suddenly awash with television lights, strode to the table with his hand outstretched. "Did you have a good rest, Grigori Mikhailovich!"

Burlane said, "He's thinking Zhukov's an asshole."

Steele pretended to be surprised at Burlane's ignorance. "Zhukov's a sodding Russian. What do you expect?"

"Did you enjoy the sights this morning, Stuart?"

"Fine, fine," said Kaplan.

Stuart Kaplan gestured for the bald eagle. Zhukov waved for Ivan Dmitrov's bust of Lenin.

Kaplan said, "I give you this American bald eagle, a symbol of our dedication to peace and freedom. It is carved from myrtle wood, found only in southwestern Oregon and in the Holy Land." He gave the eagle to Zhukov.

Zhukov smiled broadly and held the eagle out so the
cameramen could get a close-up. "It's lovely, lovely."
Zhukov put the eagle on the table and took Dmitrov's
bust from his aide and handed it to Kaplan. "You may
rest assured, Mr. Secretary Kaplan, that you Americans
need Comrade Lenin more than we do."

"Up yours, fuckhead," Burlane muttered.

One of the Russian guards, an officer who obviously
understood English, turned and stared at Burlane.

Burlane formed a V with his forefinger and middle
finger, and put this to his mouth and quickly ran his
tongue in and out, in and out between the fingers.

The officer glared.

James Burlane giggled and ran his tongue in and out
two more times.

"Your fallen comrade was a man of peace and so
honors us all," Kaplan said.

There followed two long speeches, one by Comrade
Zhukov, who called for peace and justice, and one by
Secretary Kaplan, who asked for peace and freedom.
Burlane regarded these speeches as hardly more pleasant
than having a tooth pulled or his prostate checked.

Speechifying completed, the two men signed the document and stepped back with their gifts, so that Comrade Isaak Avraamovich Ginsburg might read his poem.

As Ginsburg started forward, he gave the heavy shopping bag to Natalia.

Then Felix Jin appeared at Natalia's right shoulder.

Natalia gave the shopping bag to Nina Kabakhidze.

Burlane said, "When Ginsburg finishes his poem,
there's gonna be some action, Bob, so stay alert."

"Why, thanks." Steele, pleased at his good fortune
at falling into a story about an American spy at the
Vladivostok signing, started edging his way closer to the
retaining rope. He stopped after a couple of steps and
said, "Good luck, Yank."

Burlane gave Steele a thumbs up.

Isaak Ginsburg arrived at the microphones on the small table to begin his committee-approved poem.

"You see him in the Urals, foraging for berries,
    or loping through the taiga.
In Alaska, he pauses outside a gas station;
He paws through garbage down in Yellowstone
    while people take his picture, click, click.
That old bear's grown shaggy looking for a full belly
And a good night's sleep . . ."

James Burlane did not watch television. With rare exceptions he found television boring, intended for people whose interests and passions were less active and imaginative than his own. He did not begrudge watchers their pleasure, but rather wondered how they did it. How could they sit there with their brain cells in a state of suspended animation? Yet on this occasion, standing there on the Vladivostok airport, Burlane was never more relieved in his life than at the comforting whirring of television cameras.

The Soviets ruled by controlling everything: what their people saw and read; what they were allowed to feel and say; where they were allowed to travel. This control was insured by the barbed wire at their borders. But at Vladivostok, in their rush to score a propaganda victory over the Americans—Premier Spishkin wanted the world to see every detail—the Soviets had turned over a small bit of territory to the sovereignty of foreign television cameras. Aided by Soviet technicians and American satellites, the pictures of the exchange of gifts and Isaak Ginsburg's poem were being beamed, live, to an international audience.

All this was calculated so that everyone might enjoy the humbling of Stuart Kaplan and the inferior American war machine.

When Ginsburg finished, Burlane said, loudly, "I think I'll go for a scoop, Bob. Cheerio!"

James Burlane casually lifted the rope barrier that held the print journalists in their assigned place and strode easily in Kaplan's direction. He walked with his hands well free of his body so everybody could see that he was unarmed. He was immediately the center of attention of the television cameras.

"I wonder if I might have a word with you, Stuart. You remember me, Jim Quint, of the *New Democrat.*" Burlane grinned hugely, expansively.

No Soviet citizen would have dared be so outrageous. The Soviet security guards were momentarily confused. Should they shoot this man with the world watching on television?

Burlane turned and called back to the print journalists who stared at him in disbelief. "Hey, he promised me an exclusive on this one. I'm calling him on it."

The guards hadn't been told what to do if a Western journalist got this aggressive. No Russian journalist would dare be this brazen. Burlane's behavior was unthinkable.

Burlane said, "Stuart, you'll be pleased to know I had a wonderful train ride from Moscow. A perfectly wonderful ride. All those lovely trees."

Both Kaplan and Zhukov, stunned, stared at the large-nosed man in amazement.

"You said to look you up next time we were both in Vladivostok."

Burlane walked right up to Kaplan with the cameras recording every detail. He lowered his voice and leaned down to the shorter man. He said, "My name is James Burlane. I'm a Company man. I have three Soviet citizens who want to defect to the United States." He turned to Zhukov and whispered, "You keep your nose out of this, you miserable prick." To Kaplan, he continued, "You should consider this a direct order from the President of the United States. If you don't agree, I'll split your nuts with the arch of my foot right here in front of God and television. I did that to an Arab

terrorist once, and to a bandit in Colombia. It works."
Burlane smiled graciously.

Stuart Kaplan hesitated.

"Believe me, I don't have anything to lose," Burlane
said. "If you want to end up talking like Minnie Mouse,
try me. This is utmost, extreme, urgent priority, Mr.
Secretary."

The American secretary of state said quietly to the
Soviet foreign minister, "If you have the chutzpah to
deviate from our agreement with peace on the line, I
suppose I can too, Comrade Zhukov. Where are your
companions, Mr. Burlane?"

Burlane grinned. "Yes! My main man!" He lowered
his voice: "Hang in there." He shouted, "Isaak
Avraamovich! Mrs. Kropotkina! Nina!"

Burlane saw that Felix Jin was gone. So was the
loaded shopping bag.

Colonel Felix Jin couldn't stop his hands from shak-
ing. He was trembling like a reindeer with a belly full of
fur balls. Lighting a cigarette was a major undertaking.
He'd figured out Ginsburg's clever smuggling scheme at
the very last second. Valery Karpov wasn't joking when
he'd told the colonels they'd know what they were
looking for when they found it.

There, on a table, was the head. The wax nose and
lips and ears had taken a beating, had been battered and
flattened, had been somewhat melted by hot water, but
the face was unmistakable: V. I. Lenin.

Lenin's head had ridden across Russia in the bottom
of a samovar. The conductress must have retrieved it
from the toilet and smuggled it off the train.

Looking out the window, Jin saw that the American
party was being loaded onto the plane—along with
Ginsburg, Kropotkina, the railroad conductress, and the
American spy who called himself Jim Quint.

Jin picked up the phone and called the colonel in
charge of security. "I want the American plane held on

the ground until further instructions. Do not give the Americans permission to depart until you hear from me. Is that understood? Do I make myself clear?''

Then Jin phoned Valery Karpov's emergency number in Moscow Central and identified himself.

Karpov, who had been watching the signing and the Burlane episode on live television, said, "What's going on out there?''

"Very quickly, I will tell you I have what you are looking for on a table in front of me.''

"Describe it.''

"It has a goatee. High cheekbones.''

"Lenin's head.''

"Yes, Comrade Karpov.''

"Who knows about this, Comrade Jin?''

"Only me. Isaak Ginsburg, a woman *znachok* designer, and a railway conductress are involved. An alleged writer who is an American spy helped them defect. You probably saw that on television. They are now on the plane with the American secretary of state. I have the plane's departure on momentary hold.''

"It's all there? Everything? The teeth?''

"It's all here, comrade. It's been battered around a little, and it rode across Russia in the bottom of a samovar so the wax is quite melted, but it's all here. The features are recognizable. With a little work we can have it restored and back where it belongs.''

There was a silence on the other end.

Jin could hear Valery Karpov take a deep breath and exhale between clenched teeth as he considered his options.

Twenty-Seven

THE PILOT OF THE AIR FORCE JET SEEMED CALM ENOUGH. He said, "We are told there will be a slight delay before takeoff. We should receive permission any moment now." That was easy for the pilot to say, but the secretary of state and his party could see clearly that there was no congestion at Vladivostok. This wasn't like waiting your turn at Kennedy or La Guardia. There wasn't anything but the unpredictable Russians keeping them on the ground.

There was an uneasy, jittery calm aboard the airliner. The lanky American with the uncombed hair and the three Russians sat in isolation at the front of the cabin. If anything went wrong, it was their fault and everybody knew it. Nobody on board seriously thought the Soviets would try to force their way into the plane—not with the scene being recorded on television. The Soviets could not, would not. Would they?

The secretary of state and his aides watched in silent resentment. Their plan had been to fly from Vladivostok to the Honolulu Airport. The President would meet them in Honolulu and there would be a parade down Kalakaua Avenue. They would live it up, heroes, in the Kahala

Hilton. There would be rum punch to drink, Maui Wowie to smoke. There would be brown-skinned girls of fabulous racial combinations. The Americans waited, making light jokes, trying to act calm, but hearts fluttered. Were they being held captive by the Russians because of the defection business?

For the Soviets to hold an American secretary of state hostage was tantamount to an act of war. Stuart Kaplan couldn't imagine that a defection of three citizens could cause the Soviets to risk nuclear war. That was absurd. Preposterous.

Kaplan, who had acted out of intuition earlier, now regretted that he had not been able to ask the Company's point man what this was all about.

James Burlane accepted defeat philosophically. He had been defeated before. At least his Russian accomplices would win their freedom.

Ginsburg sat in a dazed, stunned silence. Natalia wept quietly. Nina licked her lips nervously and looked at the planeload of frightened Americans.

Burlane said, "You tried. It didn't work. Those things happen. Have you ever been out of the Soviet Union before, except for Turkey, I mean?"

"That was the only time."

"After a while, you'll forget all about Russia. Drink a little good beer, maybe. Write whatever you want to write."

"It's my home. I'll always miss it some," Ginsburg said. "Will they let us go?"

"They got what they were after, didn't they?"

"They got it."

"Then they'll let us go. What are they going to do to us with all those cameras out there?" Burlane sighed. He'd have to remember to send a first-rate case of gin to Bob Steele for keeping his mouth shut and perhaps saving Burlane's life. Burlane hoped there was plenty of booze on board. He felt like drinking himself to sleep.

Moments later the pilot said, "Well, we've been

given permission to depart. Looks like they were having a little fun with us there. No problem."

Nervous laughter fluttered down the cabin. The folks from State were clearly relieved. They had even received a bonus—the defection and the uncertain minutes waiting for permission to take off would make a wonderful story when they got back. They would be heroes.

Twenty minutes later, when they were well over the Sea of Japan, Isaak Ginsburg said, "Mr. Quint?"

"My real name's James Burlane, Isaak. Jim to you. I'm very, very sorry you didn't make it. I think I have an idea of what your plan meant to you. You came close. You did your best."

"Mr. Burlane . . . Jim. Lenin's head is inside the bust Grigori Zhukov gave to your Mr. Kaplan in the ceremony."

"What?" Burlane twisted in his seat.

Natalia Kropotkina said, "Ivan Dmitrov's bust was on display in the Hotel Rossiya at the time of the theft. I hid the head behind a patch in an air duct of the hotel that day, and we ripped it out after they had finished searching. I split my copy of the bust, put Lenin's head inside, and refinished the outside. Then I switched it with the bust on display at the Rossiya."

Burlane was amazed. "So what does Jin have down there?"

Natalia said, "We needed a diversion. What Jin has is a fake Lenin I made out of a human skull, human hair, and wax. It looks like the real thing. I made a false bottom for the samovar on the train. The fake head was under that."

"A little battered and worse for the hot water, but no doubt convincing," Ginsburg said.

"Do you mean to tell me the Soviets have had Lenin's head for three weeks, waiting to give it to Kaplan?"

"How could we possibly smuggle the head out of the country ourselves? We decided to let Comrade Zhukov do it for us. The party was eager for Zhukov to give you Americans a Lenin.''

"Natalia, you had the tools and skill to make it work.''

Natalia grinned mischievously, thinking of Ivan Dmitrov's studio. "Exactly.''

"And you needed me to draw their attention to the fake head on the train.''

"Yes. We also needed you to help us defect,'' Ginsburg said. "In that, you succeeded imaginatively, I must say. But it is the head that counts, not us. We got the head out. That's all that matters.''

"Just how is this extortion plan going to work, Isaak?''

Ginsburg told him the details.

"Oh, I like that. Humiliation. Public spectacle. Wonderful! Did you tell the Soviets what you have in mind?''

"In a note our friend, Jaan Birk, left in the mausoleum.''

Burlane glanced at Kaplan, who was receiving congratulations from his advisors. "Natalia, Isaak, you must pay attention now. Bureaucrats are the same everywhere—in Russia, the United States, Morocco, Singapore, Bolivia—it doesn't make any difference. If you ask bureaucrats for help, I guarantee they'll find a way to screw everything up. They'll steal your head, is what they'll do—with much noble sentiment—and everything you've done will have been in vain.''

"What do we do, then?'' Natalia asked.

"We tell my superiors that the Russians retrieved the head at the last second. Then I get us what we'll need to extract the year of open emigration. It won't be easy; the KGB will be scouring the planet.''

Ginsburg looked at Burlane, thinking. He started to speak, then stopped.

Burlane said, "You're wondering how I can deceive my superiors.''

"Yes, Mr. Burlane, I was.''

"They expect me to. You look surprised, Isaak. This way they can take credit later if everything works out right. If anything goes wrong, they can blame it on me, a renegade. That's understood. We'll need a whole bunch of money, by the way.''

Isaak Ginsburg marveled at James Burlane. "I was wondering about that," he said.

"Defense contractors charge the Pentagon fifteen dollars for a nickle screw and six hundred dollars for a plastic toilet seat. I'll get what we need from them, no problem. They owe the public one.''

"You will?''

"To cut the Russians' balls off? Hell, yes!''

Ginsburg grinned. "Yes, Mr. Burlane. Exactly that. Later, I'll tell you the story of Lobnoye Mesto.''

"Natalia, if I can get you Kaplan's Lenin, can you get the head out and put the bust back together without anyone being the wiser?''

"It would take a few days.''

Burlane grinned. "I'll work something out. Do not tell these people. Do not." James Burlane was elated. "Well! I think we should have a little celebration, don't you think? That's what defectors would do.'' He stood in the aisle of the plane and said loudly, "Okay, now, on your feet, Isaak Avraamovich!" He took Ginsburg by the shoulder and gave him a tug.

Ginsburg, confused, rose uncertainly.

Burlane raised his arms high with his fingers spread wide. "Okay, you Jewish dude. You slick mother. Give me ten. Let me have 'em. Don't be a stolid Russian now. Give 'em to me! That's it. Yes!''

Isaak Ginsburg let himself be shown how to give the Company's money man a magnificent, triumphant ten, in the manner of victorious athletes in the United States. Ginsburg didn't understand exactly what the giving of ten was all about, but he couldn't help but know it was a celebration.

James Burlane was unabashedly jubilant. He danced, grinning, laughing. "End zone! End zone! Hot damn! Putting it to 'em, my man! Yes! Yes! Yes!'' Burlane slammed the palms of his hands into Ginsburg's again and again, while Natalia Kropotkina, who had been weeping from joy, wept even louder. Burlane pulled Natalia to her feet and embraced her. "Come on, you too! Give me ten, Russian lady; it's your moment. You made it work. Show 'em the joy! Show 'em! You too, Nina. On your feet." Burlane embraced the joyous conductress.

Natalia Kropotkina, still crying, feeling grand, gave James Burlane ten.

Isaak Ginsburg glanced uncertainly at the American secretary of state. He turned and lifted a glass to James Burlane. "Shall we drink, then? To Jaan Birk, a hero of the people!"

"A hero of the people!" Burlane drank, wondering who Birk was.

"To Comrade Jin! A worthy foe!" Ginsburg grinned.

"To Jin!" Burlane took a hard slug.

"To Mikheyev for his inspiration. I'll tell you the story one day, James Burlane."

"Hell, yes, to Mikheyev!" Burlane said.

Natalia said, "To Leonid for his inspiration and Ivan Dmitrov for his help."

Ginsburg said, "To the coughing *zek*, and Serafim Korenkho, and my old friend, Lado Kabakhidze." He toasted and gave the weeping Nina a hug.

"To Comrade Lenin!" Burlane called up the aisle. "Mr. Secretary, we would like to drink a toast to your bust of Lenin. Will you join us?"

Stuart Kaplan grinned and held up the bust of Lenin. The cabin cheered. Kaplan stood up and took a stroll down the cabin, holding the bust of Lenin high for everybody to see.

James Burlane remembered the football spiraling his way in the darkness at Fossil . . .

Coming at him. . . .